——————————— ★ ———————————

Joan peered around him and gasped. Now she knew what had upset Helga, and it wasn't confabulation. The man crumpled in the middle of the snow did resemble Fred, or might have, if he still had a face. He looked to be about the same size, for one thing, and his blond hairline was beginning to recede. Beyond that, it was impossible to tell.

The trampled snow nearest to him looked as if it had turned into red slush and then frozen again. She had no doubt where the red had come from, though she couldn't see the weapon that must have done the damage. Or could she? She spotted what had to be blood on some branches and one baseball-sized rock. How long had it been there?

Could he possibly still be alive? She couldn't see how.

——————————— ★ ———————————

"In a surprisingly exotic setting, Sara Hoskinson Frommer has handed sensible, sexy, fortyish and newly married Joan Spencer two hard problems: murder and the challenges facing a family when a beloved elderly relative begins to fail. Joan handles both with intelligence and grace."

—S. J. Rozan, author of *Winter and Night*

Previously published Worldwide Mystery titles by
SARA HOSKINSON FROMMER

THE VANISHING VIOLINIST
MURDER & SULLIVAN
BURIED IN QUILTS
MURDER IN C MAJOR

Witness in Bishop Hill

Sara Hoskinson Frommer

WORLDWIDE®

TORONTO • NEW YORK • LONDON
AMSTERDAM • PARIS • SYDNEY • HAMBURG
STOCKHOLM • ATHENS • TOKYO • MILAN
MADRID • WARSAW • BUDAPEST • AUCKLAND

*In memory of Margaret Anne Huffman
(1941–2000)*

WITNESS IN BISHOP HILL

A Worldwide Mystery/November 2004

First published by St. Martin's Press LLC.

ISBN 0-373-26510-7

Printed in U.S.A.

Special thanks to

Donna and Lloyd Anderson
Laura Bybee
Sheriff Gib Cady
Cheryl Dunivant
Karen Foli
Richard Haseman, Lieutenant Colonel, retired
Marni Hoskinson
George Huntington
Janelle Johnson
Laura Kao
Susan Kroupa
Dory Lynch
Valerie Markley
Eileen Morey
J. D. Maxwell
Jeanne Myers
Rhonda Rieseberg
Anne Steigerwald
John Sundquist
Sharon Peterson Wexell
And to my agent, Stuart Krichevsky,
And my editor, Ben Sevier

ONE

JOAN SPENCER didn't know meeting her mother-in-law was about to lead to murder. She had married Fred Lundquist so suddenly that she hadn't met his family yet. Not that it had been a shotgun wedding, if such a thing still existed. Her children were already young adults, Andrew a junior in college and Rebecca on the verge of marriage. One minute Joan had expected to wait until everyone could be there, and the next minute waiting hadn't made sense. Not at their age. Not if she was going to worry every time Fred went to work that she might never be his wife.

Three months later, she was still glad they had gone ahead. She and Fred would get around to visiting the family soon.

EVEN BEFORE the college closed for the winter break, things were unusually quiet at the little Oliver, Indiana, police station. Detective Lieutenant Fred Lundquist was catching up on old paperwork when the phone on his desk rang.

"Lundquist."

"Fred, it's me."

"Carol?" His sister hardly ever called him, and never at work. "Are Mom and Dad all right?"

"I guess. They can't understand why you never come to see them."

He bristled. In fact, he and Joan hoped to make the trip

to northern Illinois in a few more weeks, after their first Christmas together, but he hadn't wanted to get his mother's hopes up until he was sure. "You didn't call just to tell me I'm a rotten son."

"Cut it out, Fred! I wouldn't call at all if we didn't need your help."

Laying on the guilt, he thought, just the way she used to when we were kids. He sighed. "What can I do for you?" Stretching back against the wall, he automatically caught his toes under the desk in case his old wooden swivel chair tried to dump him.

"We want to get away for a couple of weeks," Carol said. "Our neighbor has just offered us his time-share in Florida before Christmas. Right on the beach, can you imagine? We'd love to take him up on it, but we can't leave Walt alone with Mom and Dad then. It's his busiest season. He just doesn't have enough time to give them."

Fred's brother, Walter, and his wife ran a restaurant in Bishop Hill, the tiny restored Swedish community in northern Illinois where their parents lived. Carol and her husband lived in Kewanee, a small town a few miles away that was much bigger than Bishop Hill.

Their parents, Helga and Oscar Lundquist, still lived in the house in which all their children had grown up. Only Fred, the oldest surviving child, had left the area. Oscar Junior had died in infancy, a loss his mother sometimes spoke about with matter-of-fact Swedish stoicism.

Fred couldn't imagine his parents upset about not seeing Carol for a couple of weeks, even if Walt couldn't spend much time with them in his busy season. "They can't manage by themselves that long?"

"If you came around a little more, you'd know they can't." Carol's voice was as sharp as her words.

Fred bit back a retort. "I'm sorry." His family had been

more than understanding during the rough years around his divorce. If they wanted some of his time now, they had a right to ask for it.

"I'm sorry, too," Carol said quickly. "I didn't mean to be nasty."

That helped. "What do they need?"

"We look in on them at least once a day. Some days are better than others, but it's really hard, especially on Dad. He keeps expecting Mom to be the way she always was. Even on good days she repeats herself and doesn't remember where she put things."

Neither do I sometimes, Fred thought.

"On the bad days, she can't remember how to cook."

"*Mom?*" Maker of Swedish meatballs and the best apple pie he'd ever eaten? Canner of gallons of homegrown tomatoes and green beans? Carol had to be exaggerating. Still, if she'd bothered to call him, and at work... He didn't want to think about it.

Carol sighed. "She's getting old, Fred. Can you come?"

"Probably. I'll have to talk it over with my wife, of course." My wife. The words were still new on his tongue. He savored them.

"Oh...you think she'll object?" He could hear the worry in her voice.

"We'll have to work it out on this end, that's all. Give me your dates, and I'll call you back after we've had a chance to talk."

Clunking the chair forward, he took down the information with his feet on the floor. After they'd hung up, he sat without moving for a long moment, wondering how Joan would feel about it. She was so good with the old people at the Oliver Senior Citizens' Center, which she directed. And at the adult day care, with the ones who really were losing it. In those situations, she was cheerful and patient.

He hated to put her to the test with his parents. Her own had died young, and he'd never be able to reciprocate. But it wasn't fair to dump it all on Carol and Walt, either, just because they were close.

Not that he believed Carol was right about their mother. But Mom, for all her virtues, could exert pretty strong pressure on her children. If she got some bug in her ear, everybody was supposed to do what she asked. He could well believe that Walt and Carol needed relief from time to time. It was his turn. He had to make Joan understand that he had a responsibility there.

He dialed her work number, but an old woman with a southern Hoosier accent said "Joanie" would be working at the adult day care all afternoon. Was there a message?

"No, I'll talk to her this evening." He remembered only after it was out of his mouth that the woman on the other end of the line would hear "evening" as meaning four or five o'clock at the latest.

On cue she said, "She won't be finished there before five," and he thanked her.

At five the police station was swamped with half a dozen Oliver College students brought in for falsifying IDs at Jimmy's Bar. The phony IDs might have fooled someone else, but not Jimmy, after long years of owning a bar near campus.

"You gonna call my folks?" one boy asked. "Aw, man." His voice rose on "man." Blinking hard, he avoided looking at anyone.

"My father will kill me," a girl said, and big tears ran down her cheeks. She wiped at them with the hand they'd fingerprinted. Now ink and mascara smudged her face.

Fred kept his face stern for the students' benefit, and left them to Officer Jill Root, who had arrested them.

Then he dealt with a call about a man exposing himself

near the campus—a bit brisk outdoors for that. And another about a missing child, a little girl of seven. Her frantic mother said she hadn't come home from school yet. He checked his watch—almost six.

"She always comes straight home. I try not to worry, but it's dark out now, and I heard about that man. She's just a little girl." Her voice broke.

Why did people listen to police scanners, anyway?

"We'll be there right away," Fred promised, and he set the search in motion.

An hour and a half later, the little girl turned up safe at a friend's house, as he had hoped, but you couldn't mess around when it came to children. Even though nobody had made it home in time for supper, the mood at the station when Fred finally left was more of relief and rejoicing than of complaining.

By now, Joan would be long gone to orchestra rehearsal—she managed the Oliver Civic Symphony and played viola in it. As unpredictable as Fred's hours were, they'd agreed at the beginning of their marriage that anytime he didn't show up or call, she'd eat without him. Grateful for her independence, especially after his first wife's clinginess, he stopped in at Wilma's Cafe and sat in his old booth, his back to the knotty pine wall.

He waved away the menu Wilma brought. "Bring me the pot roast. Salad and coffee. And your homemade rolls, if you still have any."

She nodded. "I saved you some—figured you'd be in. I heard you found the little girl. Coulda been worse."

"Yes." He didn't want to think about how much worse. Years ago, as a big-city cop, he'd seen the victims of child molesters and kidnappers after it was too late. But not in Oliver. Not yet. He hoped he never would.

It was almost ten when Joan pulled up to her little house. The big boxes of music folders would have to wait their turn—she didn't dare leave her viola out in the cold while she carried them in. Her extra job as orchestra librarian meant carrying around the folders people didn't take home and keeping tabs on those they did take. For this short Christmas concert, they were playing Tchaikovsky's *Nutcracker Suite,* the "winter" section of Vivaldi's *Four Seasons,* and a medley of carols for an audience sing-along. All too many of the players thought they knew this music well enough not to bother practicing. They dumped it in the boxes for Joan to haul to and from rehearsals, instead.

She'd hoped her son would be home. No light in his upstairs window, though.

The front door opened, and Fred came down the walk. He bent to kiss her. "You want a little help?"

"Oh, please. Andrew seems to have vanished."

"He's a good kid." Fred and Andrew had gotten along well since they'd first met. Sometimes Joan felt they were ganging up on her, but mostly she was glad.

Fred lifted the heavy, bulky boxes out of the Civic wagon as if they were nothing and led the way to the house. "Keep that man," her mother would have said, if she'd lived long enough to meet him. Joan smiled in the dark.

He'd already shed his coat and tie for an old sweater and rumpled chinos, and he'd even made fresh coffee. She kicked off her shoes and let down her straight, still-brown hair the way he liked, and they settled together on the sofa with steaming cups. The coffee was too hot to drink right away, but they found something else to do with their mouths.

Eventually he leaned back and picked up his cup. "So how was orchestra?"

"All right. Alex didn't explode at anyone tonight. Not

even me, and I'm still struggling with the beginning of the *Nutcracker*.'' Alex, the orchestra's otherwise competent conductor, generally blew up at least once a week. Joan was glad to have escaped her wrath this time.

''Hard?''

''Just a lot of little fast notes. Not important ones, but they ought to sound clean, and I hate to have to fake them. I suppose I could do something outrageous, like practice. How was your day?'' She'd learned not to ask him what had happened. He'd tell her if he wanted to and if he could.

''Long. A little girl didn't make it home from school.''

''No.'' She waited. His brows were furrowed, but his voice gave her no idea how it had turned out.

''We found her at a friend's. Her mother was too relieved to give her a hard time.''

''Uh-huh.'' The hard time might come later, but Joan hoped the mother's anger wouldn't hide her love.

''Something else I have to tell you about.'' He leaned forward, looking down at his own big feet instead of at her.

''Oh?'' It wasn't like him to lead up to anything. Usually he'd just blurt it out, whatever it was.

''Carol called today.''

''Your sister?'' Bad news about his parents, maybe?

''Yeah. She and her husband have a chance to spend a couple of weeks in Florida before Christmas, and they want to go.''

''Good for them.'' What was he working up to?

''They want me to go help Mom and Dad while they're gone. She says Walt and Ruthie—that's Walt's wife—are too busy during the Christmas season to do what the folks need.'' He finally looked at her, as if waiting for her to clobber him.

Was he proposing to take off without her? He often told her how glad he was that she could manage without him.

But she'd hate for him to leave her now, so close to their first Christmas together. Rebecca, her daughter, had even hinted that she might come home to be with them all. And they'd been planning to go see his folks afterward.

"Of course you said you would." She kicked herself mentally. How could I say that? How's he supposed to know what I feel if I don't tell him?

"I said I'd talk it over with you. Bishop Hill is just a wide spot in the road, even compared to Oliver. You'll probably be bored."

"Not half as bored as I'd be if you went without me." She held her breath.

"I wouldn't do that." He smiled, and those wonderful blue eyes crinkled down at her.

She stretched up and kissed him. "I'd love to go. We were talking about visiting them soon anyway. Might as well be useful. Tell me about them. You never talk about your family."

He hesitated. "Well, you know about Dad."

"His name is Oscar, I know that. And he taught you to bake that great sourdough bread. And popovers." She smiled, remembering the day she and Fred had met.

"Dad was a baker most of his life. Had a little bakery right there in Bishop Hill. Sold it some years back, but he sometimes still helps out in the busy season. At least he used to. I'm not sure what he does these days."

"Bishop Hill has a busy season?"

Fred smiled at her obvious doubt. "These days it does. It's turned into a tourist attraction. The Heritage Association folks have restored a bunch of the old buildings and told the world to come visit."

"How old can they be in northern Illinois?"

"Mid-nineteenth century. A group of Swedes founded the place as a religious commune, and a lot of the people who live there now are descended from those original settlers.''

''Your family?''

''Could be. I'm not sure.''

It made her want to giggle to think of Fred as coming out of a religious commune. But why not? ''So they weren't celibate, like the Shakers.''

''No, but they didn't last as long. The colony dissolved a few years after the founder was murdered.''

''*Murdered?* Who killed him? Do they know?''

''It wasn't a mystery. The guy walked right up to him and shot him. Best I remember, it was over a woman. You don't hear people talk about that much, though.''

''Do they talk about him at all?''

''Sure. His name was Eric Janson.'' He pronounced the *J* the Swedish way, like a *Y*.

''Janson?'' She pronounced it in English. ''I think I've heard of the Jansonists. A small sect?''

''That's right. As I said, they didn't last all that long, but they were amazingly productive for a few years, anyway. They made and sold linen and brooms and bricks, and of course they farmed. One old man told me Janson got so rich he used to light his cigars with dollar bills. No idea whether it's true, but it's a good story.''

''What does this have to do with the bakery's busy season?''

''Bishop Hill celebrates some of the traditional Swedish holidays, probably more than they ever did back then. It brings in the tourists, and that's what the place mostly lives on. The Christmas market at the beginning of December, especially. And Lucia Day, a week or two later.''

''I've heard of that. Something with candles?''

''That's right. A daughter wears a crown of candles in her hair while she serves her family breakfast coffee and sweet breads. Nowadays the shops and museums have girls who wear them.''

"Real candles? In their hair?" It horrified her.

He laughed. "You should see the look on your face. Those girls don't use real ones, but that's the tradition.''

She tried to rearrange her face, but from the amused expression on his, she might as well not have bothered. "Never mind. Tell me about your mother.''

That hesitation again. "Carol says she's forgetting things. Sometimes she can't remember how to cook.'' He shook his head. "It doesn't seem possible. Mom is...was...the best cook in Henry County. Well, one of them. She and Ingrid Friberg used to fight it out at the county fair every year.''

"They didn't!"

He grinned. "No, they didn't. They were always good friends. But I'm glad I never had to be a judge at the food tent. Though back when I was about ten, I thought that would be the best job in the whole world.''

"And now Carol says she can't do it." Joan shook her head. She wished she didn't know as much as she did about what that could mean. She wasn't usually grateful that her parents had died young, but over at the adult day care she saw how hard the dementia of elderly parents could be for the whole family.

"Carol always was a worrywart." He said it lightly, but the concern showed on his face. "She's probably blown some little thing all out of proportion. Mom sounds fine when we talk on the phone.''

Fred in denial? She didn't argue. They'd know soon enough.

TWO

WHEN JOAN TOLD Andrew at breakfast, he asked to go along. Tall and thin, he was still wearing the sweats he'd slept in and probably would wear for an early morning bike ride. He obviously hadn't so much as run a comb through his dark, curly hair.

"Why would you want to go to Bishop Hill?" Fred asked.

"It sounds interesting. Besides, I've had my nose in a book all semester. And you know how dead Oliver is over the break. I don't even have exams this semester."

"How'd you manage that?" Joan said.

"Some of the profs hate 'em, too. I have to write a paper, but I don't have to stay in this dump to do it." He looked at her face. "Sorry, Mom, I don't mean this house. I'm...I just..."

Stir-crazy, that's what you are. "You just want out." And you can't swing a trip to Cancún.

"True. And I might go on into Chicago. One of my friends has been after me to visit. He knows some great places to hear live jazz."

Andrew was a good kid, she knew, and having him live at home was the only way he'd been able to afford Oliver College, even with his scholarship and lab assistant job. Joan enjoyed his company and didn't begrudge him anything. Still, this would be her first trip with her husband since their wedding in September. Who wanted her son along on her honeymoon? They'd be back in time to spend Christmas with him.

The night before, after they'd said yes to Carol, Fred had phoned and booked them into the only bed and breakfast in the village, to give them more privacy than staying with his folks. "Mom might carry on," he'd said. "But she'll survive."

"If Carol's right, she might not even notice."

"She'll notice, all right. I'll tell her it's our honeymoon. It may be as close as we get to a real one."

Joan had felt cherished.

But now Fred said, "Sure, Andrew, why don't you come?"

She could have kicked him. Don't I get a say in this? she yelled silently.

"You don't mind?" Andrew said, more to Fred than to her. She didn't usually mind that he took her for granted, but this was getting to her.

"If you don't mind driving," Fred told him, and turned to Joan. "Just on the off chance that I get called back to Oliver, it would be good to have two cars. You and I can go in mine, and Andrew can follow in yours."

She was stunned that he said it so casually, that he even could think such a thing.

"You might get called back? You'd just leave me there?" With your mother falling apart? Or do you truly not believe there's anything to that?

"It's such a remote possibility I wasn't even going to mention it. But if I don't have to uproot Mom and Dad, I can do whatever needs doing here and be back there in no time."

"I hope you're right." She fought the bite in her voice. Helping his elderly parents was one thing, but Andrew was perfectly capable of spending some time alone. "Were you planning to put Andrew up with us, too?"

Fred smiled with his eyes. "No, I had something else in mind. Andrew, would you be willing to stay in my old room? That would keep my mom happy, and she'd leave us in peace."

"Glad to."

That put a different light on it. Maybe it wasn't such a bad plan at that. If Fred has to leave me to cope with his parents, Joan thought, I might even be glad to have Andrew along.

THE DRIVE TO Bishop Hill was uneventful. From the front passenger seat of Fred's Chevy, Joan watched the hills of southern Indiana change to the flat land around Indianapolis. Then the interstate gave everything a sameness for several hours until they left it beyond Peoria to drive through farming country and little towns Fred probably knew well. There were several inches on the ground up here, with a dusting of new snow on top, though the roads were clear.

"It looks so clean." She waved at the gleaming crystals.

"The gift shops love it. And Walt's restaurant feeds the Christmas shoppers, from November on."

"You can help your folks shovel snow."

He laughed. "They won't need that kind of help. Not unless there's something Carol didn't tell me, anyway. Mom's every bit as strong as Dad, and she does a lot of the outside work."

They drove through Galva, even smaller than Oliver. Many of its houses were decorated for Christmas in everything from subdued evergreens and bows to blinking lights, plastic Santas, and Rudolphs.

"There's my school." Fred pointed. Had he gone out of

his way to show it to her? It felt like it. "Bishop Hill doesn't have a school anymore. But you'll see the old ones. The Old Colony Schoolhouse was built right after Eric Janson was killed."

A few miles out of Galva he turned north, and suddenly they were there.

"Don't blink, or you'll miss it," he said. But he slowed to a crawl. A few light flakes were falling now, as if to welcome them. "You can check out all the old buildings later."

But she already saw them, and her feet itched to explore them and the shops in some of them, with Swedish flags and banners everywhere. She was charmed by the park they faced.

"You didn't tell me about the park." With a fence of narrow, solid white pickets, it featured trees, benches, and an octagonal bandstand and gave a restful quality to the center of the village. Noticing first one tall monument and then another, she asked, "Or is it a graveyard?"

"You mean the monuments? They're historical. The cemetery is east of town." He pointed ahead to a two-story yellow frame house with American and Swedish flags flying out in front. "There's the bed and breakfast. It used to be the old hospital." He turned right, drove a long block past it, and pulled up to the last house on the left, a white house trimmed in dark green. With a low front porch and window boxes filled with evergreen boughs, it stood across from an ordinary-looking house that had a sign proclaiming it a historic site of some kind. "And this is home."

Joan thought she saw someone flick the white curtains in a front window. Then the door opened and a woman ran out, her arms wide.

"Son! Why didn't you tell me you were coming?" Taller and bigger boned than most of the little old ladies at the

Oliver Senior Citizens' Center, she might have been a blue-eyed blonde before she went white. Her hair was cropped to a smooth white crown.

Fred picked her up and hugged her. Then he set her down and turned. "Mom, this is Joan, my wife."

"Mrs. Lundquist, I'm so happy to meet you," Joan said, and watched her face light up. "Or should I call you Mother Lundquist?" She was determined to get past "hey, you" right now.

"Call me Helga!" Helga hugged Joan with arms that still had a lot of strength, and called back to the open front door, "Oscar, come meet Fred's wife!"

"Let's go inside first, okay?" Fred said.

"Where are my manners? Come in, come in." Apparently oblivious to the cold, even with only a sweater to protect her, she stood back to shoo them into the house, but it was Fred who closed the door.

Oscar Lundquist had the frazzled look of a man just waking up from a nap. He wasn't quite as big a man as Fred. His white hair was thicker, but his eyes crinkled just like Fred's. He shook Joan's hand vigorously. "Fred didn't tell me you were such a looker!"

"She is, isn't she, Dad?" Fred said, and Joan felt her face go hot.

"I heard Helga. You call me Oscar. Do I get to kiss the bride?"

Joan offered her cheek, but he greeted her full on the lips with a kiss that was oddly familiar, if a little less closely shaven around the lips.

"Welcome to the family," he said. "Son, this time I think you picked a good one."

"That's what I've been telling you." Fred smiled broadly, and Joan could see the relief in his eyes. As nervous as she'd been feeling about how they would accept her, it hadn't occurred to her that he'd be worried, too.

She took his hand. "I can't wait to meet your brother and sister."

"If Walt kisses you like that, his wife will skin him alive," Fred said.

They all laughed, and Joan was glad to see that her mother-in-law showed no such insecurity. She remembered when her first husband, a minister, had begun marrying couples, early in their own marriage.

"Will you be upset if I kiss the bride?" Ken had asked her before the first wedding at which he'd officiated.

"Not if you kiss all of them," she'd said, and meant it. It still amused her that he'd never done it.

"I'll have to go up and put clean sheets on your old bed," Helga said now. "I don't know why no one told me you were coming."

Fred exchanged a look with his father. "I thought Walt or Carol would tell you," he said. "I guess I should have called."

Joan knew he had called. So Carol was right about their mother, who might already have changed those sheets, if someone hadn't done it for her.

"You have a lovely home," she said, and meant it. The clean lines of the furniture had to be Swedish—all but an ugly skirted recliner that must be Oscar's. Swedish candlesticks and painted wooden horses on the mantelpiece proclaimed their heritage more obviously, and green plants flourished near the front windows. But the place wasn't full of knickknacks, like the houses of so many of the old people she visited in Oliver.

"Thank you," Helga said. "I try to keep it nice. Would you like to see the upstairs?"

"Oh, Mother, she doesn't want a tour of our little house," Oscar said.

Joan smiled at her. "I'd love to."

"Men don't understand," Helga said, and climbed the steep steps with apparent ease.

"But they're good to have around the house."

Helga laughed. Joan was glad to see that her sense of humor was intact.

The upstairs echoed the simplicity she'd seen downstairs. Plain wooden beds, except for the carved headboard in the master bedroom, and only slightly faded handmade quilts Rebecca would have loved—and been able to name, Joan was sure. If it wasn't a star, a nine-patch, or a double wedding ring, she herself was a little foggy about such things. Fred's old bed was indeed freshly made—Helga turned down the quilt to check it.

"Wonderful," Joan said. "My son really likes Fred. He'll get a kick out of sleeping in the bed Fred slept in when he was a boy."

"Your son? Didn't you and Fred just get married?"

Joan could see her rethinking that big kiss from Oscar. "Yes, we did. But before I met Fred, I was married to a minister, and we had a daughter, Rebecca, and a son, Andrew. Andrew is coming here today, too."

Frowning, Helga went straight to the point. "What happened to the pastor?"

"He died young."

"I'm so sorry." But she smiled broadly.

Joan smiled back. "It was a long time ago. And then Fred came along. I love him very much, Helga. I want to be a good wife to him." No point in subtlety. Besides, she meant every word. "Fred says your cooking has won prizes. I'd love to learn how to make some Swedish dishes. I hope you'll share some of your special recipes with me."

Helga beamed. "I will show you."

They went downstairs, united, to find the living room crowded with men. Andrew had arrived. Looking like a black sheep in this flock of blond Swedes, he was already involved in a lively conversation with Fred's dad and a younger man who had to be Fred's brother, another six-footer with the same stocky build, receding blond hairline and amazing blue eyes.

Fred looked up. "Mom, Joan. Come meet Andrew and Walt."

"I know Walter!" Helga said.

"Yes, but I don't," Joan told her. "And I'd like to introduce my son, Andrew. Andrew, this is Fred's mother, Helga Lundquist."

"How do you do, Mrs. Lundquist," he said, and waited for her to offer her hand, which she promptly did.

"Such a polite young man." She smiled at him. "But we're all Fred's family. You can call me Helga."

"Thank you, Helga," he said.

"You don't look a bit like your mother. Are you adopted?"

"No, ma'am. I look like my father. He died when I was little." Joan couldn't remember when he'd last called anyone "ma'am." Good job, Andrew. She was suddenly very glad he had come.

"Well," Helga said, and let it rest. Joan recognized the all-purpose reply used in awkward situations by some of the declining old folks at the adult day care program housed at the senior center. Helga had probably already forgotten about Andrew's father.

Walt didn't kiss her, but he gave Joan a quick hug and welcomed her to the family. "You ready to go to supper?"

"Supper's nowhere near ready yet," Helga said. "I haven't even started."

"That's good, Mom." Walt hugged her, too. "You're all my guests at the restaurant tonight."

"Well, now, isn't that nice?" she asked nobody in particular and went to the closet for her coat.

"I'll drop off our luggage on the way," Fred said, "and the car."

Walt claimed Joan, and they walked down the street past lighted windows toward the bed and breakfast. It would feel funny, she thought, to sleep in a hospital that was all fancied up. Fred had shown her pictures on the Web site. He'd chosen a good-sized room, he said, one big enough to spend time in if she wanted to while he was visiting his parents, "so you and Mom won't have to be on top of each other every day." She blessed his thoughtfulness.

With Andrew and the senior Lundquists lagging behind them, Joan asked Walt cautiously about his mother.

"Today's one of her good days," he said. "She might even have been able to put that supper on the table, with a little help from Dad."

"Have you had her evaluated?"

"Why bother? There's nothing they can do for it." His voice was matter-of-fact, but a muscle in his jaw gave away his feelings.

"Oh, Walt, that may not be true."

He avoided her eyes. "She'd never go."

Butt out, Joan, she told herself, but it didn't come naturally. "Tell me about your restaurant," she said. "Have you always had it?"

"Ruthie started it a few years ago," he said. "My wife. At first she was only open at noon, but business was good enough that we finally took the plunge to keep it open for dinner as well. That's when I quit my old retail job and joined her. People who spend the day in Bishop Hill shouldn't have to go somewhere else for dinner."

"Is it working out that way?"

"It's seasonal, like everything else. But we're gradually picking up some regulars who come to us for fine food all year round. Not just Swedish specialties, though of course we feature those." His voice became more lively as he talked. "And here we are."

They had turned a corner past the old hospital, where Fred's Chevy was now parked. A slender woman in a blue and gold apron hurried out of the restaurant, which only the hand-lettered LUNDQUISTS sign over the door distinguished from a house.

"I'm Ruthie," she said, and her voice was as friendly as her smile. "You must be Joan. Welcome to the family!"

Joan shook hands. "Thank you for having us."

"We're grateful to you and Fred for coming. We really were a little worried about losing Carol just now."

The others caught up to them and the greetings continued while they made their way past diners in the main part of the restaurant. Walt and Ruthie greeted most of them by name as they led the family into a private back room. There Walt seated them at a big round table with comfortable wooden chairs and real china and silver. Fresh holly filled the vase in the center of the white linen tablecloth.

Walt lit the candles on the table. "I ordered for us. I hope you don't mind."

He'd put Joan next to Fred, and Andrew across from her. An empty chair next to Andrew made Joan wonder whether someone else would be joining them, but before she could ask, the already dim lights dimmed still further, and the voices of young women singing a familiar tune filled the room. But the Swedish words were not familiar until she heard *"Sankta Lucia, Sankta Lucia."* How had a Neapolitan boat song ever traveled to Sweden?

"Look!" Andrew said.

Behind her, Joan heard a sweet young voice singing along with the piped-in music. She turned to see a very blond girl about Andrew's age in a long white robe with a red sash. She was bearing a plate of fragrant rolls and gingersnaps. It wasn't the food that had made him exclaim, she was sure, or even the girl's lovely face or singing, but the crown of lighted candles above her braids. The flames flickered only a little as she glided into the room. Joan held her breath.

No one else seemed surprised, but Walt's face shone with more than the reflected candlelight, and he led the applause when the song ended. The girl came first to Ruthie and then to each of them in turn, bending her knees and keeping her back straight to offer her plate without dripping wax on anyone. When Joan took a roll, the smell of burning wax blended with the sweet smell of the bread. But not the smell of burning hair, at least not so far.

"Thank you, Kierstin," Walt said when she had finished. "Come back and join us."

"Okay," she said. She smiled at them all and glided back out.

Joan let out her breath.

Across the table, Andrew was agog. "Is she your daughter?" he finally managed to ask.

Ruthie laughed. "She's our only chicken."

"Why was she wearing candles in her hair?"

"It's an old Swedish tradition on Lucia Day, which comes later this week. In Sweden the daughter takes breakfast in bed to her family. In Bishop Hill, though, we celebrate Lucia Nights. You'll see on Friday."

Kierstin, minus the candles and robe, came back to the table in a sweater and neat blue jeans.

"Sit there, by Andrew," her mother said. "Kierstin, meet Andrew Spencer and his mother, Joan, Uncle Fred's wife."

Kierstin nodded to them. "Andrew, Aunt Joan." Aunt Joan. It hadn't crossed Joan's mind that she might have nieces and nephews, and Fred hadn't mentioned any.

"Does that make us cousins?" Andrew asked Kierstin as she slid in between him and Oscar.

"Only by marriage. I don't think that really counts, do you?"

Andrew didn't have a chance. This girl even had dimples.

The rest of the meal was as pleasant as the beginning, if not as startling. Joan was surprised by the sweet taste of the cabbage roll with Swedish cream sauce. And the coffee with her pumpkin cheesecake reminded her of the "Swede coffee" she'd tasted in a mobile home outside Oliver.

"Do you make your coffee with egg in the grounds?" she asked.

"I didn't know you knew about Swedish cooking," Ruthie said.

"I don't. I ran into it by accident in southern Indiana."

"We Swedes get around," Oscar said. He'd been very quiet, but the food and coffee seemed to have revived him.

"Can't we go home now?" Helga asked suddenly in a loud voice.

"Sure, sweetheart," Oscar said. "Soon as I finish my coffee."

"Want me to walk you home, Mom?" Fred offered.

"No, I want Oscar." She tightened her lips and folded her arms.

"I'm right here," Oscar said. He finished the coffee, thanked Ruthie and Walt, and helped Helga slide her chair back. "Don't you all get up. We'll find our own way home."

Walt murmured, "They'll be all right," into Joan's left ear. But he stood and helped his mother into her coat.

"We're so glad you could come," Ruthie told them.

"See you tomorrow," Fred said, and then they were gone.

Walt rejoined them at the table, but the mood was broken.

"I'm sorry we didn't get to meet Carol and her husband, too," Joan said. "When do they leave?"

"First thing in the morning," Ruthie said. "We're driving them up to O'Hare." She glanced at her watch.

"Tell them to have a safe trip," Fred said. "And don't worry about Mom and Dad. You have enough on your hands."

"We won't," Walt said. "Not with you here. What could possibly go wrong?"

Never say a thing like that, Joan thought.

Andrew and Kierstin had kept their heads together throughout most of the evening. Now she told her parents she was going to walk around town with him. "You know, kind of show him the sights."

The Bishop Hill high life? Joan wondered. She hadn't seen so much as a movie theater.

"We may already be in bed when you come home—we're going to fold early," Ruthie said. "And, Kierstin, if you need anything while we're gone tomorrow, Uncle Fred and Aunt Joan will be here, and Farfar and Farmor, of course."

"Farfar…?" Joan asked.

"Swedish for father's father," Walt said.

"And Farmor is my father's mother," Kierstin told her. "People here don't speak Swedish, but we like to use a few words in the family."

"I'll take good care of her tonight," Andrew said, and she dimpled up at him.

"Don't stay out late," Ruthie reminded her. "She has to catch the school bus tomorrow," she told Andrew.

School bus? This child was younger than she looked. "What year are you, Kierstin?" Joan asked.

"I'm a senior." Thank God for small favors. "I'm planning to go to the U of I in Champaign next year."

"Let me tell you about a little school in Indiana," Andrew said in the friendliest possible way that somehow came just short of a leer.

She's in high school, Andrew! Joan thought.

This could be a long couple of weeks.

THREE

IN THE MORNING, Joan and Fred luxuriated in the knowledge that neither of them had to go to work for two whole weeks. At half past eight, lured by aromas that slipped around the edges of their door, they collected their basket of warm, fresh-baked blueberry muffins and cranberry scones and Swedish rusks from the hall table and carried it up to the second floor to breakfast by the wood stove in the upstairs common room, instead of at the gateleg table in their own spacious room, the Dr. Vannice room. All the guests' rooms were named for early settlers, their hostess had told them the night before, most of them for doctors, but two for pastors. She had shown them the porches on the back of the hospital, where long-ago patients had sunned themselves and breathed fresh air. Here and there ancient crutches, wheelchairs, and bedpans planted with green vines reminded them that the place really had been a hospital.

It wasn't as if they were a real honeymoon couple, Joan thought as she climbed the stairs to the common room, not after several months of marriage. But this morning she couldn't help being glad they had the whole place to themselves, not counting their hosts, of course, who lived on the second floor, across from the common room.

"This place will be full over the weekend," Fred said.

Joan raised her eyebrows, her mouth too full of heavenly light-buttered scone to ask why.

"Lucia Nights, remember?"

Hard to believe the quiet village she'd seen last night would be that different in a couple of days, but he ought to know.

Back in their room, the sun was pouring through the white tab curtains, and it was a pleasure to cover the bed with its double wedding ring quilt. She'd have to tell Rebecca that this one had an eight-point star in the middle of each ring. Rebecca would know whether that was unusual.

Eventually they strolled down to Helga and Oscar's and found Helga teaching Andrew to make Swedish pancakes. Must be one of her good days. Clearly, they weren't needed.

Joan could feel relief oozing out of Fred. He'd been worrying a lot more about his mother than he'd been letting on, she was sure. But pumping him about it wasn't likely to help. When he was ready, if he ever was ready, she'd hear about it. She only hoped she'd know how to respond.

He proposed a bike ride.

"Bikes?" Joan said. Could even Fred conjure up bikes in Bishop Hill?

"Mountain bikes—one of the little services the bed and breakfast provides."

"Why not, then? It's flat enough around here, and right now the roads are clear of snow." Joan looked up at the clouds overhead and sniffed the air. It had a familiar dusty smell. More snow coming.

After one circuit of the park they headed south to a museum that displayed oil paintings of the dour Swedes who had founded the place, and of rows of women planting corn and men harvesting it with scythes for the women to tie into bundles, assembly-line fashion.

"It's almost as if they'd had a photographer on the spot," Joan said, reading about Olof Krans, the artist who had documented the colony at the time.

Fred nodded. "Only a lot slower."

"Let's come back another time. I'd like to get out and just ride while we can."

And so they rode to Galva, where they stopped to thaw out and eat a leisurely lunch before turning back. A few rolling hills Joan hadn't noticed from the car proved more of a challenge than she had expected, but she managed. Nothing like southern Indiana hills, of course.

Back in Bishop Hill, Fred said, "Time to check on the folks again," and Joan agreed, already wondering how stiff she was going to be the next day. Though she walked regularly, her bicycling muscles hadn't pedaled miles like that for some time. They parked the bikes in the shed behind the old hospital. Setting off down the long block hand in hand, they saw a man running toward them from the other end. He seemed to be yelling something.

Suddenly Joan recognized Andrew. "Something must be wrong at your folks'!" She started running.

Fred passed her in a few strides.

Now she could hear Andrew's words: "Mom, Fred! Hurry!" She ran harder.

Fred reached him first and grabbed his parka. "What's wrong?"

Andrew stood panting in his grasp. "It's Helga. She's missing."

"When?"

"She was gone when Oscar woke up from his nap."

Fred dropped the parka. "When was that?" His voice was calmer now.

"After lunch, more than an hour ago. I was out poking

around some of the little shops. He hadn't gone to sleep when I left, and when I came back, he was all upset.''

"You sure she didn't just take a walk?''

"That's what Oscar thought at first, but when she didn't come back in a few minutes, we went looking for her. We've been looking ever since, but we can't find her anywhere.''

"Let's go talk to Dad,'' Fred said. When Andrew took off running, he said quietly to Joan, "It's probably going to be nothing, like the little girl in Oliver. Mom has friends all over Bishop Hill. If she ran into someone while she was out walking and went in for a cup of coffee...'' But she could hear the worry behind the words.

Joan put her arm back into his. "Does your dad panic easily?''

"He didn't used to.'' He frowned and walked faster.

Oscar met them at the door. "She's gone. My Helga's gone.'' He looked exhausted and a little shaky on his feet. Joan hugged him and kept hold of his hand, as much for physical support as for encouragement.

"Let's sit here on the sofa together, Oscar, while you tell us all about it. And, Andrew, could you make us something hot to drink? And bring something sweet to go with it?'' He was sure to know his way around the kitchen by now.

"Sure, Mom.'' He shed his jacket and disappeared.

Oscar collapsed onto the sofa. His eyes, the blue already cloudy, were moist, but she couldn't tell whether he'd been weeping or it was only the rheumy discharge of old age.

"All I did was take a nap.'' His voice rose.

"Of course you did,'' Joan said, and squeezed his hand. "Has she disappeared like this before?''

"Not for so long. Never this long.'' So it had happened more than once. Typical of so many Alzheimer's patients.

Even without a diagnosis she couldn't help thinking of Helga that way now.

"Where did you find her before?" Fred said. Joan could imagine how much it was costing him not to jump down his father's throat.

"Someone usually brings her home. She goes off without a coat, and the neighbors see her."

"Uh-huh." Joan remembered how Helga had run out to them in a sweater. "Did you look for her coat?"

"It's not here," Andrew called from the kitchen.

"Neither are her mittens, hat, and boots," Oscar said. "I looked."

"Good. That explains why no one brought her home. And it means she's not going to freeze." Not unless she's fallen out there, anyway. Joan offered Oscar her handkerchief, and he blew his nose loudly.

He pocketed the handkerchief absently. "I never thought of that."

"Did you ask her friends?" Fred said.

"Not at first." Andrew carried in a tray with steaming mugs of hot chocolate and a plate of cookies. He set it on the coffee table in front of them. "At first we just looked outdoors."

"We asked everyone we saw," Oscar said. He picked up a mug and a handful of cookies.

"Then we went in the shops, and finally we started knocking on doors," Andrew said. Sitting down, he reached for the cookies.

"Whose doors?"

Oscar rattled off a list of names that meant nothing to Joan, but Fred nodded. Old Bishop Hill people, then.

"But nobody saw her today," Oscar said.

"You didn't ask anyone you didn't know?" Joan asked. Oscar just looked at her.

Fred raised an eyebrow. "You think there's someone in Bishop Hill he doesn't know?"

Right. "So where should we look now?"

"Dad should stay home, in case she comes back while we're out."

Oscar looked relieved and seemed to sink farther into the sofa. "Don't worry, son. I'll be right here."

"Andrew, we'll get you a bike, too," Joan said. "The three of us can ride around the edges of town, in case she took a wrong turn and got lost." She hoped Fred wouldn't mind her horning in, but he didn't seem to.

They deposited their mugs on the table, took turns in the only bathroom the old house possessed, and wrapped up again. Even though the sun had finally come out, the air would be plenty cold. Oscar wasn't wrong to worry about Helga.

Hurrying back to the bed and breakfast for the bikes, Fred said, "We'll make one more good pass around town. If we don't find her this time, we'll have to call the sheriff for help. He wouldn't come if you or I had been missing for such a short time, but losing someone like Mom is like losing a child."

He's no longer in denial, Joan thought. He knows what's happening to her.

"How could she get lost in a place this small?" Andrew asked.

Fred just shook his head.

She's hurt, Joan thought. She has to be. And cold by now. Already feeling the chill, she hugged herself.

They sent Andrew toward the cemetery. "We didn't see her on the road to Galva," Fred told him. "But maybe she went to visit some of her old friends in the cemetery. Go east on Main Street and past the church. Then make a big circle. Look in all the little roads. Ask at houses, too. You know where you've already asked."

Andrew nodded and pedaled off.

"Where do you want me to go?" Joan asked.

"Stick with me. We'll go up past Mom and Dad's, check out the woods first. She used to like those woods." He shook his head. "I didn't believe Carol. Mom seems so normal most of the time."

"A lot of people do," Joan said. "And they hide it as long as they can. It's everybody's nightmare."

"But Mom? Wandering around without a coat so the neighbors bring her home?" He shook his head again. "Why didn't Carol tell me that?"

"Maybe she didn't know. Would your dad even have mentioned it if she hadn't been lost?"

"Stubborn old man."

"He was trying to protect her. People don't want to lose control—have their children take over."

He just shook his head.

They parked the bikes outside the Lundquists' house and crossed the road toward the snowy open field with the wooded ravine behind it. Joan blessed her good boots. She'd need them down in that ravine.

"No one's gone through the fence recently," she said. The snow in the field was obviously untouched, its top crystals glistening in the sunlight.

"But look up there!" A few yards ahead, the snow beside the road was churned up.

Joan could see easily where someone had waded from the road to the fence and along the fence line down into the woods.

Fred reached the spot first, but waited for her. "Can't see any footprints—it's a mess. And watch yourself. It's tricky walking in here."

He was right. Not only the snow, but things hidden under it made the going rough. Following him, Joan struggled forward past the fence and down the steep hill into the ravine. After tripping and picking herself up more than once, she slowed down and managed to keep her footing. Then she heard a faint sound off to the right and forgot all caution.

"Where are you going?" Fred yelled.

Breaking through drifted and crusted snow, with bare branches whipping her face, Joan called back, "She's hurt. Can't you hear her?" She stood still. Now the crying was unmistakable.

"Mom!" Fred called. "Mom, is that you?" They listened together. The crying had stopped. He raised his hands to his mouth and shouted. "Mom, it's Fred!" Now he looked and sounded as worried as Joan was sure he felt.

The crying started up again, louder this time, beyond some thick underbrush.

Joan was almost on top of her before she spotted her, curled up into a ball with her back to them, shivering and sobbing. She had burrowed into a kind of nest in the deep brush. Her brown coat and knitted hat blended with the brown twigs, like a deer hiding in the forest. In fact, looking at the spot she had chosen, Joan was sure that deer had used it first. A deer trail, which Helga's tracks had joined, led right past it. It would have given her an easier time than plowing through the woods herself.

"Helga!" Joan knelt down and reached out to her. "Oh, Helga! Are you all right?"

"No!" Helga wailed. "Fred's dead! He killed him! I saw it!" And she wouldn't budge.

Poor baby. I didn't think she was that far gone. Joan stroked her back and exchanged concerned glances with Fred.

He squatted down beside them and spoke softly. "I'm right here, Mom, see? I'm all right. Nobody killed me."

Helga finally turned, and now Joan could see congealed blood in the scratches on her contorted face. "Helga, you're hurt!"

Helga didn't seem to notice. "He killed Fred!" she wailed again, and rocked back and forth in the snow. Then she whispered, "Come in here. Keep quiet so he won't kill you, too."

"It's all right," Joan told her. "He's gone now. You're safe." She hoped she was telling the truth. But what was she thinking? There was no one here but the three of them.

"See, Mom? I'm fine," Fred said. "Let's take you home. Dad's worried about you. He thinks you got lost."

"Dad?" She looked around vaguely. "Dad's here?"

Joan wondered whether she was thinking of her own father. "Oscar's at home," she told her. "Oscar misses you."

"Well." Helga crawled out of the bushes and stood up. "I have to go home now. It's time to fix Oscar his supper."

Suddenly all business, she brushed the snow off her knees with red mittens, snowflakes knitted into the backs. Fred crooked his arm, and she took it as if he were escorting her on a date.

They walked her out of the woods the way they had come in, both ready to support her if she fell, but she had less trouble than Joan. Fred must be right, Joan thought—she must come into these woods often, as close as they are to the house. Does that mean this kind of thing is going to keep happening? How can we protect her if she's going to wander? And what really happened today, to terrify her like that? What did she see? Why did she think Fred was dead?

FOUR

WONDERFUL ODORS met them at the door—yeast and cin
namon and some spice she couldn't identify. Oscar mus
have recovered enough to bake something. Maybe that'
what he did when he was really upset.

He greeted them with mingled joy and concern. "Wher
were you?" he scolded Helga. "And what happened to
your face?"

"My face?" She reached up to the bloody scratches
"I'll wash it off, and then I'll make you supper." She
turned to Joan. "That man! Always hungry."

"Let me help you," Joan said, and followed her up to
the bathroom. With most of the blood washed off, the
scratches weren't as bad as they had looked in the woods
but Helga winced and clearly wouldn't have cleaned them
out on her own. After letting Joan smear on a little antibi
otic ointment, she put her foot down at anything more.

"I don't have time for this," she said. "I have to cool
supper."

A few of those scratches might bleed a little more, Joan
thought, but you'll do.

When they went back downstairs, Andrew had arrived
The three men had their heads together, and Joan could see
that Andrew was eager to take off with Fred. No fair, guys
she thought. You're not leaving me here to mama-sit. Os-

car's wide awake now, and Helga's too busy to take off again. Besides, Andrew's turning into a good cook.

"Andrew, good you're here. Could you help Helga and Oscar get supper ready? I want to go back out to the woods with Fred before the light's gone." It was already four o'clock, and December sunset came early here, so near the eastern edge of the Central time zone.

He gave her a put-upon look she didn't blame him for, but didn't fight it.

"You play dirty," Fred said when they were outside again.

She grinned. "I did, didn't I? But whatever your mother thought she saw, she was sure you were dead. I need to be out here with you. Andrew can't protect you the way I can."

He laughed, as she had meant him to do, but then all humor left his face. "We don't know what we're getting into." He looked into her eyes. "Promise me you'll be careful. If I say jump, I need to know you'll jump."

She nodded. "Of course. But you're not expecting trouble, are you?"

"No. She probably imagined the whole thing. Even if she did see anybody, he's long gone, after all the noise we made getting Mom out."

"Still…"

"Exactly."

No longer so worried about his mother, they followed the tracks that had led them down into the ravine. This time they stuck with the tracks past where Joan had veered off the first time, when she'd heard Helga crying. Fred walked deliberately and paused frequently. Joan, following in his footsteps, tried to see what he was looking at, but it all looked the same to her—mostly undisturbed snow on the ground, snow on the tree trunks and branches, occasional footprints of birds and small animals—nothing to suggest why Helga had panicked. No deer along here.

The air was crisp and clear, the sun low in the western sky, and the temperature dropping. If it weren't for their concern about Helga's confusion, this could be pure delight, to be out walking in the snowy woods with the man she loved.

Now, for the first time, she thought she saw another set of tracks mixed with Helga's. And more of those tracks coming down from a spot she'd seen up by the road, with a sign that gave permission to burn leaves and brush only to local residents. Mostly they were a blur of someone slogging through the snow that had drifted in the ravine, not clear footprints. But they looked wider than Helga's.

"See those?" Joan said, pointing. The raking light made deep shadows inside the tracks. But it gave little warmth, and her bones felt the cold.

Fred nodded.

The new tracks joined the old ones, or was it the other way around? Had Helga seen this person come into the woods and gone in after him? Or her, of course. But she'd talked about a man, and she thought he'd killed Fred. Were there two men? Or just footprints from which Helga had imagined the men and the rest of it?

"You know, don't you, that people…" she didn't want to say "people with Alzheimer's," but didn't know how to go on. "That people tend to confabulate stories out of very little."

Fred pointed to the tracks. "You think Mom confabulated these into a man killing me?"

"Something like that."

The trees opened into a clearing, and suddenly Fred stopped and put his arm out.

Joan peered around him and gasped. Now she knew what

had upset Helga, and it wasn't confabulation. The man crumpled in the middle of the snow did resemble Fred, or might have, if he'd still had a face. He looked to be about the same size, for one thing, and his blond hairline was beginning to recede. Beyond that, it was impossible to tell.

The trampled snow nearest to him looked as if it had turned into red slush and then frozen again. She had no doubt where the red had come from, though she couldn't see the weapon that must have done the damage. Or could she? She spotted what had to be blood on some branches and one baseball-sized rock. How long had it been there?

Could he possibly still be alive? She couldn't see how.

She didn't need Fred to tell her to stay back, but noticed that he walked carefully around the bloodstained wood and rock to kneel and check the pulse at the man's neck. Shaking his head, he stood up and returned in his own footsteps. The pulse in Fred's neck was pounding so hard that Joan could see the beats when he stood beside her again.

"I didn't expect to find anything here at all," he said. "I guess Mom's not as mixed up as she seems."

"You can see where she went off toward where we found her," Joan said. "You think the killer went after her?" She was itching to find out. Anything to keep her eyes from being drawn to that bloody pulp that once had been a face. Who in little Bishop Hill could do such a thing?

"Maybe," Fred said, but he stayed put. "He didn't go anywhere else unless he went back where he came from. No other tracks out of this clearing."

Except the ones we're on, she thought.

"If she was right about this, maybe she was right that he was after her." The moment the words were out of her mouth, she regretted them.

"Yeah." His lips were tight. "I want you to go back to

the house and call the sheriff—just dial 911. I left my cell phone in our room.''

"You're not coming?''

"I'll walk you up to where I can see the road. Then I'll come back here to protect the crime scene.''

He was right, she knew, but she hated the idea of leaving him there. They started off together, following their own tracks back until they could see both the road and the clearing through the leafless trees.

"I'll watch you to the road from here,'' Fred said.

"Maybe I'd better call from the bed and breakfast,'' she said. "If I have to describe the scene, it might set your mom off again.''

"Good. Then come back as far as the house and wait for them. You can show them where we went in.''

"Where should I tell them to come?''

"To the ravine on the north edge of town, across the road from the old Janson house.'' This time he said it with a *J*. Probably the sheriff would, too. "That's the house across from ours, on Olson Street. I don't remember the name of the other road—we didn't use to have street signs in Bishop Hill. But he'll know.''

"Got it.''

"And try not to make any new tracks. When they arrive, lead them in the same way we came.''

As if you needed to tell me that. "Right.'' She reached up and hugged him, hard. "I'm so glad it wasn't you.''

"No gladder than I am.''

She wondered. That poor man was out of his misery. Joan, on the other hand, knew the pain of surviving the death of one life partner. She had coped, but she couldn't imagine having to deal with this kind of horror. Her heart went out to whatever poor woman cared about the dead man.

"Hurry!"

She hurried the best she could on feet numb from the cold that had seeped through her boots, all the time hating every step she took away from him. What if the killer came back? Ordinarily, Fred could take care of himself. But the man dead in the snow looked plenty strong, and it hadn't helped him against a brutality that was hard to imagine in this peaceful setting.

Unable to keep from worrying, Joan struggled on. The last bit was the easiest, because not only Helga, but she and Fred had already made a path in the snow on their way into and out of the woods. Once on the road, she turned and waved back to him. Then she ran to the Lundquists' yard, grabbed her bike, and rode furiously back to the old colony hospital. Glad not to see anyone, she felt safe using the phone in the hall outside their room, rather than messing with Fred's cell phone. Panting, she punched 911.

"911 emergency," a pleasant woman's voice answered.

"I want to report a murder."

FIVE

RESISTING THE TEMPTATION to pace, Fred leaned against a tree and looked down at the crumpled body. That's all the sheriff would need, him fouling up the evidence. Male Caucasian—could be a Swede, especially considering where he was found—about six feet, stocky build, beginning to bald, small earlobes, face unrecognizable. Might have been Walt, except for those earlobes. Sheepskin jacket, covered in blood, a suede glove on the hand flung out to one side. No hat, unless it was under him.

Let's hope he's carrying identification. Hate to have to ask anyone to ID him. Better the sheriff than me.

Bloody branches and rocks frozen into the snow suggested that the killer had picked up weapons where he'd found them. With the cold, the blood hadn't lost its bright red color as it would have in summer.

Without moving closer, Fred studied the tracks leading away from the scene. His and Joan's led off to the south, not that he could distinguish individual footprints there. But he thought he recognized his mother's on one side. And a man's large boot on the other. So he had been following her, or maybe just her tracks. Had he seen her? In either case, why hadn't he caught up to her? Maybe he'd followed the deer trail past her spot. If she'd stayed quiet enough, she would have been almost invisible.

Till we scared him off.

It was possible. Hard to believe the man who did that kind of damage had left so easily.

But if the killer knows what she looks like, what's to keep him from coming after her?

For the moment, she'd be safe in her own house, surrounded by potential witnesses. Until that fiend was caught, they wouldn't dare leave her alone.

He heard sirens in the distance. That was quick. Maybe they came from Galva. The flashing lights stopped at the top of the hill. They'd pulled up at the Bishop Hill burn site at the top of the ravine, where piles of branches and yard waste were stacked to burn. It made a handy flat spot where they could avoid blocking the road. All the vehicles would attract the locals and maybe even a few early tourists. He hoped they would leave someone up there to keep the gawkers at bay. More sirens.

Joan and the EMTs arrived first. She stepped to one side at the edge of the clearing while the EMTs ran forward, checked the body for signs of life, and shook their heads. Then they, too, waited at the edge of the clearing.

Right behind them was a young woman, well bundled against the cold. "Kate Buker, deputy sheriff," she said when she reached him. Up close, he guessed her to be about thirty, neither heavy nor slender, though it was hard to tell through her padded uniform jacket. Probably all muscles. Her voice sounded younger than she looked, or probably wanted to sound. There were advantages to a low voice when you wanted someone to take you seriously.

"Fred Lundquist," he said, resisting the temptation to pull rank. He had no standing here, miles from Indiana, much less Oliver.

"Related to the restaurant Lundquist?" She didn't smile.

"My brother."

"You look like him." She looked at the body on the

other side of the clearing. "And a lot like this guy. You related to him, too?"

"No."

"You were with her when she found him?" She jerked her head at Joan.

"Yes."

She sighed. "You walked around a lot, I see."

"No, ma'am," Fred said. "It was like that when we arrived, and already frozen. I checked his pulse and came straight back here."

"What else did you disturb?" Hands on her hips, one resting on her gun belt.

Cold and worried again about his mother, he suddenly lost patience. "Not a damn thing. Didn't even unbutton his coat. I only stayed to preserve the crime scene." He pulled his badge out of his pocket and passed it to her.

"Sorry, Lieutenant," she said, and handed it back. "I appreciate what you've done. But we'll take it from here."

"Sheriff too busy?" he asked mildly.

"Out of town. Family emergency."

"I should tell you—"

"I said we'd handle it." She glared at him.

"We...there may be an eyewitness."

The glare turned to a glower. "You let an eyewitness leave the scene?"

"My mother. She's at home, just across the road. She's an old lady, Deputy Buker. And her mind is failing." He couldn't fool himself about that anymore.

"What did she tell you?"

"She said she saw a man kill me."

Her eyebrows rose.

"When we found her, she was hiding from him, terrified. She kept saying it even after she saw me alive. We didn't take her seriously, but we came back to look around, maybe see what had frightened her. This is what we found."

"And you think he saw her?"

"It's possible. I didn't follow her tracks, because I didn't want to destroy evidence, but if you look over there, you can see where she went." He pointed. "We found her hiding in some bushes down the ravine from here, along a deer trail. Best I can see from here, a man's boots followed her. Unless it was the other way around. I couldn't tell."

Kate Buker nodded slowly. "You asking for protection?" Fred couldn't tell whether she still had her back up or was just finding out what she was up against.

"We won't leave her alone. But I couldn't bring a gun into Illinois."

"I'm sure we can do something. Given the circumstances."

Her back was settling down. Good. "Thanks," he said. "All right if we go to her now?"

"Sure. Which house is it?"

"White house across from the old Janson house."

"Thanks, Lieutenant. A sheriff's investigator will want to talk to you later, and to your mother."

Joan had stood silent throughout the whole exchange. He took her mittened hand and helped her make her way up the hill. The sun was setting. Soon the flashers would be joined by powerful lights to illuminate the clearing while the crime scene people searched for evidence. They hadn't arrived yet, but already he heard more sirens in the distance. Up at the burn site, the crowd was gathering, drawn by the sirens and lights. More deputies were ordering them back.

A few flakes of snow had begun to fall. If they amounted to anything, they would obscure the tracks. Not his problem, he told himself. When they reached the house, though, he wasn't ready to face the family. He picked up the bike he had left there. "Where's yours?" he asked Joan.

"I left it at the bed and breakfast."

"Good. I'll walk mine back."

"I'll come along."

He steered with one hand and put the other arm around her, glad to feel her body against his, even through all the layers. Her cheeks and nose were red, and her eyes sparkled with the snowflakes landing on her lashes, but she was no longer shivering, as she had been while Deputy Buker was giving him the once-over.

"Remind me to treat witnesses better than that," he said.

"You wouldn't act like that. Not to a friendly witness."

"I probably have, especially when I was in over my head."

"You think that's her problem?"

"Could be. She's young." He tried not to think of some of his own youthful insecurities.

"You can be intimidating, you know," Joan said, not looking intimidated.

"It's useful at times."

"Try not to use it when the investigator comes."

"Yes, ma'am." Although he was teasing her, he knew she was right about that. For his mother's sake, he needed to get the sheriff's investigator firmly on their side.

SIX

CHILLED CLEAR THROUGH now, Joan was glad to reach the warm house. Inside, the yeasty fragrance of whatever Oscar had been baking still lingered. But now it blended with spicy vegetable smells and a steaminess that she hoped meant hot soup. She stripped off her coat, mittens, and boots and wished for a fireplace. Even Fred was blowing on his fingers.

Helga hurried out of the kitchen. "Go wash your hands, everybody. Supper's ready!"

Joan wasn't surprised to see Andrew leave the kitchen and follow Fred upstairs. She knew he'd want to pump Fred about what they had found. They left Oscar snoring gently in his big recliner. Following Helga back into the kitchen to soak her hands in warm water at the sink, Joan asked her, "Want me to wake Oscar up?"

"That man! He'd sleep right through supper if we let him." Helga's cheeks were bright. With a houseful of family to feed, she was in her element, almost as if nothing had happened to her.

Joan dried her hands on her jeans and went back to the living room. "Oscar? Oscar, suppertime."

He jerked. "I'm awake. Just closed my eyes for a minute."

The way he did when Helga took off, Joan thought.

They sat down together at the round table, as Fred must

have sat there with his parents and brother and sister when he was growing up.

Oscar, sitting by Helga, reached out his hands, and they held hands around the table. *"I Jesus namn till bords vi ga, välsigna gud den mat vi fa,"* he prayed, and smiled broadly. "Joan, that means, 'In Jesus's name to the table we go, God's blessings on the food we have.'" Then he served up the soup in big, flat bowls with stiff Swedish horses painted on the rim while Andrew, next to Joan, started Oscar's fresh bread and butter around the table.

"This is heaven!" Joan said. "I was so cold out there."

"Oh?" Helga said. "Where did you go?"

"To the woods," Fred told her. "With me."

Helga's face clouded over. "But...but you're dead! I saw him kill you!" She grabbed Oscar's arm. "He killed our boy!" Tears welled up in her eyes. "It was awful!"

"No, Mom," Fred said, and took her other hand. "He didn't kill me. I'm right here, see? I'm fine. But you did see someone. Someone else."

Good, Joan thought. He's getting her ready for the investigator. And he's being careful not to put words in her mouth. He's a good cop.

"Someone else got killed? You sure?"

"I'm sure."

"Oh, that poor man." But even as she said it, Helga was dredging up a smile.

"Yes, Mom."

"Well, then, eat some more soup."

"You'll be a star witness, Helga," Andrew said. "Everyone will want to ask you all about it."

He was too far away to kick under the table. Helga doesn't need that, Joan telegraphed with a frown and a tiny shake of her head. He subsided.

Helga looked confused for a moment, but she didn't respond, and they made it through supper without upsetting her again. Catastrophic reactions were all too common when Alzheimer's patients experienced too much stress. For Helga's sake, and for her family's sake, they were worth avoiding.

Joan watched her confusion increase while helping her with the dishes and thought, she's fading fast. Like last night. The director of the adult day care in Oliver called it sundowning, and it fit, as if the light had gone out of her. It was hard to imagine her being much help to the investigator now.

The knock, when it came, startled Joan more than it did Helga. She heard Fred go to the door.

"Deputy Buker," he said. "Come in."

"And this is Greg Peterson, the sheriff's investigator," said the voice of the young woman who had bearded Fred in the woods.

"May I speak to your mother?" asked a much deeper, male voice. Joan hoped it wouldn't frighten Helga. For the moment, though, washing the last of the dishes by hand, she seemed oblivious to what was happening in the living room.

"Yes, of course," Fred said. "But I don't know how much she'll be able to help you."

"She might. It looks as if she did see it, and whether he saw her or not, the killer did follow her. We tracked them out of that clearing and found some places where his footprints were clearly on top of hers. But he followed the deer path past her. She must have stayed very still. I'll try not to upset her, but I have to ask her a few questions."

"I'll get her," Fred said.

"There's someone here to see you," Joan told Helga. "Let's go in the living room."

Fred stuck his head in the kitchen door. "Mom, you have company."

"But…" Helga's voice trailed off as she looked at the dishes Joan had dried.

"We'll come back and put them away."

"All right, then."

Fred went back into the living room. But Helga dried her own soapy hands on the dish towel, emptied the sink, and wiped it dry with the towel before she would follow. Checking her appearance in the little mirror beside the kitchen door, she patted down her short white hair and smoothed it back over her ears. Her color was high from standing over the hot dishwater, but as far as Joan could tell, she never bothered with makeup even when it wasn't.

Joan waited with her. It was faster, she was sure, than trying to rush her.

"Mom?" Fred called.

"I'm coming." Helga moved slowly now, not like the brisk woman who had climbed out of the woods to feed Oscar his supper.

The interview was mercifully brief. After preliminary introductions, during which Helga's hostess sense seemed to revive and sustain her, they all sat down. Greg Peterson, a big bear of a man wearing a brown tweed suit, not a uniform, filled an upholstered chair. His face seemed gentle. Joan hoped he really would be. He looked to be about her own age, in his early forties, younger than Fred, but with several years on the deputy, who found a straight chair near the door. Oscar leaned back in his big chair, and Andrew straddled one from the dining room.

Looking at Peterson rather than at Helga, Joan said quietly, as if she were making pleasant conversation, "Short and direct works best." She hoped he would understand.

Peterson nodded, his brown eyes warm. "I have a grand-nother.'' He turned to Helga and spoke softly. ''Mrs. Lundquist, I hear you went to the woods today.''

Helga looked surprised. ''I did?''

''We all did, Mom, remember?'' Fred said.

''If you say so.'' She smiled at Peterson, but her eyebrows made an uncertain peak.

''Did something there scare you?''

The gentle question erased Helga's uncertainty. Her eyes filled up. ''Oh! Oh! He killed Fred! He killed my boy! It was awful!'' She turned to Fred. ''He killed you!''

This time he didn't try to correct or comfort her.

''You say 'he,''' Peterson said. ''Was it a man?''

''Yes, a big man. He killed him!'' Tears streaming now, she rocked forward and back.

''We want to catch that man,'' Peterson said. ''You say he's big. That helps us. What kind of big? Tall? Fat?''

''He was big.'' She kept rocking. ''With a big coat. He just kept hitting him.''

''What did he look like? Was he white or black?''

Helga only shook her head.

''Will you know him if you see him again? We won't let him hurt you, I promise.''

She kept shaking her head, but Joan couldn't tell whether it was a ''no'' this time or just distress.

''He killed my boy!''

Peterson shook his head, too. His eyes mirrored Helga's distress, but his voice was calm. ''Thank you, Mrs. Lundquist. I'm sorry I upset you.''

Now Fred spoke. ''Mom, it's all right. Here I am. The man killed someone else, not me.''

''He did?'' Her mouth quivered, and so did her voice.

''Yes.''

''You're all right?''

''I'm just fine.''

She still looked troubled.

"Your son is right," Peterson said. "The man who die was a serviceman." He turned to Fred. "Wearing dog tag that matched the ID in his wallet. No local address in hi wallet, but we'll get one from the military, if he has one Name's Gustaf Friberg."

Oscar came to life, thudding the recliner up so hard th ruffles wobbled. "Gus Friberg's dead?"

"Yes, sir. You know him?" Peterson looked hopeful.

No wonder, Joan thought. It sounded as if Oscar wa going to save him lots of time.

"I didn't even know he was home."

"The Fribergs are our neighbors," Fred said. "Gus i their youngest child. Must be in his forties by now. He's career Army man. Has a couple of older sisters."

"Their names?" Peterson whipped out a notebook an pen. If he'd been from Bishop Hill, he would have know them, Joan was sure.

"Hanna York and Christina Swanson. The parents ar Nels and Ingrid. They live just down the road—the parents not the daughters." He pointed. "In the first house past th dead-end sign—the one on the left."

"We were there today!" Andrew said.

"Doing what?" Peterson looked hard at him.

"Looking…looking for Helga." He lowered his voic just in time. He was catching on. "But Mrs. Friberg hadn' seen her."

"Ingrid and Helga are good friends," Oscar said. "She' going to take this hard."

"Ingrid? What's the matter with Ingrid?" Helga de manded, but with less agitation than when she believed Fre was dead. Joan hoped that belief would fade with time "Why doesn't anyone tell me anything?"

"Ingrid's all right," Oscar said. "It's her boy, Gus."

"I know Gus. A sweet boy."

"Yes," Fred said, and stopped.

Good, Joan thought. Don't tell her. She's had enough.

"Have you notified them?" Fred asked Peterson.

"I didn't know where to find them. I'll notify them now." He looked as if he were dreading it. He looked exhausted, too. Probably cold and hungry. Joan wished they hadn't put all the leftovers away.

"Want me to come along?" Fred offered.

"Thanks, we can do it." He nodded at Buker. "You happen to know anyone close to them?"

"The girls," Fred said. "But you'll have to ask Ingrid and Nels where they are."

"I expect we're as close as anyone," Oscar said. "We'd better go over."

"By tomorrow the whole town will be there," Fred said. "But we can stay tonight until the girls show up."

"That's good," Peterson said. "Give us a few minutes with the parents first. I'll need to ask someone in the family to ID the body. He had a surgical scar that might help."

"On his right wrist?" Fred said.

"Yes. You know something about that?"

"Then it's Gus. Gutsy kid. He fell during a junior high track meet and smashed it. They had to go in there and piece it back together. He ran the rest of the season with a long-arm cast."

"Thank you. I hate to put his folks through any more than I have to." Peterson stood up. Fred and Oscar got to their feet, as did Andrew, who had sat silent since he arrived. "I'm sorry to bring you such bad news. I know this is going to hit you all hard." He turned to Fred. "Be sure to keep a close eye on your mother. The man who did this may not know how little she can tell us."

"He won't think she can tell you anything if he didn't

see her and if you don't tell anyone she was there,'' Fred said.

A big if, Joan thought. She'd managed to hide, but had he seen her well enough to recognize her?

"Don't count on it,'' Peterson said. "He might already know who she is. But I'll do everything I can to help. And we'll have a deputy nearby, watching. Deputy Buker here will be the first.''

"I'm glad to do it,'' Buker said, and actually smiled.

Joan was inclined to believe her. It was hard to recognize this pleasant woman as the insecure deputy who had raked Fred over the coals.

"Thank you for your time, Mrs. Lundquist,'' she told Helga now.

"Come again when you can stay longer.'' Helga smiled as if they'd come over for coffee. As soon as Oscar closed the door, she asked him, "Who were those people?''

"The sheriff's people,'' he said. "They say Gus Friberg is dead.''

"Gus? Oh, no! Gus was such a sweet little boy.'' She didn't ask what had happened to him. "We need to go see his mama. Now let me see, what can I take over to her?'' She hurried back into the kitchen.

Oscar followed her. "I'll help her. You stay with your folks,'' he told Andrew on the way out. "You did more than your share today.''

"Yeah,'' Andrew said. He winked at Fred. No wonder he and Fred were such a pair. Fred had never had a son, and Andrew hadn't had a father for so many years. They were both making up for lost time.

"Sit down a minute,'' Fred said. Andrew sat back down, and Fred lowered his voice. "I'm sure you got the gist of it. A man who grew up just down the road was brutally murdered this afternoon, and it seems that my mom saw it happen. If not, she at least found the body.''

Joan shuddered, seeing what was left of that face again. "That would be enough.''

Fred squeezed her hand. "Yes. And we're not sure whether the killer knows who she is or what she saw. If he knows she saw him, she could be in real danger.''

"She can't tell us anything about him,'' Andrew said.

"But Peterson is right,'' Joan said. "He doesn't know that.''

"If he knows her, he does.''

"Maybe not even then. People can be out of it one day and clear the next. It can change from moment to moment. Besides, she still has good social manners. I don't know how much people in Bishop Hill can tell.''

"Oscar says people bring her home when she goes out without a coat.''

"You're right,'' Joan said. "I forgot that. Still, the killer might not know her at all, and even if he does, he can't count on her not letting something slip. She did tell us she'd seen a murder.''

"We'll have to watch her,'' Fred said.

"We could take her back home with us,'' Joan said slowly. She wondered how she'd cope with all five of them in her little house. "But it might be hard on her.'' Not to mention me.

Andrew, for all he was a good kid, left things where they fell, and privacy was hard to come by even without in-laws. She'd heard of the sandwich generation. With Andrew in the house and Helga confused after a long trip, she thought she'd feel like squashed peanut butter and jelly.

"I don't think she's in much danger in the middle of Bishop Hill,'' Fred said.

The way Gus wasn't? Joan thought.

"Not if she's surrounded by people, anyway," Fred said. "I don't think we can count on Dad to stay awake, but the three of us can keep her surrounded. And keep her at home or in public places."

"She wants to go to their house tonight," Andrew said.

"Trust me, the minute the news gets around, the Fribergs' house will be a very public place. And in Bishop Hill, a squad car outside it will spread the word faster than you can imagine. You'll see. We may not even be the first people to arrive."

"But what's to keep him from breaking in here and killing her in her sleep?" Joan couldn't help it.

"I'll be here," Andrew said.

"Sure," she said. "Sound asleep." Fred would want to sleep upstairs, and how could she say no? Good-bye to the honeymoon retreat. They couldn't risk it.

"I'm a night owl, you know that," Andrew said. "I'll listen."

Fred looked at him. "How late can you stay awake?"

"I pull all-nighters when I have to." He said it matter-of-factly. Joan tried to remember the last time she'd managed to stay awake all night, but couldn't.

Fred leaned forward. "Are you willing to sit up after Mom and Dad go to bed? I'll come relieve you about four."

Andrew shrugged. "Six would do, if I can sleep till noon once I crash."

"Five, then. Mom will be awake by six, and she'll worry if she sees your bed wasn't slept in. But she won't think anything of it if I show up early for breakfast."

Andrew ran his fingers through his hair. "I'll go up to bed when they do. Put my pajamas on, mess up the bed, and come back down here until you show."

Is this my child? "Thank you, Andrew," Joan said.

"Sure, Mom."

"And if there's any trouble—if you spot anything at all, you call 911 immediately," Fred said. "They promise to have a deputy close, so you won't have to wait for help. Then call me."

SEVEN

FRED DREADED introducing Joan to old friends in Bishop Hill during the kind of visit they were about to have. Holding her coat for her, he dropped a kiss on her hair.

"You all right?" she asked, as if she could read his mind.

"Not my favorite activity, but I'll live. I'm glad you're here."

"I'm such an outsider. I hate to horn in at a time like this."

"You're my wife."

"Yes." Her smile melted him.

"You two lovebirds about ready?" his dad asked.

"Just about," Fred said. "There's something we all need to talk about, though, and it's important."

"What's important?" his mom asked.

"You know we're going to see the Fribergs."

"Their boy Gus died," she said. "We're taking over some of Dad's fresh rolls."

"That's right. So let's not worry them with anything that happened to us." He was pussyfooting around it, not wanting to put into her head the very things he hoped she could forget to talk about.

"You don't need to tell your mother how to act!" She looked hurt.

"I'm sorry, Mom." He couldn't push her any further, or he'd provoke the very reaction he was hoping to avoid.

"Did you know Gus?" she asked Joan.

"No, I didn't."

"That's too bad. He was a sweet boy."

"You're good friends with his mother, aren't you?" Joan asked her. "Tell me about her on the way over." They set out arm in arm.

Mom's walking confidently, Fred thought. She still knows her way to Ingrid's, at least. His dad followed a step or two behind her, carrying his rolls and a flashlight and shining the beam on her path.

"Come on, Andrew," Fred said. "You might as well. They met you this afternoon."

"Okay." Andrew grabbed his jacket and closed the door behind him.

At the last minute Fred went back and locked it. Then he set off with Andrew, down the dead-end road. The Fribergs lived on the south side of the road, directly behind the Lundquists, but with a field separating them. The dogs across the road started barking before his mom and Joan passed their house. They must be downwind.

He recognized the sheriff's car outside their big house, but its lights weren't flashing. All the obvious activity was still up the road to the east, at the burn site and in the ravine. They were showing respect for the family's feelings. He liked that.

He and Joan stood back while his father rang the doorbell. Peterson opened the door. "I'm glad you're here," he said. "They're taking it pretty hard."

White haired and stony faced, Nels and Ingrid sat side by side in two chairs that matched their sofa. Fred couldn't ever remember seeing them sit in those chairs together. Like his mom, Ingrid Friberg had always seemed to be cooking something. When she sat down, it was usually with a lap full of peas to shell or beans to snap. Nels hadn't spent a lot of time just sitting, either. A house painter all his working days, he'd been more likely to repaint a room in his own house than to take his ease in it. Even now, the long arms sticking out of his shirtsleeves showed wiry muscles that had to have come from all those years of brushing paint on walls and woodwork. The walls around him looked clean, as if he'd kept painting even in retirement.

Tonight they both looked old and defeated, and their big Swedish bodies seemed to have shrunk. Fred wondered how they had looked an hour earlier, before they'd heard about Gus. It was so long since he'd seen them—did they always look so old these days? Ingrid's eyes were swollen, and her arthritic hands, swollen in a different way, twisted a large white handkerchief, probably one of Nels's. The lines in Nels's face looked as if he'd never smile again.

They stood slowly when Fred's parents went over to them. His dad and Nels shook hands, and his mom embraced Ingrid as if they were sisters. In many ways they were. Ingrid was only a few years younger, and they had mothered each other's children. Almost the same size, they looked like sisters, but Ingrid's timid spirit had never been a match for his mom's toughness. What would this blow do to her?

"He was so young!" Ingrid cried, and then wept on his mom's shoulder, not bothering with the handkerchief.

"Such a sweet boy," Fred's mother said. She probably thought it was the first time she'd said it. How did his dad stand it, day after day? She stood shoulder to shoulder with Ingrid, holding her left hand. Fred introduced Joan and Andrew, and Ingrid made no attempt to free that hand while she shook hands with her right.

"You were here this afternoon," Ingrid said to Andrew.

"Yes," he said. "Looking for Helga."

Fred didn't think his mother even noticed. She seemed to tune in and out of conversation.

Ingrid smiled at him through her tears. "I'm glad you found her. I need her tonight."

"Are your girls coming?" Fred asked.

"Yes. The sheriff's people had to tell them," and she nodded at Peterson and Buker, standing quietly near the door. "I couldn't."

Fred turned to Joan. "Hanna's just a little younger than I am. She married a guy a year behind me in school, Tim York. They have a hog farm over by Galva. Christina, the younger girl, married Bengt Swanson, a fellow from Kewanee—from Wethersfield, actually. They live there. Bengt sells cars south of town."

"Used cars," Nels said. Almost snapped. Fred couldn't tell whether it was a criticism or just all he could make himself say at the moment.

"Gus was my baby," Ingrid said, and her voice broke on "baby."

"There, there, Mother." Nels patted her shoulder awkwardly.

Fred's mom embraced her again. "You just cry it out."

She did—no question who was giving her more comfort. Fred hoped her daughters could do as well as his mother. From what he remembered of them, he doubted their husbands would be any more use than their father. Tim, Hanna's husband, had excelled in Future Farmers. Always won prizes for his hogs in 4-H. He did the hardest work himself—you had to give him that. He had a crooked grin that attracted the girls, but he had a cold streak too. Fred had never forgotten the day Tim had bragged to the guys at school about helping his father castrate dozens of pigs, one after the other. He'd had to help, Fred was sure. But the way he told it, glorying in the details and watching all those guys squirm—he wasn't just going on about a hard day's work.

Fred didn't know Bengt as well, but he'd never seen anything to suggest that he would reach out to anyone, except maybe Christina in bed. Handsome as a young man, Bengt had played high school football for Wethersfield against Galva, and the girls had crowded around him. No wonder he kept pennants of nearby high school teams flying over his used car lot. He was attentive to his customers, Fred knew, and responsive to their requests. Probably about as truthful as a used car salesman could be and survive. Fred's parents had insisted on buying their last car at Bengt's, because, as his mom said, Bengt was almost in the family. He wondered idly what had happened to that car. Maybe Kierstin was driving it these days. He hoped neither of his parents was driving, period. Hadn't even asked.

Carol was right when she chewed me out, Fred thought. I really have been out of it. I had no idea what their life was like.

He was going to have to pay more attention, and not stay away so long next time. If there even would be a next time.

He tuned back in to his surroundings. Ingrid and Nels had gone back to their chairs, and his mom had pulled a rocker up near Ingrid. His dad had carried his rolls out to the kitchen, where Fred knew they soon would be joined by masses of food from other neighbors. Why was food supposed to cure grief? Or was it just that friends felt helpless to do anything else?

He stood next to Joan, who was sitting on the sofa with Andrew.

"Tell me about your son," she was saying to the Fribergs. "I only wish I could have known him."

"He was a sweet boy," Fred's mother said. "Wasn't he, Ingrid?"

Ingrid nodded.

"I heard he was in the service," Joan said.

It was Nels's turn to nod. "Army," he said.

"He was a master sergeant," Ingrid said, and straightened up in her rocker as if a sergeant had ordered her to.

"Do you have pictures of him?" Andrew asked.

Ingrid went over to a small bookcase in the corner and pulled out a family album. Joan and Andrew scooted apart on the sofa, and she sat down between them, opened the book to the middle, and flipped several pages. Fred sat on the sofa arm and looked over Joan's shoulder.

"Here's his first baby picture, with his big sisters." Ingrid turned a page. "And there they are, rocking him in their doll cradle. They were so proud of him." The tears threatened again, but she ignored them. Flipping pages, she took them through his life—more shots of little Gus with his sisters, then pudgy Gus in a Cub Scout uniform, slim Gus in track shorts and shoes, spiffed-up Gus with a girl at the junior prom, and Gus in his Army uniform, holding a duffel bag. Fred remembered Gus better as he had looked in the younger pictures than in the later ones, though he remembered when the boy began running track—and when he broke that wrist. Later on, after he himself had left home, he'd had less and less contact with the Fribergs' youngest. The last picture in the album, of Gus in a flannel shirt and jeans, showed a stronger, more mature man's body, like the body in the woods, except that in the picture he was smiling and holding a Christmas tree over his shoulder.

"This was last Christmas. He went out and cut us a little tree. He was going to do it again this year." Ingrid waved at the room, which showed no signs of the holidays.

"Would you like me to cut you a tree?" Andrew offered.

Ingrid hesitated and looked at Nels, but he avoided her eyes.

"Thank you," she said. "After…"

"Whenever you're ready," Andrew said when she couldn't go on. "I'm staying here for a while, with Oscar and Helga."

Joan's eyes shone. Fred squeezed her shoulder.

But he couldn't focus on pictures or Christmas trees. Who had killed Gus, and why? He wished he could ask Ingrid and Nels when Gus had arrived in Bishop Hill, and about the people he'd been in touch with. Not with his mom in the room. Maybe tomorrow. Would Peterson let him help? Since they'd arrived, he and Buker had been standing near the door, observing the family, but not interfering in any way.

Fred hoped he would at least already have asked them. He felt torn between wanting to dive into the investigation with the risk of having his efforts resented, and knowing that his first responsibility was to protect his mother.

Best way to protect her is catch the guy.

He hoped it wouldn't be long until the girls and their husbands arrived. Not that he looked forward to spending time with them, but it meant that after a decent interval, he could take his family home and go to bed early. Both his mom and dad looked as if they could fold at any moment. And five a.m. would come much too early for him.

Hanna and Tim burst in first, not bothering to knock. Hanna looked like a younger, less beaten-down version of her mother, though her eyes, too, were swollen. Tim, tall and dark, with bushy eyebrows, looked only vaguely like the teenager Fred remembered from school. He'd put meat on those bones in the ensuing years. Close behind them was a well-groomed woman in trim black slacks and a white silky blouse, her face drawn and pale under a cloud of dark hair loosely restrained by some kind of tie that matched her blouse. It took Fred a few moments to recognize her as

Tim's unmarried sister, Debbie York. He had taken her out a few times during high school, though they'd never been serious. She didn't look like a high school girl anymore, but she was still attractive and had been good company the last time they'd met, some years ago now. It still surprised him that she'd never married. He didn't think it was for lack of interest in the opposite sex. He remembered some passionate kisses on her front porch. Unless he'd been fooling himself, the passion hadn't all come from him.

Hanna gave her father a formal kiss on the cheek. Then she embraced Ingrid, and they wept together while the men shook hands.

Fred introduced Joan and Andrew. Debbie told Joan, "We've all looked forward to meeting you. But not like this!"

"You still on the farm?" Fred asked her.

"Living, not working. I teach high school English in Galva." Then, when Hanna finally stepped back, Debbie hugged Ingrid. "Oh, Ingrid!" She didn't spoil it by blabbing on about herself or telling her it was God's will, but listened to Ingrid, who was speaking softly now.

Christina and Bengt were not far behind. Christina, though she'd gained weight and colored her hair, might have been Hanna's twin. Bengt's football muscles had gone to flab, and he was nearly bald, but Fred had no trouble recognizing both of them.

The embraces and handshakes were repeated. Then the sisters fell on each other and told each other how horrified they were, and what they'd been doing when the phone had rung with the terrible news.

Tim and Bengt stood around looking awkward.

"How're they doing?" Tim asked Fred, jerking his head at Nels and Ingrid, but not waiting to hear. "This'll about kill them. They talk like the sun rises and sets on Gus."

"Did they even know he was coming home?" Bengt asked. "This is the first I heard, not that I've been around much to hear, but Christina talks to her mother. I try to get her not to do it when she's in the office, but you know women."

"She works for you?" Fred said.

"When we're shorthanded. It's hard to keep good help."

"So I've heard."

"I guess cops don't have to worry. All you guys have to do is write your quota of tickets and collect a steady paycheck." Bengt flashed a grin he probably thought sold cars.

Tim laughed.

Buker came over to him. "Can you spare us a moment, sir?" she asked.

"What about?"

"Just routine." She led him into the dining room, where Peterson waited.

"Is that for real?" Bengt asked Fred. "That 'just routine' business?" He was playing it cool, but Fred heard the nervousness in his tone.

"I'm sure it is. They'll want to talk to everyone they can about Gus."

"They talk to you?"

"Yes."

"Tell you anything?"

"I doubt that they know much yet."

Bengt subsided and said little until it was his turn. Peterson took each family member separately into the dining room, while Buker stayed by the door. Fred itched to hear what they said, but couldn't stretch his ears that far, and they didn't talk about it when they returned.

Then the first neighbor knocked on the door carrying some kind of covered dish that had to have set a record for speed cooking—or thawing, more like it—and another was close behind.

The Lundquists were no longer needed. Fred collected his family, and they made their farewells and left. On the way out, he told Peterson, "Anything I can do, just call me," and Peterson thanked him as if he meant it.

EIGHT

When the alarm went off in the morning, Fred wasn't ready. Raising one eyelid and seeing only darkness, he rolled over to go back to sleep. Then, maybe because the bed felt wrong and the room didn't smell like home, he remembered. This wasn't Oliver. And this was no normal morning. He dragged himself out of bed and pulled on his pants.

"What time is it?" Joan mumbled.

"Five. I told Andrew I'd be there by now."

"I'll get dressed." But she didn't move.

"Don't bother. I'll take advantage of Dad's recliner till Mom wakes up."

"You're sure?" She opened her eyes.

"I'm sure. If you're awake in a couple of hours, you might wander over for breakfast. But don't worry about it."

"Mmm." She rolled over, barely returning his kiss.

The cold air woke him thoroughly. He didn't bother with a flashlight, but walked down the middle of the street, unworried about meeting traffic at this hour. The squad car facing him in front of his parents' house was a comforting presence. The deputy in the driver's seat lowered the window and aimed a flashlight beam at him. "You going somewhere?"

"To my mother's. Fred Lundquist." He held his badge in the beam.

"Just checking, Lieutenant." The light clicked off.

"Thanks. I appreciate it." Fred went on in, glad to have to use his key on the front door.

Andrew was on his feet in a flash.

"Just me, Andrew. Everything quiet?"

"It's a creaky old house—scared me a couple of times." He yawned. "I made coffee a while ago. Left you some."

"Thanks. I'll see you for lunch."

Andrew nodded sleepily and climbed the stairs.

Fred left the lukewarm coffee, figuring he might heat it later. He didn't expect to have any trouble staying awake, even in his dad's comfortable chair. He'd just shut his eyes.

His mother's voice startled him, all the more because it came from the kitchen. How could he have fallen asleep!

Was she wandering in the night now? Kicking himself for passing up Andrew's coffee, he got out of the recliner and ran into the kitchen.

The room was icy—even in the dark, he saw in dismay that the back door stood wide open. Oh, no, he thought. She's really lost it now. "Mom! What are you doing, wandering around in the dark like this? It's way too early to get up. And too cold to leave the door open like that."

Then he saw the dim outline of a tall figure running out the door, and he ran after it. On the way to the door, though, he collided with his mother, who was brandishing a broom over her head. By the time he could untangle himself, a motor had started up in the street behind the house. It drove off in the direction of the woods and the road to Kewanee.

"Mom, come with me," he told her, and pulled her into the living room. Opening the front door, he called to the deputy. But he already knew it was hopeless. With his squad car facing away from the back of the house, the deputy wouldn't have seen the other vehicle. And Fred couldn't even describe it.

"Where are you taking me?" his mother cried. "Leave me alone!" She was stronger than he expected, but he held on, afraid she would run outside.

"Mom, it's all right. It's me, Fred." Hanging on to her, he reached for a light switch.

She stopped pulling and squinted in the sudden glare. "Fred?"

"What happened?" he said. "Who was that man?"

"What man? What are you talking about?" She pushed him away. "And why is it so cold in here?"

"The man in your kitchen. You remember!"

"I don't know what you're talking about. There's no man in my kitchen. It's the middle of the night."

"Mom, you're not trying!" He wanted to shake her. "Come on, try! You've got to remember this. It's really important!"

"Leave me alone!" She burst into tears.

Fred's father roared down the stairs into the living room, stopped dead, and reached out his arms to her. "What's the matter, sweetheart?" he asked softly, glaring at Fred over her head.

At the same time, the deputy came in the front door, which Fred had left ajar. "What happened?"

"We had an intruder," Fred said. "He ran out the back door—probably got in that way, too." Leaving his mother in his father's arms, he turned the kitchen light on.

The deputy shone his flashlight on the back door and its frame. "Broke in." He reached for the cell phone on his belt and spoke into it. "Which way did he go?"

"He drove off toward the ravine."

"In...?"

"I don't know. I didn't see it. Just heard the motor start. Sounded like a pickup."

The deputy nodded. He'd probably heard it, too.

"At least shut that door," Fred's dad said. Standing in the door to the living room, he had an arm around her now.

"Do you have any plastic wrap?" the deputy asked. "Don't want to mess up any fingerprints."

"We've got disposable gloves. Get him some gloves, Helga."

She reached under the sink and offered the deputy a box of plastic gloves without a word. Fred couldn't imagine why she had them. Maybe for some messy cooking job.

The deputy took one and pulled the door to. "That's the best I can do for now. You're going to have to get someone to fix the door after we've looked at it."

"What's the matter with the door?" Fred's mother asked. "Is that why we're so cold?"

"Yes," his dad told her. "But we'll fix it in a little while."

The deputy was looking around the kitchen. "There's a drawer open." He looked in without touching it. "Mrs. Lundquist, were you looking for a knife?"

"In the middle of the night?" she said. "Don't be silly."

A chill went down Fred's backbone. She'd picked up a broom, not a knife. It had to have been the intruder.

"Go back to bed, Helga," his dad said. "We'll take care of this."

"All right, Oscar."

Fred watched her walk to the stairs, aching for her.

The moment she disappeared, his father waved his finger under Fred's nose. "As for you, I don't *ever* want to hear you talk like that to your mother again. She does the best she can. She can't remember things anymore, and shouting at her isn't going to bring them back."

"I just—"

"She was already scared, and you just made it worse. Never again, you hear?"

"Yes, Dad. I'm sorry." He felt about ten years old. Aside from being unkind to his mother, he knew better than to jump down the throat of a witness like that. Now it was too late. Odds of her being able to retrieve anything about the intruder had dropped to nil. He'd made sure of that.

"All right," his father said. "What happened?"

Fred told him, knowing he'd have to tell it again.

"You think he wanted to hurt her?" the deputy asked.

With the knife drawer open like that? "Yes." That's why I behaved like a fool.

"No idea who it was?"

"He was tall. That's all I could tell."

"But you're sure it was a man?"

He nodded slowly. "I'm sure. I never saw a woman move like that."

NINE

JOAN BARELY FELT his kiss before drowning in sleep again. When she woke for the second time, the sun was in her eyes and her stomach was growling. She decided to walk over for breakfast. Even if they'd already eaten, odds were good that Helga would be glad to make more. Like most people with Alzheimer's, she seemed to be at her best in the morning, as she had been yesterday. This morning called for comfort food, food eaten with family. Maybe someone else would like the scones and muffins the bed and breakfast had set out for her and Fred. She carried their fragrant basket from the table outside their room upstairs to the common room.

She should have known better. The other guests were full of the terrible news. Joan, having avoided watching it on television, tried to leave her basket for them and slip out, but one woman grabbed her coat sleeve to keep her from leaving before she'd had an earful.

"Did you hear about the murder right here in Bishop Hill? Isn't it awful?"

Joan cut her off. "The victim's family and ours are close friends," she said in as frosty a tone as she could dredge up. She had no intention of feeding people's curiosity with the gruesome details she was sure they'd love.

"I had no idea," the woman said and released her sleeve. "I'm so sorry."

Joan gave her a sad smile she was sure Miss Manners would have applauded, pulled on her hat and mittens, and left.

Walking the long block to the house, she heard someone behind her calling her name. She turned. It was Walt, trotting to catch up with her. She waited, feeling guilty for not having filled him and Ruthie in. They shouldn't have had to learn it with everyone else, not with their family involved.

"I can't believe it!" His heavy breathing made clouds in front of his face. "Murder in Bishop Hill. And Gus Friberg, of all people. Makes you feel nobody's safe. Are you all right?"

"Me?" What an odd question. But he meant well. Maybe her name had been on the news. "I'm fine. We should have told you, but we all went over to the Fribergs' last night. Stayed until after their daughters arrived."

"I hoped you had. Mom and Ingrid have been close for so long."

"Your mom was wonderful with her."

"She would be."

"But we're concerned about her."

"Ingrid?"

"No, your mother."

"What does Mom have to do with it?"

Joan told him where they'd found her, and the shape she'd been in. "She said she saw it happen, and Fred and the sheriff's investigator agree that she probably did."

"Who's that? Greg Peterson?"

"How'd you know?"

"Greg works most of the cases around here. Not that we have a lot of murders, you understand. Not even much shoplifting. But go on about Mom."

"If the killer saw her, too, as she thought he did, she's

in danger until he's caught, even though she can't tell a coherent story and probably couldn't identify him if she saw him. All she could say was that he was a big man, and she was sure it was Fred she saw murdered, even when Fred was standing right there talking to her.''

"She was upset."

"Yes." Walt had no idea how upset.

"We can't tell her to stay home."

"No. She wouldn't remember why, and it would terrify her all over again every time we told her. She wouldn't be safe at home alone anyway. They said a deputy would be nearby, but we're just going to have to take turns making sure someone's with her. Someone besides your dad—he can't seem to help falling asleep."

"I suppose I could ask her to help in the restaurant," Walt said slowly.

"Could she? And would you want her to?"

"Sometimes she cuts up vegetables for us, or fixes salads. She enjoys feeling helpful. But I can't watch her every minute."

"It's all right. Fred and Andrew and I will split up the time. That's what we came for, so you could do what you have to do without worrying about her."

"Kierstin can help after school."

"Is she responsible?"

"Very. And she loves Mom."

"Talk it over with Fred, won't you? I'll distract your mom. And, Walt, we haven't told anyone, not even the Fribergs, that your mother is a witness. Greg Peterson promised not to, either. She'll be safer if the word doesn't get out. Be sure Ruthie and Kierstin know that."

He nodded soberly, and they walked together to the house.

Helga came to the door in the same wool slacks and

sweater she'd worn for two days. Was that a problem already? They'd have to pay attention. Maybe Oscar was making sure her clothes were clean, though that seemed unlikely. So far, though, she smelled clean enough. And the scratches on her face showed no sign of infection. She must be washing.

"Walter! Come in, come in. It's cold out there. And this is…?" She looked at Joan pleasantly, but with no sign of recognition.

"I'm Joan, Fred's new wife. Walter and I hope you still have some breakfast for us."

"I made Swedish pancakes for Oscar and Fred. You two come right in, and I'll make some for you."

They went into the house and hung up their things. The aroma of baked ham greeted Joan's nostrils. Baked ham for breakfast, too? she wondered. Helga disappeared into the kitchen.

"Hi, Dad," Walt said. "Hi, Fred. I hear you've had some excitement."

"We're going over to their house later today," Oscar said. "Your mother has a ham baking."

Of course, Joan thought. It's for the Fribergs. And Helga can do that. Nothing complicated about a baked ham. I should probably go help with the pancakes, though.

"Do they have any?" Walt cut himself off.

"Who did it?" Fred said. Still standing, as Walt was, he was amazingly awake, though his eyes gave away his lack of sleep. "We haven't talked to anyone yet this morning."

"I'd put my money on Mark Balter, myself."

Joan couldn't make herself leave. Standing by the kitchen door, she watched Helga, just in case. Helga seemed to be moving competently. She might measure the salt wrong, but Oscar didn't look worried. Not that he had anything to worry about. He'd already eaten.

"Mark Balter?" Fred said. "In my class?"

"He's just out of prison," Walt said. "Served time for auto theft, and he wasn't just going for a joy ride. They finally caught up with him in Las Vegas."

"I remember he cheated on tests," Fred said. "But I don't remember that he was ever violent like that."

Joan saw again the horrible red pulp that had been Gus's face, and shuddered.

"You pick him because he's an ex-con?" Fred asked.

"No, because his wife divorced him while he was in prison."

"It happens."

"And Gus Friberg was dating her."

Fred raised an eyebrow. "Who'd Mark marry, anyway?"

"You remember Gerri Holm? A few years behind you?"

"There were a bunch of Holm girls, all blond and kind of scrawny. Nothing to get excited about." He looked sideways at Joan as if to say, not like you. She smiled at him.

"Gerri's Gus's age," Walt said. "She may have been scrawny when you left home, but not now. Gorgeous woman. Mark's nuts about her. Always has been. I hear he was furious at Gus."

"You think Gerri and Gus were doing more than dating?"

"She's home visiting her parents. Hard to believe it's a coincidence that Gus was visiting his. He's practically never come home."

Joan wondered what Nels and Ingrid knew about Gerri Balter. And did it matter whether Gerri was serious about Gus, if Mark thought she was?

"Pancakes!" Helga called. "Come eat."

Oscar, who had been leaning back in his recliner, opened one eye. "Your mother says 'eat,' you better eat."

The pancakes, rolled up like crepes, were excellent, light

in texture, with an unexpected tartness—did she put lemon in them?—that begged for the maple syrup and homemade strawberry-rhubarb jam Helga kept urging on them. Good enough to make almost anyone but this family forget for a little while that Gus Friberg had been murdered.

Not quite good enough to make Joan forget that Helga was at risk of sharing his fate. Walt, either, apparently.

"You two want to see a little of Bishop Hill this morning?" he said. "Do a little Christmas shopping, maybe? I thought I'd stick around and visit the folks until that ham is ready."

"That ham is not for you, Walter Lundquist," his mother said. "I'm taking it to Ingrid."

"I know, Mom, but it smells great."

"Feel like a little walk?" Fred asked Joan.

"Sure." She thanked Helga for breakfast and promised to be back soon.

"Take your time," Walt said. "And tell Fred about Kierstin."

"I will," Joan promised. "That was good of him," she said when the door closed behind them. Without discussing where to go, they set off arm in arm past the woods and the ball field, away from the bed and breakfast and away from the Fribergs' house. Joan avoided looking at the mess of tracks by the woods and squinched her eyes against the bright sunshine reflecting off the snow. She hoped it would help against the cold.

"I take it you told Walt about Mom," Fred said. He didn't seem to mind.

"Yes. And I warned him to keep it in the family. He thinks Kierstin can spend some time with her."

"Mom would probably love that."

"He hadn't heard a word about your mom. That must mean the newscasts didn't mention her."

"I didn't expect them to. Peterson wouldn't leak it to them. Not just for Mom's sake, either. The less you tell, the bigger your advantage over the man you're after."

"You're sure it was a man?"

"I am now." He took a deep breath. "We had some more excitement last night—well, early this morning, while it was still dark. A man broke into the house."

"Oh, no! You saw him?"

"Just an outline."

"What happened?"

"Nothing, really. Mom was set to run him off with a broom, but when he saw me, he ran. Got away in some kind of car or truck."

"She must have been terrified."

"She was—but she forgot it a lot sooner than I did. Joan, the knife drawer was open."

"You think she was going to fight back?"

"Maybe, though when I got there she was waving a broom, instead. Maybe he was going to use one on her, or maybe just scare her with it. But we can't count on that."

"Oh, Fred!"

"Dad will tell Walt when he gets a chance. We don't want to scare her all over again."

"So he knows who she is."

"Looks like it. Could be a coincidence, of course—some stranger breaking in—but I'm not big on coincidences."

"We can't fight a knife-wielding murderer!"

"All we have to do is not leave her alone. As I said, he ran the minute he saw me. The deputies are going to stay a lot closer from now on. And be sure they can see the whole house, not just the front."

They turned south at the old Colony Church building and walked toward the park on their right. Across Bishop Hill Street from the park was a row of stores in old buildings.

"There's Dad's old bakery," Fred said. Several layers of brown paint were peeling off its walls, and two benches stood in front of its windows.

Through the windows, trimmed in white, Joan could see fresh loaves stacked on shelves behind the counter. "If I weren't so full of pancakes, I'd have a hard time walking past it."

"Want to go in? Maggie's an old friend."

"Sure." She followed him into the warm bakery, and one whiff told her it really was a good thing she wasn't hungry. All those different kinds of bread stacked in neatly labeled bins on the wall behind the counter, more varieties than she'd ever seen in Oliver—onion, dill, sunflower seed, sourdough, and Swedish rye. They would have been impossible to resist, not to mention the sweet rolls, cookies, cakes, and pies inside glass shelves. Could little Bishop Hill consume all that? Or did people from other nearby towns come this far for it? Probably the bakery counted on selling extra during this tourist season. Small tables and chairs invited them to eat their purchases on the spot, and a row of coffeepots lined a shelf on a wall at the far end of the room.

"Well, hi, Fred. Good to see you. It's been a long time." A tall, bony woman with bright blue eyes and a face full of wrinkles came through a door behind the counter. She was wearing a rough white cotton apron over short sleeves, and her hair was hidden under a white kerchief.

"Maggie, meet my wife, Joan Spencer. Joan, this is Maggie Lund. She was Dad's right hand for years. Now she owns the bakery."

Maggie shook her hand. "Welcome to Bishop Hill, Joan. I think I met your son yesterday. Nice-looking boy. He was looking for Helga—I take it you found her."

"Oh, sure," Joan said, returning her smile as if there weren't a thing to worry about.

"Oscar was pretty excited when he heard you were coming. But you picked a terrible week to do it. Poor Gus. And his poor parents."

"Yes."

"How is your mother taking it?"

"My mother?" Fred sounded as if he'd never heard of her. Was he wondering whether the word had leaked out about her finding the body? But did that even matter after this morning?

"Helga and Ingrid are such good friends," Maggie said. "I was afraid it might hit her hard."

"It did," Fred said. "But she's doing all right this morning."

"She was wonderful with Ingrid last night," Joan said, picking up on his cue.

"She comes by almost every day, you know. Sometimes she seems to think your dad still owns the bakery. I don't let on. If she walks out without paying, I just put it on your dad's tab."

"Thanks, Maggie."

"Was Gus in yesterday, by any chance?" Joan asked.

"No. I didn't even know he was home."

"I just wondered. The sheriff is going to have to trace his movements." She wasn't sure it was true, but it sounded likely.

"If I knew anything, I'd tell him."

An old-fashioned bell tinkled when the door opened, and a woman with five children filled the room as much with noise as with bodies.

"How much are your cookies?" the woman asked Maggie. Obviously not local.

"See you, Maggie," Fred said, and they left her to deal with paying customers. Outside, he told Joan, "Sometime you'll have to ask her to show you the coffin factory."

Joan stared at him. "The what?"

"A long time ago, there was a coffin factory in the cellar. They brought the coffins up through a hole in the floor. It's covered up, but Maggie can show you."

"This was the undertaker's? With those front windows?" It felt all wrong.

"Maybe. I don't know that they even had undertakers at first, though. I think they laid people out at home. They must have had some system when they lived in dormitories, though."

"Dormitories?"

"Sure. They lived communally. The Big Brick, a dormitory where the ball field is now, was the biggest brick building west of Chicago. But before that, there were so many deaths in the first year that those people didn't even have coffins, and neither did the ones who died in the cholera epidemic a few years later. They wrapped them in cloth, instead. But in normal times, they did."

Joan remembered the paintings of the workers in the field and imagined lines of carpenters making coffins. They'd have to be short lines, she thought, if they did it all in this building.

"We'd better head back," Fred said. "Walt's going to be pacing the floor, especially if Dad told him about last night."

"Some honeymoon." As soon as it slipped out, Joan was sorry she'd said it. She squeezed his hand.

"Want to go sit in the gazebo for a few minutes?" He gestured toward the bandstand in the snow-covered park.

Feeling her warm toes inside her dry boots, Joan laughed. "I think I had enough of plowing through snow yesterday."

"What kind of Swede are you!" He bent down and kissed her.

"Right here in front of God and everybody!"

"Who's looking?" He put an arm around her, and they started walking back.

But someone had been looking. "Fred! Fred Lundquist!" The tall man coming toward them had a wide smile on his angular face. And a five o'clock shadow, this early in the morning.

Fred looked puzzled.

"Don't worry about introducing me," Joan told him.

"But I almost can. It's—" Then his face cleared. "Mark, is that you?" They met, and the two men shook hands. "Joan, this is Mark Balter, my classmate. Mark, how are you doing?" As if he hadn't heard a word about Mark's past.

"Never better." So Mark was a bluffer, too. Didn't he think they'd find out? "Oh, hell, Fred, that's not true. I'm just getting my feet back on the ground. I did some time in prison."

"I'm sorry to hear that. Still on parole, or are you past that?"

"I have to keep my nose clean for a couple of years. But hey, there's no way I'm going back. Is this the wife? I heard you got married again."

"Yes, Joan and I were married this fall."

"So, Joan, what do you think of our metropolis?" Mark waved his hand at the park.

"I like it, as much as I've seen. We just got here night before last."

"And you got mixed up with Gus Friberg yesterday, I hear." From the tension in his mouth, Joan thought more anger than phony grief had wiped out his smile.

"Afraid so," Fred said. "I barely remember Gus. He was just a kid when we were in school."

"He hightailed it out of here the minute he graduated. Couldn't get away fast enough. But he came back to try to beat my time with *my* wife.'' No mistaking his bitterness now. He was clenching one fist. ''I suppose you heard that.''

''Someone mentioned her,'' Fred said. ''Gerri Holm, was it?''

The muscles in Mark's face softened. ''Gerri couldn't stick it out, me being in prison and all, but hey, now that I'm out, I figure I've got a chance.''

Now that Gus is dead, you mean, Joan thought.

''God, we were in love! We could hardly keep our hands off each other.''

''I haven't seen Gerri since she was a kid,'' Fred said. ''Don't imagine I'd know her.''

''You wouldn't forget her now.'' Mark hiked up his padded jacket to haul his wallet out of his jeans pocket. He pulled out a worn snapshot and showed it to them without letting go of it. ''Tell me she's not the most beautiful woman you ever saw.''

Joan studied a fresh-faced blonde smiling in the very bandstand beside them, her hair lifted by a light breeze. Her skimpy sundress showed off her tan and slim figure. ''She's lovely.''

''She certainly improved with age,'' Fred said.

''You better believe it!'' Mark returned the picture to his pocket. ''I'll let you go, but maybe we could have a drink together while you're home, talk about old times.''

''Maybe,'' Fred said. ''But I came to help my folks while my sister's out of town. We're spending a lot of time with Mom. She's having trouble with her memory. We can't trust anything she says anymore.''

Good move, Fred, Joan thought. Especially if Walt is right about Mark.

''Well, good to see you, anyway. Nice to meet you, Joan.''

They parted as amiably as any old school friends might.

"You think he did it?" Joan said when they were well out of earshot.

"He was furious at Gus, and he didn't mind shooting off his mouth about how glad he is to have him out of the picture, dead, even. I put some of that down to the urge to show off the beautiful woman he married, even if she did divorce him. Testosterone speaking. But was he furious enough?" He shook his head. "I have no idea."

TEN

WALT WAS STANDING on the porch when they walked up. "Mom shooed me out. I figured I'd do her as much good out here as in there."

"We're set for now," Fred said. "If Kierstin has time, maybe she and Andrew could take a shift this afternoon. Make it seem natural."

"She'll make time, especially after what Dad just told me." Walt's jaw clenched. "Are you sure it's safe to leave her with the kids like that?"

"Plus the sheriff's deputies. Walt, the man ran the minute he saw me. I'm sure he's afraid to be seen."

"If you say so." Walt frowned. "But it's intolerable to have to stand guard over her like this in Bishop Hill, of all places."

It's just a matter of time before someone will have to stay with her anyway, Joan thought, but he's right, not like this. Then she spotted the squad car parked across the road, facing the house. Good.

Walt took off for the restaurant, and they went in. The ham smelled done. Should she check it? Or suggest it to Helga?

"Mom, Dad!" Fred called. "I brought Joan to see you."

Helga came into the living room from the kitchen. "Well, hello. I didn't know you were coming."

Good fake, Helga. You probably didn't even remember

we were in town, much less who I am. "We had a nice walk," Joan said. "Fred took me to see Oscar's old bakery. Maggie said you like to go there to see her, too."

"Maggie's a hard worker. Isn't she, Oscar?"

Pen in hand, Oscar looked up from the crossword puzzle he was working in the paper. Confident man, to work it in ink. "She always was. She say she needed any help today?"

Fred shook his head. "Want to go ask her?"

"Not particularly." His eyes strayed back to the paper.

"Don't you go anywhere!" Helga put her hands on her hips. "You promised you'd carry the ham over to Ingrid and Nels."

"I will," Oscar said.

"And we can't just drop it and run out on them. We have to stay."

"Are you ready?" He made no move.

"I am, but you need to put your boots on. Then wash your hands."

He felt for the boots, which had retreated behind the skirt of the hideous recliner, fished them out, and pulled them on. "See how she makes me work?" But he was smiling.

"He doesn't mean it," Helga told them. "He's such a big tease."

A good sign, Joan thought, that she still could tell the difference, especially this morning.

Eventually, bundled up, they set off for the Fribergs' with Oscar carrying the ham.

Joan and Fred strolled along a few paces behind his parents and Andrew, who had dragged out of bed in time to join them. Fred seemed amazingly relaxed for someone supposed to be watching for a man who was after his mother, but Joan couldn't help scanning the woods beyond the field to their right. Had Fred mastered the art of looking without turning his head?

"Maybe she'll be safe in a crowd," she said. "But what if he shoots her from behind a tree?"

"This is no sniper. And Gus wasn't shot."

"How could you tell, with all that blood?"

"I couldn't, but Greg Peterson called this morning, before you came over. They didn't find any evidence of it at the autopsy. Gus was battered to death, they know now. They found blood of his type on a length of branch, and traces of…" He stopped when he looked at her face. I'm probably turning green, she thought, and wished she could forget what she had seen. Banish it from her mind. All she could do was distract herself with other thoughts.

"That doesn't mean the guy doesn't have a gun," she said.

"Sure. Maybe even a rifle."

She thought about it. "But you think it was spur of the moment, killing Gus. And he wouldn't be likely to stalk Helga with a gun."

"Which doesn't mean he wouldn't kill her."

"You think he'd do to her what he did to Gus?" Somehow, until now, she'd imagined a quick, easy death for Helga, if murder ever was easy. What Fred was suggesting would be a thousand times worse. Not to mention the knife drawer. But that, too, would have been spur of the moment.

"Not if we surround her with witnesses."

She glared at him. "That's not what I asked."

"It's hard to believe anyone would do that in cold blood, but…" His eyes lost their focus. What horror was he remembering from some other time and place? Or was he, too, picturing his mother without a face?

"You have to help them catch him."

"If they let me," he said bleakly.

"They won't let you?"

"Let's just say cops tend to get a little turfy sometimes. And they don't like family members getting involved. I have to respect that. At least Peterson called. I'll talk to him again today. Give him space to work."

"He doesn't have to know everything."

"Yes, he does. Anything you find out, you tell him right away."

"Or you?"

"Well…"

"That's what I thought." Privately, she intended to tell Fred anything she learned if it was possible, and go to the investigator only as a last resort. "Any idea when the sheriff himself will be back?"

"Peterson didn't say. He's playing it pretty close to his vest. He may not know. I suspect he'd work this case anyway."

In the daylight, the Fribergs' house turned out to be painted in what Joan thought might be traditional Swedish colors, its walls flowerpot red, with woodwork a soft gray-green trimmed in creamy white. It would have been easy to paint the whole house the same color, but each separate bit of edging outlining the window frames had been painted precisely, and Joan found the contrasts restful, rather than fussy.

"It's beautiful!" she said.

"Nels is a house painter," Fred said, as if that explained it. "A good one."

"I see that." More than that, he had taste. Or was that Ingrid's taste? Somehow, she doubted it. Ingrid probably would defer such decisions to her husband. Not like Helga, who clearly ruled Oscar's roost.

"He may have had to get permission to use those col-

ors.'' This didn't sound like family authority he was talking
about.

''Whose permission?''

''Technically, the state's, if theirs is one of the old
houses, because all of Bishop Hill is a state historic site.
Some of the buildings even belong to the state. But actually,
the village acts for the state when it comes to things like
that.''

''Do they ever say no?''

''Oh, sure, if you want to do something that isn't in keeping with how it used to be. I'm not sure Nels's colors would
be allowed, but their house may not be old enough to matter.''

''Aren't you coming in?'' Helga said from the Fribergs'
porch.

''Yes, Mom,'' he said, and sighed.

Today Nels and Ingrid were not sitting numbly in the
living room. ''Come have a drink,'' Nels called to Oscar
and Fred from a back room. Still a few months underage,
Andrew shrugged and followed them into the room, where
Joan could see other men with glasses in their hands. It
would be his decision—she didn't watch his every move in
Oliver, either.

Ingrid looked a little lost, even while thanking Helga for
the ham, as if she didn't know what to do with it. Maybe
she didn't. Their refrigerator probably was overflowing by
now. Even now, someone else was coming in the door,
probably with more food. Or were people finally arriving
to eat it? Those men were going to need something before
long if they kept tossing them back.

''I'll take that for you.'' A slender dark-haired woman
they had met the night before reached for the ham Oscar
had passed to Helga.

"Thank you, Debbie," Ingrid said, and Debbie disappeared into the kitchen.

"I know I met her last night." Joan put a question into it. "Is Debbie one of your daughters?"

"Not yet," Ingrid said, and then the sweet smile on her face dissolved. "Not ever," she whispered, blinking away sudden tears.

Debbie returned and embraced her. "I'll always feel like your daughter, Ingrid."

"Because of your brother?" Now Joan remembered. Debbie was the sister of Hanna Friberg's husband, Tim York.

"No, because Gus and I would have been married someday." Now Debbie was the one blinking hard. For the first time, Joan saw how swollen her eyes were.

"You would not!" Coming out of nowhere, a blond fury in a parka launched herself at Debbie. Startled, Joan recognized the woman she had seen only a little while earlier, smiling in Mark Balter's snapshot. Now Gerri Balter's face was contorted and her eyes wild. She had a handful of Debbie's black hair wrapped around her fist.

"Help!" With one hand Debbie grabbed at the hair Gerri was pulling, and with the other, she scratched at Gerri's face. "Get her off me!"

Joan seemed to have grown roots into the floor. Fred and Andrew came running toward them from the back room, though the other men scarcely moved. But it wasn't men who broke up the fight.

"Stop that!" Helga grabbed both women's arms and jerked them apart. "Have some respect! This is a house of mourning."

Immediately, Gerri stood still, dark strands of Debbie's hair fluttering from her hand to the floor. Looking stunned,

Debbie watched them fall. The hair still attached to her head stood out in all directions.

A few feet away, Andrew skidded into Fred's out-stretched arm. Fred murmured something to him that Joan couldn't hear, but she was glad. Helga was doing fine on her own.

"Are you all right?" Helga asked Ingrid, who looked almost as stunned as Debbie.

She found her voice. "Thank you, Helga."

"I'm sorry," Gerri told Debbie. "Please forgive me," she said to Ingrid. "I had no right. I was upset."

"You think we're not?" Ingrid said. "But why go after Debbie? And what did you mean, she wouldn't have married my Gus?" She put her arm around Debbie, who was still trembling, whether with fear or anger, Joan couldn't tell. It crossed her mind that this timid, fragile-looking woman had brought up daughters. Maybe she could have broken up the fight without Helga's help, but Joan doubted it.

"Gus and I had been seeing each other," Gerri said. "And calling and E-mailing each other constantly, no matter where we were. We came home this week because we wanted to be married in Bishop Hill. But this…this…We wanted to tell you together." Her eyes filled. The scratches on her face had begun to ooze thin lines of blood, though not as much as the big scratches on Helga's face, which by now had scabbed over. Like Helga, Gerri didn't seem to notice them.

"It's not true," Debbie said, but her voice was flat. Joan's heart went out to her, hit not only by the death of the man she loved but also by the death of his love for her.

"I had no idea," Ingrid said. "I thought…" She looked at Debbie.

"Gus thought so, too," Gerri said. "He said he always thought someday he'd go home and marry Debbie."

"He told you that?" Debbie said, still in that empty-sounding voice.

Joan could see why Debbie wouldn't believe Gerri. It didn't sound like the kind of thing a man would tell the woman he loved about someone else.

Gerri nodded. "We didn't mean to fall in love. It just—just happened."

Joan thought she sounded like a teenager explaining why she was pregnant. But this was a mature woman talking about the man she'd thought she was about to marry, to a woman who had believed for years that Gus would be hers. If one of them had murdered the other, it would make sense. But now they'd both lost out. Still, she couldn't help wondering how committed Gerri was to Gus. How recent was this sudden love?

Ingrid turned to Joan. "Joan, this is Gerri Balter," she said.

"I know," Joan said. "I met Mark today. He showed us her picture."

"Who?" Ingrid asked.

"Mark Balter, her ex-husband. Fred said they went to school together."

"Him!" Gerri's tone left nothing to the imagination.

Joan plowed ahead. "He sounded like a man in love. Didn't he know you were about to marry Gus?"

"He knew."

"He seemed to think he could get you back."

"After Gus?" Scorn dripped from the words.

Debbie gasped. "You don't think he…"

"He might have. He just might have. He had this crazy idea I'd go back to him once he was out of prison." Gerri's eyes flashed. "I can't imagine why I married him in the first place. It's not been too hard to stay away from him—he's still on parole and can't leave Henry County. But whenever I come home, he follows me everywhere. I've told him to leave me alone, but he won't listen. If he thinks I'll have anything to do with him now, he's wrong."

"Have you talked to the sheriff?" Joan asked quietly.

"I will."

Joan didn't know whether to believe her or not. "So you're staying with your parents?"

"Only until Gus is decently buried."

Joan's eyes met Fred's. He'd tell Greg Peterson, she knew. And Peterson wasn't likely to let Gerri Balter leave Bishop Hill. Not yet.

ELEVEN

NEITHER GERRI BALTER nor Debbie York hung around the Fribergs' very long after their fight. While Joan felt for both of them, she ached for Ingrid, left without the support and comfort of a woman who, but for Gus's murder, would have been her daughter-in-law. Debbie had just been bumped out of the family, but Gerri, after bumping her, clearly had no intention of playing a devoted Ruth to Ingrid's Naomi, if she even knew the Bible story.

According to Fred, Ingrid's own daughters had left the nest young. Joan wondered how often they came home, even as close as they lived to Bishop Hill. They hadn't shown up yet today.

Ingrid, Helga's good friend, was losing her mind. And Nels, her husband, didn't seem able to offer much comfort. Be fair, Joan thought. Gus was his son, too. Who's comforting Nels?

In the back room, the alcohol was flowing freely again, comfort of a different sort. Time to feed those men. With Debbie gone, Joan figured she'd better offer to help.

"Ingrid, should we set out some lunch?"

"Oh…yes," Ingrid said, looking around vaguely. "I don't know what we have in the house. People keep bringing things."

"I'll help," Helga said. She seemed to know her way

around Ingrid's kitchen and found plates in the cupboards and Oscar's rolls in the bread drawer.

Joan pulled Helga's ham back out of the refrigerator and sliced it. She and Helga laid platters of ham, deviled eggs, potato salad, and cheese on the kitchen table. Cholesterol special, no greens or fruit in sight. Never mind, she thought. This was comfort food. She rejected several casseroles that looked big enough to feed an army at suppertime or maybe after the funeral, if an army of mourners showed up then. Who knew when Gus's body would be available for a funeral? Soon, maybe, if Peterson already had given Fred the autopsy report. For that matter, who knew how long it would be before his mother felt normal enough to cook again?

At first Ingrid merely watched them, but then she said, ''I'd better make coffee. Those men...'' Her gnarled hands set a kettle of water on the stove, measured the beans into the grinder, and ground their fragrance into the room. ''We'll need mugs, too.'' Grabbing handles, she set out a bunch of mugs. As she moved through the familiar tasks, Joan saw color returning to her pale face.

The men—even Fred and Oscar—dug in as if they hadn't eaten in days. Sitting around Ingrid's kitchen table, no one said much. Joan didn't know two of the men, but when no one introduced them, she didn't ask. Fred would tell her later if it mattered who they were, she thought.

''Your girls coming back today?'' she asked, as much to break the silence as because she wanted to know.

''They didn't say,'' Ingrid said. ''Hanna's pretty busy on the farm, you know.'' She subsided into gloom and picked at the scant food on her plate.

Too busy to visit her parents? Joan thought. The day after her brother was killed? And you didn't even invent an excuse for Christina.

"You're not eating," Helga scolded her friend. "You have to keep your strength up." She ladled a spoonful of potato salad onto Ingrid's plate. "Try this, I made it myself."

Ingrid had to know it wasn't true, but she smiled and patted Helga's hand. "Thank you, Helga." She put a forkful into her mouth, and Helga beamed.

Nels was eating, but he looked as if he'd like to make them all disappear.

Joan tried again. "Nels, your house is so beautiful. Fred said you painted it yourself."

"Thank you." He smiled for the first time, a smile she thought must have charmed local housewives.

"Do you paint most of the houses in Bishop Hill?"

The smile faded. "Not anymore. They think I'm too old to climb a ladder."

"Are you?"

"Did our house last summer." He scowled and chomped fiercely on a ham sandwich.

Joan suddenly couldn't bear another minute with these grieving parents. Let's get out of here! she cried silently to Fred. But she couldn't abandon Ingrid to clean up alone. Forget the small talk, she told herself. No one's up to it, and Nels isn't like Fred and Andrew anyway. I can't imagine him doing dishes.

Her thoughts took a turn. If it had been Andrew…it hurt even to look at Andrew with that thought in mind. She hoped Gus's parents had not seen his battered face. But the scar on his wrist should have spared them that. And his dental records could prove his identity, if there was any doubt at all. Or the Army could.

Finally the last dish was washed, the leftovers tucked back into the refrigerator. Time to leave, as Nels's cronies already had done. Only Helga was doing anyone any good, but of course she couldn't stay there without them, and they couldn't explain why.

The doorbell rang while they were putting their coats on.

"It's the pastor," Ingrid said. "About Gus's…" But she couldn't get out the word.

"You talk to him," Nels said, and stalked into the back room.

"Nels never did go to church much," Ingrid apologized for him. She introduced them all to the Reverend Phil Vincent, a man with a shining face, who looked to be about seventy. She said he served several small communities.

He wouldn't have to come up with a new sermon every week, Joan thought. Every three, maybe. Makes sense, as long as he can drive, anyhow.

"Pastor, I want the service in the church," Ingrid told him. "Not in a funeral home. I know nobody's buried from the church anymore, but that's what I want for my family."

"Let's talk it over," said Pastor Vincent. "And tell me about your son."

"You don't need us," Oscar said. "Good to see you, Pastor."

Helga hugged Ingrid one more time, and they left her alone with him.

Walking home, Oscar already was yawning. It figured. Andrew left them to go on a run. He needed the exercise, he said, but promised to be back by four when Kierstin would come to spend some time with him and Helga. Joan figured he'd had about as much family as he could take.

The phone was ringing when they opened the door. Helga easily beat Oscar to it and picked it up, breathless.

"Hello…hello? Speak up, I can't understand you." She listened for a moment or two more and put the receiver down in disgust. "I don't know why people bother to call if they don't talk so you can hear them."

"If it's important they'll call back," Joan said.

Fred grinned. "Or if they're selling something."

"I can't bother with them," Helga said. "I have to make supper."

Joan and Fred looked at each other.

"Not yet, Mom," he said. "I'm still full of that great lunch you and Ingrid laid out for us. If you feed us again now, I won't do it justice."

"Pretty soon," she said. "You know your father gets hungry early."

"Only thing I'm hungry for is a nap," Oscar said. "Come upstairs and take a nap with me." He stroked her cheek.

In that instant her face shed a dozen years. "Really, Oscar! In front of the children!"

"Leave them down here," he said. "You and I will go upstairs, where they won't see us." He held out his hand, and she took it.

"If you think it's all right."

"After you, my love." They climbed the stairs like young lovers.

Bless his heart, Joan thought, he loves her, and he's mastered the art of distraction. "What a gift."

"To all of us." Fred shook his head. Sitting down on the sofa, he patted the cushion beside him. "He has to keep this up day after day. I don't have his patience—this morning I actually yelled at her. No wonder he wears out sometimes."

She curled up in his arms. "And then she takes off, or does who knows what. I've been thinking about what we do know."

"Not much."

"We know it was a man. She's never wavered in that.

And she's never mentioned more than one. Neither did Peterson.''

"Who got a good look at the tracks he left. I wish…" His frustration showed in his face. Fred was used to being in the know when it came to police investigations. This role had to be hard for him.

"You'll wear him down. Your mom's sure she saw it happen.''

"I think she did.''

"That means it was quite a while after lunch, because you know she cleaned up the kitchen and put every last plate away before she went out. When Buker and Peterson arrived last night, it was hard to get her to stop.''

"Ask Andrew,'' he said. "He'll know when she left.''

"Even so, we don't know how much after that Gus was killed. Or did Peterson give you an idea? Wouldn't they have taken his temperature on the spot?''

"He didn't tell me—yet." He looked hopeful. "But he was cold when I checked for a pulse. Even in that weather, he had to have been there half an hour, anyhow. Probably more—Andrew said they were out hunting Mom for an hour.''

"She was well wrapped, and her blood was circulating, but she was plenty chilly, especially not moving like that.''

"She's lucky we found her when we did.''

"Yeah." Or is she? Joan wondered. Is anybody lucky to be spared a quick, easy death, only to live through the ravages of Alzheimer's? But there's still enough of her in there that nobody's ready to lose her.

"I know what you're thinking.''

He probably did. She reached up and stroked his cheek, as Oscar had stroked Helga's. "Okay,'' she said, "some other things we know. Andrew and Oscar covered a lot of ground in that hour, but nobody remembered seeing her.

That might mean she went straight from the house to the woods. Only the people in the old Janson house had a chance of seeing her, unless she passed someone on the road.''

"You think she followed someone in there?" he asked.

"No, don't you remember? Those other tracks came from that place where people can burn stuff.''

He nodded. "The burn site. You're right, they did.''

"And hers joined them," Joan said. "Only we don't know in what order.''

"Peterson was sure the killer chased after her. So was Mom.''

"Yeah. But you think maybe she'd already left the clearing when he came in and killed Gus? She could have heard them and watched from behind a tree or bush or something, and only then started running, when she got scared.''

"The length of her stride ought to tell where she started running," Fred said. "I'll ask.''

"Maybe she and Gus were chatting when the killer arrived. He fought with Gus and killed him while she got away. Maybe Gus yelled at her to run and saved her life.''

"A lot of maybes. They don't get us very far.''

"No," she said. "But we know some suspects. Mark Balter, for one.''

"And for two?''

She hesitated. "If Debbie York already knew about Gerri, if she knew Gus was dumping her…''

"You think she'd turn on him?" Clearly, from his tone, he didn't think so.

"Not really. I'd think she'd take it out on the other woman, instead.''

"Gerri attacked her first," Fred said.

"Gus was already dead by then, whoever killed him.''

"It's not a womanly crime," he said. "I can't see her going after him with a branch. Not the Deb I knew."

"Oh, ho." She raised an eyebrow at him, and he blushed. Fair as he was, she couldn't remember ever having seen him blush before, but the red ran right up his neck to the tops of his ears. She waited.

"We dated," he said. "Some. In high school."

"And now she teaches where you both went to school?"

"I guess so."

"Maybe I could ask her about you back then." She grinned, enjoying his embarrassment. "Worm my way into her confidence."

"Go ahead. Not that I think it was Deb. Mom was so sure it was a man."

"She was sure he killed you, too."

Fred winced.

Joan took pity on him. "I don't really think Debbie did it, either. She ought to have been teaching school at that hour with plenty of witnesses, but anybody can call in sick. Kierstin might know."

"Good thought. We'll ask her when she comes over. I won't mind if you spend the afternoon in the gift shops, either."

"You want me to?"

"You'll probably learn more from those folks by yourself than with me tagging along. I don't want you to feel completely tied to Mom, either. I'll stick with her."

"Until Andrew and Kierstin come? Do you think they'll be enough? Kierstin's a child, and Andrew's only twenty. Could they defend her?" Could anybody defend her against the kind of attack that killed Gus?

"It won't come to that, especially with a deputy looking out for her. The only thing this man has to fear from Mom is exposure. It would defeat his purpose to do anything with witnesses around. That's why he ran this morning, before I could get a look at him.''

"I suppose so." She thought a moment. "So, if I'm doing the shops, and Andrew and Kierstin and a deputy are with your mom, does that mean you have plans?''

"I might drive up to Cambridge." He tossed it off casually, as if it didn't mean he'd be abandoning her in Bishop Hill.

"I'll bite. What's Cambridge?''

"County seat, where the sheriff's office is. I thought I'd cruise around and look for Peterson. Time to see what I can get out of him. Did they check Gus's service record? What has he done to make enemies? Even if there's nothing negative on his record, did they get in touch with his commanding officer and ask whether anyone with a grudge could have followed him here?''

"You think?" she said.

"Could be.''

"And if he won't tell you?''

"I'll ask Nels and Ingrid. Nels couldn't think of anyone, but he'll know where Gus was stationed, and I can go from there.''

"Will the Army tell you?" She found that hard to believe.

"Not officially. But I'm not official, remember? I'll find somebody who knows somebody who knows somebody. Lay it on thick how worried I am about my poor elderly mother.''

That was the truth. "You have someone in mind?''

"You have any idea how many cops are vets?''

"Oh.''

"But first I'll try to persuade Peterson. Right now, you go spend money. Support Bishop Hill.''

"Yes, sir.''

TWELVE

JOAN FOLLOWED the same path they'd taken after breakfast, past the ravine and the Colony Church to the bakery and the shops they hadn't visited. The temperature had risen perceptibly, and with afternoon sunshine on her face she walked along comfortably. This time she passed by Oscar's old bakery, but she returned the greeting when Maggie Lund waved at her through the window. She wondered how long it would take to become acquainted in such a small place. It would probably help, of course, to have married into an old Bishop Hill family.

Next to the bakery, but set back from the street, stood an old barn. The date 1882 was painted at the bottom of a little structure on top of the roof, like a mini-building, with its own pointy roof. She supposed that was a cupola, though somehow she had always thought cupolas were round. Shoppers were emerging from the barn with baskets and wreaths of dried flowers and herbs. From the look of the garden out front, now mulched for the winter, Joan suspected that at least the herbs were local products. She stuck her head in the door, but the place was doing so much business that she hated to interrupt.

I'd never make a cop. Besides, I promised Fred I'd spend money.

A large basket caught her eye, not only handsome, but

perfect to carry the other things she would blow Fred's money on. The price made her blink.

"They're really strong," the shopkeeper at her elbow told her. She whacked the shopping basket against the wall to demonstrate.

Joan remembered her mission. "I'll take it. My husband sent me shopping to support his hometown."

"Oh? Who is your husband?"

And they were off. This woman remembered that Maggie had bought the bakery from Oscar, but she herself was not a native of Bishop Hill. Still, she had heard all about Gus—hadn't everyone? Terrible, just terrible. No, she'd never met the man. Well, yes, it was possible that he had come into the shop that day, but she didn't remember. She was sure that if she sold him anything, she didn't get his name. And she didn't recognize the photograph they'd shown on TV. A nice-looking young man. She'd heard they were going to need a closed casket at the funeral, his face was so bad. Such a shame. No, it didn't seem to be cutting into her sales. Not yet, anyway. She worried what would happen this weekend if they didn't find the killer by then. "Or, heaven forbid, if he strikes again. A serial killer loose in Bishop Hill..." She shuddered.

Joan agreed and made her escape.

Her forays into other shops produced little more information, though other people seemed more fearful than the basket lady. No one remembered having seen Gus, alone or with anyone else. She weighed down her new basket with stoneware for Margaret Duffy, the old teacher who had persuaded the board of the Oliver Senior Citizens' Center to hire her. At the Steeple Building she bought a book she'd loved as a child, *Snip, Snap, Snur and the Red Shoes*, both in English and, just for fun, in the original Swedish, for Laura Putnam, the little girl she had once rescued from a tornado. She hadn't decided yet about Annie Jordan, who had taken Joan under her wing at the senior center. Maybe Annie would like some of the many wooden Swedish candlesticks, or the basket for her ever-present knitting. It would be an insult to take her one of the beautiful sweaters from the artisans' shop. Some of that handmade paper might be nice, though, or a handblown glass ornament.

Looking for gifts for Oscar and Helga so close to home made little sense, but there had to be something for Fred and Andrew. Why were men so hard? Rebecca, her daughter, would be easy. She would love something from the quilt shop Joan hadn't visited yet.

But that's not why I'm doing this, she had to keep reminding herself and make herself dive into still another conversation about Gus Friberg.

"I feel so sorry for his poor mother," one woman told her. "Ingrid never misses church and always looks so lonely. She doesn't speak much. Hurries home like she has to cook dinner for a big family. But they've all long flown the nest, you know? She rattles around in that big house."

As if Nels didn't exist. "And her husband?" Joan said.

"I suppose he was a good enough house painter." The woman didn't sniff, but her dismissal couldn't have been plainer. No one else had much to say about him, either, not even the woodworkers and broom maker selling their wares. Nels seemed to be right. In spite of his obvious craftsmanship, he'd outlived whatever reputation he once had enjoyed.

Joan's feet ached. Why people enjoyed spending a day shopping always escaped her, but more of them seemed to be on the streets today than yesterday, when they'd seen so few people that Fred had kissed her right out on the sidewalk.

"Is something happening here today?" she asked in the Colony Store.

"No, but tomorrow is the first Lucia Night," a tired-looking older woman behind the counter told her. Under her all-too-blond hair, her face sagged. She wore rings on all her fingers, though she had bitten her nails to the quick. "Tomorrow night every window in town will have a candle in it, and we'll have special music. Our Lucia here in the store will give you cider and sweets. Where do you come from?"

"Indiana," Joan said. "I'm visiting family here."

"Oh? Who?"

"Oscar and Helga Lundquist. I married their son Fred."

"Fred Lundquist…I think he went to school with my oldest daughter."

"What was her name?"

"Vicki Holm, same as mine."

Joan looked more closely at her face and thought she saw a resemblance. "Are you Gerri's mother, too? Gerri Balter?" Mark had said Gerri was a Holm.

Vicki's eyes opened wide. "How do you know Gerri?"

"I met her this morning, at the Fribergs' house. I'm so sorry for her loss."

"Her loss?" Vicki sounded genuinely surprised.

"Gerri told us she and Gus had come home to be married."

Vicki's whole body stiffened. "You have the wrong person. My Gerri had one disastrous marriage. She's not about to make that mistake again."

She hadn't told her mother! Or was it possible that she hadn't really been engaged to Gus at all? Had she made the whole thing up after he died? And then gone so far as to attack Debbie? Surely not. Gerri had said they wanted to be married in Bishop Hill. Had she mentioned who would marry them? Or where? Joan couldn't remember. The Fribergs' pastor had come to the house today, but that was for Ingrid. It didn't say anything about Gus, much less Gerri. Maybe they would want their wedding in the church, whether they were churchgoers or not. Still, they might have planned a quick wedding before a judge or the county clerk.

Vicki Holm glared at her. "You going to buy that or not?"

Joan looked down at the Lucia doll she had picked up unconsciously. "Yes, please," she said meekly, although she had no idea what she would do with it. She watched Vicki wrap it in tissue and brown paper in silence and slap the receipt down on it.

The county clerk, that's who would know whether they at least had gone in for a license. Did it even matter, at this point, to anyone but Gerri?

"Merry Christmas," Vicki told her as if she didn't mean it, and she turned to her next customer.

What would make Gerri's mother think Gus Friberg would be as disastrous a husband as Mark Balter had been? Did she know something about Gus? Too late to ask her now. For that matter, it was close to four, when Andrew and Kierstin were supposed to take over staying with Helga. Joan wanted to be there when they did, if they even remembered.

She went back by way of the bed and breakfast to stash her purchases in their room. When she arrived at the house, Andrew met her at the door. "You probably thought I'd forget."

"Who, me? Where is everyone?"

"Oscar's upstairs, and Helga's on the phone."

"And Fred?" But then she saw him, stretched out in his

father's chair, snoring softly. She smiled. He hadn't had much sleep.

"He was wide awake when I got here," Andrew said. He and Fred stood up for each other.

"I'm sure he was."

"Don't keep calling me!" Helga slammed down the kitchen phone and came into the living room. "Why do they do that, anyway?"

"Who?" Andrew said.

"I don't know who. He never says."

"What does he say?" Joan asked.

"Nothing that makes any sense. I hung up on him." And that was all they could get out of her.

"You don't think..." Andrew said.

"Oh, Andrew, no!" Joan said.

"What are you talking about?" Helga asked them.

"Andrew wondered whether that was someone who's been worrying me," Joan said, truthfully enough. "Would it be all right for me to answer your phone the next time?"

"Be my guest!"

"Speaking of guests," Andrew said, "there's Kierstin, coming up the walk."

Helga flew to the door and threw it open. "Child, come in out of the cold!"

"Farmor!" Kierstin, her cheeks red, hugged her, while Andrew quietly closed the door behind her. She pulled off her hat and let her braids come tumbling down. "How are you?"

"I'm glad to see you. I haven't seen you for much too long."

"I should come by more often." Good for Kierstin, Joan thought. She knows better than to upset her grandmother by reminding her how recently they ate supper together.

"Dad wants us all to go to the restaurant for supper. Is that all right with you?"

"Dad?" Helga looked foggy.

"My dad. Your son Walter." Kierstin had the hang of keeping it simple and straightforward for her, and she cut to the heart of what Helga was confused about.

"Of course. You tell Walter we'll be glad to come." Helga turned to Joan. "It's good to have a restaurant in the family. Wait until you see it!"

"I look forward to it. I'll tell Fred when he wakes up."

"Just resting my eyes," he murmured from the recliner.

"Noisily." She smiled down at his receding hairline. "Did you hear the part about eating at Walt and Ruthie's?"

"I'll be back in plenty of time."

"Where are you going?" his mother asked.

He opened his eyes. "Not far. Over to Cambridge." He waved toward the window that had to be in the direction of Cambridge.

"Drive carefully."

"Yes, Mom." He sighed and shut his eyes again. Fred was a good driver. That restraint had to have cost him something.

Joan said, "And while you're there, would you mind checking something?"

"Sure, what?"

"You know I went shopping this afternoon." That was for Helga's benefit, mostly. "I had the oddest conversation in the Colony Store. The woman who sold me something was Vicki Holm."

"I went to school with Vicki."

"Her mother."

He nodded. "I remember her. All those Holm girls looked like their mother."

"She remembered you, too," Joan said, and smiled at

Helga. "Anyhow, I said something sympathetic about Gerri, because of Gus, you know. And she just hit the ceiling. Said Gerri wasn't about to make the mistake of getting married again, that her first husband had been a disaster. Gerri obviously hadn't said a word about it to her, or if she had, this lady wasn't buying it. I began to wonder whether it was all in her head—Gerri's, I mean."

"They hadn't told Gus's parents yet. It's not so odd that Gerri hadn't told her mother."

"Maybe. It's probably nothing. She may just have been overreacting, after the crummy first husband. But while you're in the county seat, you might find out whether they even got around to buying a license."

"Okay. You want to come along?"

"I don't think so. That recliner looks pretty good to me right now."

He leaned forward and thwacked his feet on the floor. "It's all yours." Standing tall now, he looked down at Kierstin, though Andrew could look him in the eye. "You two have a good time with Mom."

"We always have a good time, don't we, Farmor?" Kierstin said.

"We sure do." Helga smiled at her, and reached out to take her hand. "And this young man is...?"

"Andrew. My mom is Joan, Fred's new wife." He pointed her out. How had Andrew caught on so quickly to the technique of reintroducing her to people she couldn't remember?

"That's right," Helga said to him, without looking at Joan. "So you're family now."

"On my first visit to Bishop Hill."

"Let's go for a walk, then. I'll show it to you."

Joan settled into the recliner, glad to put her feet up and release the hair clasp that would have hurt the back of her head when she leaned it against the chair. Fred stroked her long, straight hair gently. "I'll be back soon," he said.

After what seemed like mere seconds, she woke alone in a dim room.

Then she heard the phone. Maybe that's what woke me, she thought, and struggled out of the chair to answer it.

"Hello?"

Even though the words were something between a whisper and a mutter, she was somehow sure the speaker was a man. "Don't tell what you saw. You hear me? Don't tell anyone."

THIRTEEN

THE DRIVE FROM Bishop Hill to Cambridge was short, all on back roads so familiar that Fred didn't have to think about the right-angle turns along the way. Just being able to see the horizon gave him a sense of peace after the years he'd spent in Oliver, where the horizon always hid behind the next hill. Years. Not possible. No wonder his sister had pressured him to come home. Good thing somebody had.

The little town had fewer trees than he remembered, but they still lined the streets. He parked near the big new building that connected the jail and sheriff's office to the old courthouse. Should ease the perennial security problems involved in moving prisoners to and from court. He'd promised Joan that he'd check with the county clerk about Gus Friberg's marriage license, and he didn't know how late that office would stay open. Better take care of that first.

Even for the clerk's office, he had to go through the main security door and pass through a metal detector, where a uniformed deputy directed him up a flight of steps and left, into the old part of the building.

"Yes, sir?" a pretty young woman behind the counter greeted him. "What can I do for you?"

"You heard about Gus Friberg, the man who was murdered over in Bishop Hill."

She looked startled, then appropriately somber. "Wasn't

it awful? But you want the sheriff, upstairs. This is the clerk's office. We don't do murders.''

"I know. I want to know whether Gus took out a marriage license in the couple of days before he died.''

"Are you a reporter?'' she asked, wide-eyed. "We don't get a lot of reporters in here.''

"No. Gus was our neighbor.'' He'd leave it at that. She seemed willing enough.

"I'm so sorry.'' She hauled down one of the heavy record books. "That would be sometime this week?''

"Probably. I don't think he'd been home more than a day or two.''

"Isn't that the saddest thing?'' Flipping pages, she found it quickly and turned the volume so that he could read where her finger was pointing. "Gustaf Friberg and Gerri Holm Balter—I remember them. We don't get many couples in here that old.''

With her fresh young face, she looked about sixteen, though he supposed she had to be at least in her twenties. Running his hand over his high forehead, he wondered what she'd think if he told her he had been married only three months.

Probably thinks really old people like us don't do it anymore. She ought to see Mom and Dad going upstairs.

"Thank you,'' he said with a straight face. Who knew what was bugging Vicki Holm? At least Gerri hadn't invented the whole thing.

"Did they have time to get married first?'' the child clerk asked.

"No.'' Not even to tell their parents.

"Ohhhh. That's so sad, you know? She looked really radiant, like a bride should. And now she'll probably never be one.''

"She was married before.'' Why did he tell her that?

"Did he die, too?"

"No." Shut up, Lundquist, he told himself, but he knew their life stories would line the birdcage soon enough. Nothing about a murder victim's life stayed private very long. "Thanks for your help."

"No problem." She flashed him a smile that was anything but flirtatious and slid the book back into its place on the shelf.

Feeling his age, Fred strolled up to the sheriff's office. I should have called, he thought. Probably drove over here for nothing. Almost nothing. At least he had found out about the license.

But Kate Buker met him at the door. "Lieutenant," she said. "I'm glad to see you."

"Oh?"

Her smile transformed her into a real person. Still in uniform, she didn't exactly project femininity, but she seemed more confident, more professional than the uptight, defensive woman he'd first met at the crime scene. "Greg Peterson was going to call you. Let me get him for you."

"You're not parked out there this afternoon, watching Mom?"

She smiled again. "Not my turn this afternoon. But I'll go back." She spoke into the phone. "He'll be right with you."

Peterson had changed his brown tweeds for gray flannel, with a blue sweater underneath that looked like something Joan's friend Annie might have knitted. He still looked like a bear, Fred thought. A bear in a sweater.

"I take it you didn't catch our morning intruder."

"We didn't so much as see a moving vehicle within a mile of the house," Peterson said. "He probably holed up somewhere local."

"Figures. This has to be the man Mom saw kill Gus."

"I agree," Peterson said. "I spoke with Friberg's commanding officer, a Colonel Newcomb. He says he'll probably turn it over to their Criminal Investigation Division, and he's promised full cooperation. Of course, they'll want everything we can give them, too. The way they look at it, Friberg was one of their own, and they owe it to him to find out what happened to him. They have resources we can only dream of."

"Good work, Peterson," he said, as if the man had been under his command.

"Thanks. But I didn't have much to do with it. He could just as easily have turned me down cold."

No wonder Peterson was glad to see him. He wanted to pick Fred's brain.

He smiled that gentle smile that had put Fred's mom at ease. "Let's go to my office. Can I give you a cup of coffee?"

"Sure." Fred followed him to a square office with a U-shaped desk and chairs that put his own cubicle and old wooden swivel chair to shame. Peterson showed him to a chair and went for the coffee, which turned out to be surprisingly good, not like the stuff he drank in Oliver, which sometimes sat on the warmer far too long.

Fred swallowed appreciatively. "You've met the family," he said.

"No obvious conflicts there."

"Nothing that sticks out," Fred agreed.

"You've known them long?"

"We were all kids together, except for Bengt Swanson, Christina's husband. Saw him some when our high schools played each other. He was quite an athlete back then. Packed a wallop on the football field." Fred had been on the receiving end of some of those wallops.

"So he'd be strong enough," Peterson said. He chewed on his lower lip.

"He still looks in pretty good shape."

Peterson nodded. "And the other son-in-law?"

"Tim? Went to school with him. He's a hog farmer, and yes, I'm sure he's strong enough, too." He hesitated. "And maybe mean enough, though I can't think why he'd go after Gus."

Peterson jumped on it. "Mean enough? What makes you think that?"

"The way he used to talk with the guys—nothing worth mentioning, really. I don't know how he turned out. Until the other night I hadn't seen him for years."

He nodded.

"You hear about Mark Balter?" Fred asked him.

"A relative?"

"No. A classmate of mine, so years older than Gus. Excon, with motive."

"Oh?"

"Gus Friberg and Balter's ex-wife were engaged to be married, and Mark wanted her back in the worst way."

"You're sure?" Peterson leaned forward. No wonder— Mark Balter fit.

"I'm sure. Met him on the street. If you'd heard him— seen his face..."

"Any history of violence?"

"Not that I know of."

"I'd better talk with him," Peterson said.

"Yeah. And with his ex-wife, Gerri." Fred spelled it for him.

"Where is she?"

"In Bishop Hill, visiting her mother, Vicki Holm. The mother works at the Colony Store, and according to my wife she didn't know about the engagement. Very negative about it. Claimed Gerri wouldn't marry again."

Peterson's ears perked up at that. "You sure she would?"

"My wife wondered the same thing, but I just came from the county clerk. They took out a license the day Gus was killed."

"You think the ex knew?"

"No idea. But someone else didn't want that marriage."

"The mother?"

"Sounds like it, but I was thinking of Tim York's sister." Fred hated to say it. "Seems she expected Gus to come home sometime and marry her. When Gerri flew at her—"

"What?"

"Gerri walked into the Fribergs' house when Debbie York was saying something about marrying Gus. Attacked her for it."

"Physically?" Amusement fought the control Peterson was just barely keeping over his face.

"Yeah. Grabbed her by the hair. For a minute there, I thought I was going to have to pull them apart."

"But?"

"Would you believe it, my mother beat me to it."

Peterson said, "You'd think the one who lost out would have gone after the other one."

"You'd never think Deb would do such a thing." Not Deb. Not the Deb he knew. "She wasn't a violent person back when I knew her."

"And Gerri was?"

"I didn't know her, not really. She's a lot younger, more Gus's age."

Peterson had been making notes. Names, mostly, Fred suspected. He would have been, in his place.

"One more thing."

"Yes?" Peterson asked.

"Gerri said she was leaving town as soon as Gus was buried."

"Thanks."

"So, what did you learn from Colonel Newcomb?"

"Not much," Peterson admitted.

"Maybe we could prime the pump a little."

"For instance?" He didn't object to the "we." A good sign, Fred thought.

"Since Colonel Newcomb promised full cooperation, give him all the information you've dug up about Gus's local contacts, but ask about conflicts he had there. Can Newcomb think of anyone who might hate Gus enough to follow him here? Or feel threatened by him? Or harbor a grudge?"

"I'll ask him. Thank you for your help, Lieutenant."

Would wonders never cease? "You're welcome," Fred said. "Let me know if I can help in any way. And call me Fred, won't you?"

"Sure, Fred. I'm Greg. Is someone with your mother? Closer than our squad car, I mean."

"My niece, Kierstin, and Andrew, my wife's son. Last I heard, Mom was going to give them the guided tour of Bishop Hill. She doesn't remember that Kierstin has lived there all her life."

The door to the office opened, and a young woman stuck her head in. "Pardon me for interrupting, but if you're Fred Lundquist, there's a call for you."

"Thanks, Tracy," Peterson said and held the phone out to Fred.

It had to be about Mom. Why else would anyone ask for him? "Yes?"

"Fred, it's me." Joan's voice trembled. "He's calling."

"Who's calling?" But he knew what she would answer before the words were out of his mouth.

"It has to be the killer. You know those phone calls your mom has been getting? The ones she hangs up on because he won't speak up?"

He nodded, as if she could hear him. "Uh-huh."

"I'm sure it was a man, but he whispered, sort of."

"What did he say? Word for word, if you can." He made writing gestures in the air, and Peterson immediately brought over a notepad and pen.

"That's why I'm sure it was the man who killed Gus. He said, in this spooky kind of Peter Lorre half voice, 'Don't tell what you saw. You hear me? Don't tell anyone.'"

He scribbled it down and showed it to Peterson. "That's all? Nothing else?"

"That's all. He hung up before I could say anything."

"And you didn't recognize his voice? Or the way he said the words?"

"No."

"Could you hear anything in the background?"

She hesitated. "No, but it was so quick. Maybe I missed it."

"Joan, are you all right?"

"It scared me." But her voice was calmer now. "Fred, all I said was hello. I'm sure he thought he was talking to your mother. If he's in Bishop Hill and he sees her on the street, he's going to know it was someone else on the phone."

He shivered. "Only if he saw her immediately after he hung up. Give her a couple of minutes on foot, and she could be anywhere in Bishop Hill. He'd know that."

"I hope so. At least, I think I do. Does it make any difference?"

"I don't know. I'll be there in a few minutes, okay?"

"Okay."

He hung up and turned to Peterson. "My wife."

"I gathered that."

"My mother's been bothered by phone calls she said she couldn't hear. We figured they were some persistent telephone sales rep. Only this time Mom was out with Andrew and Kierstin, and Joan answered the phone. She thinks it was a man, half whispering. She didn't recognize the voice, but she doesn't know much of anyone around here."

"Next time, tell her to dial star fifty-seven. The phone company will charge you a few bucks, but they'll ID the last caller and notify us. And I'll get a warrant so you can record them. We ought to be able to get a voiceprint."

"Thank you. I'll need to buy a tape recorder."

"We can provide one. Let's hope he calls back."

"He'll probably use a pay phone."

"Not if he's calling from Bishop Hill," Peterson said. "There aren't any."

"I've got to get back there." No question now about whether the killer saw Mom—and recognized her. For the first time, Fred felt truly afraid.

FOURTEEN

JOAN WAS AMAZED at how fast Fred made it back from Cambridge. She'd rummaged shamelessly in Helga's kitchen until she found a pad of paper under the cheese grater and a pencil in the knife drawer. She parked them by the telephone, in case the killer called again. But when it did ring, it was only Walt, checking to be sure Kierstin had arrived as promised.

"I would have called sooner," he said, "but we've been busy here. Tomorrow night all the Bishop Hill restaurants will serve supper, but we're it tonight, and the traffic is already picking up."

It wouldn't be fair to worry him about the other call. Fred would be back soon. She hardly had time to pace. When the Chevy pulled up, she ran outside, not bothering with her coat. Just like Helga, she thought.

He swept her into a bear hug. "Is she all right?"

"I don't know. I mean, I'm sure she is, but it's getting dark. Oh, Fred, let's go find them—your mom and the kids."

He walked her into the house. "Before I forget, if you answer another one of those calls, push star fifty-seven to tell the sheriff who it was."

"Fred, it's an old dial phone, not a push button. There isn't any star on it. And there's no place to plug in a new phone. I looked. This one's wired right into the wall."

"We don't have time to rewire it," Fred said. "Peterson's getting a warrant so we can at least record the next call. He lent me a tape recorder." He pulled it out of his coat pocket and took it into the kitchen.

"Do we have to wait for the warrant?"

"If we don't, the guy could get off."

"Oh." Right now she hardly cared what happened later. She just wanted him caught. This call had really scared her. But she knew better. She'd feel even worse if that violent killer got away with it and was turned loose to kill again because of something she did.

"Nothing's really changed; you know that. If anything, this may be our first lead on him."

"I know." She reached for her coat anyway.

"Let me tell Dad." He took the stairs two at a time.

He's as worried as I am, she thought.

Arm in arm, they walked toward the bed and breakfast and turned toward the shops.

Joan scanned the growing number of pedestrians when they reached the main shopping area. No sign of Helga, but she didn't see Andrew or Kierstin, either. "They wouldn't leave her alone."

"No. They probably went indoors somewhere."

"I'm surprised she's not agitating to go home and cook."

"The kids know we're going to Walt and Ruthie's."

"Right." Where's my head? Joan thought, and then she saw Andrew on the tiny porch of the bakery, holding up the wall with one outstretched arm while bending his dark curls toward a golden head that had to be Kierstin's.

"Fred, there they are." Courting. And no sign of Helga. "I don't see Mom."

"She must be in the bakery." Joan hurried faster, annoyed that Andrew could be outside with all his attention on Kierstin instead of sticking like a burr to Helga.

Fred didn't say anything, but pulled her along even faster.

"Hey, you two!" Joan called when she came close enough not to be suspected of accosting some stranger. No response.

"Andrew! Kierstin!" Fred shouted, and they turned.

"Hi, Fred, Mom," Andrew said, obviously unconcerned.

Now they were face-to-face. "Where's Helga?" Joan said.

"In there," Andrew said, and pointed airily at the bakery. "She wanted to take some bread to Walt."

"How long ago?" Fred asked.

Kierstin blushed, and Andrew looked flustered. "A few minutes," he said. "What time is it, anyway?"

"Andrew Spencer, you were supposed to stick with her!"

"We did, Mom. I told you—she's in there with Maggie."

Fred was already through the door, narrowly avoiding a woman coming out with a full shopping bag. A paper sack with a loaf of bread rode on the top of her load.

"That's not good enough, do you hear?" Joan said. She heard her tone, but she didn't care. "We trusted you two to take care of her, not moon over each other."

Kierstin hung her head.

"Helga's pretty stubborn," Andrew said. "But next time we'll go in with her, okay?" His voice had taken on a defensive edge.

"If there is a next time. I don't think you have any idea how much danger she's in. Someone broke into the house this morning. She's already forgotten it, of course. We didn't want to tell you in front of her and scare her."

"Broke in! While I was sleeping?"

"Yes, after Fred got there."

"But she's all right! I mean…"

She let him worry for a moment. "You're right. She was. And it's our job to keep her that way." Turning her back on them, she went in.

Fred, his shoulders sagging, stood in front of the counter. "She left," he told her. "But Maggie didn't see where she went. She's checking the bathroom."

Maggie came through the door behind the counter, shaking her head. "Not in there."

"So walk us through it again, please," Fred said, suddenly shifting from worried son to professional cop.

"There's not much to tell," Maggie said. "Your mom came in here maybe ten or fifteen minutes ago and bought a couple of loaves of Swedish rye. Said they were for Walt's restaurant. I didn't tell her how much bread we'd already baked for Walt today."

"And then?"

"She was kind of looking at the pies and such, and I let her look while I waited on other customers. By the time I was finished, she'd left. I charged the bread to Oscar's account and didn't think another thing about it. She does that all the time, and he settles up at the end of the month. I figured she probably went to the restaurant. She was looking out the front window, too, and I saw Kierstin out there."

"Thank you, Maggie," Fred said. "We're a little anxious about her these days."

"I understand. It's so hard to see her fail like this." She glanced out the window. "There's Kierstin now."

"And my son," Joan said. "They must have missed her." Easy to see how. She fumed.

"If you see her, or if you think of anything else, give us a call," Fred said. "Here's my cell phone number." He handed Maggie his card.

"I sure will." She tucked it into her apron pocket.

They returned to the porch. "What now?" Joan asked Fred, but she was glaring at Andrew and Kierstin.

"I'm so sorry!" Kierstin said. Her eyes brimmed, just short of spilling tears. "I love her!"

"I know you do," Fred said. "But she's so quick—you can't look away like that when you're responsible for her safety. Give her a moment, and she's past you."

"It's my fault," Andrew said. "I thought sure we'd see her."

"You're right," Joan told him. "It is."

His face fell.

Am I being too hard on him? she thought. I wouldn't give Oscar such a hard time.

"Doesn't matter whose fault it is," Fred said. "She's long gone. We just have to figure where."

For now, Joan thought, he's thinking optimistically. Or maybe he doesn't think we should scare the kids. In her heart of hearts, she thought it was too late to worry about scaring them. She thought it was too late for Helga, period.

"Would she go home?" Kierstin asked.

"She bought bread for your dad," Joan said. "I'll bet she took it to the restaurant." Unless Gus's killer got her. But where would he take her? He couldn't kill her right there in front of all those people.

Fred nodded. "Good a guess as any. We'll go there, and you kids go back to the house and check with Dad. If she's not there, leave the house open and the lights on, and take Dad over to the restaurant for supper. Call Walt, but don't let on Mom isn't with us if Dad can hear you. Got it?"

"Yessir," Andrew said. "Come on, Kierstin." They set off at a trot.

Fred still seemed amazingly calm. "We'll find her," he said as if he believed it.

"I hope so. I hope…" She couldn't tell him her worst fears. This was *his* mother.

"I know." Still standing on the porch, he pulled the phone out of his pocket. "Lieutenant Lundquist calling Greg Peterson, please. No, not tomorrow. Tell him the woman we talked about today is missing—trust me, he'll want to know. I'm checking two places right now, and I'll report back immediately." He left his number. "Now let's march." He tucked Joan's hand in the curve of his arm.

The phone rang before they reached the restaurant. Fred didn't slow his pace to answer it. "Yes. Less than half an hour ago, from the bakery. The kids who'd been with her have gone back to check the house, and we're on our way to the restaurant—she bought some bread she said was for my brother. Right. Thanks."

"That was Peterson?" Joan asked.

"Yes."

"I'm glad. Fred, that man was so scary!" She hadn't meant to say it, but it slipped out of her. "I'm sorry."

He squeezed her arm. "I know. The hell of it is, we don't know what he looks like. The killer could be any one of these men." He waved at the crowd.

"If he is, she's probably okay. He'd hardly have had time to get her and blend back into the crowd."

For the first time, Fred smiled. "You're right. Anyhow, Peterson said he's got a photo of a man Gus had some problems with in the Army—he was discharged a few months ago after he was convicted in a civilian trial."

"Did he say what for?" Surely he'd mention it if the guy was convicted of an ax murder.

"No."

Walt met them at the door. "I just had the oddest call from Kierstin," he said. "She said she was bringing Dad over, but not a word about Mom. I asked, and she just said she'd tell me all about that when they got here.''

Joan's heart sank. In spite of herself, she had hoped they would find Helga at home.

''She's not here?'' Fred said.

''Mom? No, I thought she'd be with you.''

''She got away from Andrew and Kierstin a few minutes back. I sent them to the house, but told them not to let on to Dad.''

Walt's face clouded over. ''That's why Kierstin wouldn't tell me. How could they let Mom—''

Fred interrupted him. ''Walt, you know better. We never should have asked those kids to watch her. She's so quick and so stubborn, they couldn't stand up to her. We've already called the sheriff's office.''

He pulled out the phone and punched in numbers that must have been to Peterson's cell phone, because he got an immediate answer. ''Greg, Fred. She's not here at the restaurant or the house, either one. I'll wait.'' He pocketed the phone and said to Walt, ''He's sending a deputy for me.''

''What should we do?'' Walt said.

''Act as normal as possible. Feed the family in the back room—no point in alarming the whole restaurant if Dad falls apart. I'll wait for the deputy. Joan, you stick with Dad, keep him as calm as you can.''

''All right,'' she promised, even though everything in her screamed to go with him.

''I'll have Ruthie pack you something,'' Walt said.

''Thanks, Walt.''

Joan was grateful, too. She hated to picture Fred out searching for Helga while the rest of them were filling their faces.

''You want me to send something for the other guy?''

''He won't object. And coffee.''

Walt nodded and disappeared into the kitchen, but Joan wondered how any of them would be able to eat.

WHEN HIS DAD ARRIVED with Kierstin and Andrew, Fred welcomed them to Walt and Ruthie's place as if it were his own. "Joan's waiting for you in the back room," he told them, not mentioning his mom.

"Won't you eat with us?" his dad asked.

"No, Dad, I'm waiting for the deputy sheriff. Ruthie's fixing us a sack lunch." He'd no sooner said it than Ruthie appeared in the kitchen door with a substantial basket.

"It's hot," she warned him.

"Thanks, Ruthie." He took it and inhaled. "It smells great." And he'd be able to warm his hands over it.

"Come on back, Dad," Ruthie said, taking his arm. "And you kids. Walt's coming in a minute."

Fred went to wait by the front door. He set the basket on the floor beside him and, with the family out of the way, let the worry wash over him. And the guilt. How had he not seen it coming? He heard himself this afternoon, assuring Peterson how responsible those kids were. Bad enough when Mom disappeared during Dad's naps, but that was before they knew what danger she was in. They had to find her before the killer did. If he knew her phone number, he knew her. This was no tourist, no stranger. He was more likely to be someone local, probably someone she'd feel safe with, and he wouldn't have any trouble persuading her to go with him. Just tell her Oscar needs her, and she'd go anywhere.

The door opened to admit an attractive young woman in a slim black coat and a short black velvet dress, her brown hair waving around her face. It took Fred a moment to recognize Kate Buker out of uniform. He'd interrupted a date.

"I got here as fast as I could," she said. "Any word?"

He shook his head. "Thank you for coming."

She waved it off. "Everyone's looking for her. Greg sent me to take you up to our command central. Meanwhile, he said to tell you Colonel Newcomb mentioned a Royal Funkhouse."

"Roy Funkhouse?" Walt had materialized, a menu in his hand.

"You know him?" Fred said.

"Sure. He works at the garage we use over in Galva. Been there a couple of months."

"Know anything about him?"

"Not much," Walt said. "He's a mechanic. Worked on our car a couple of times. Seemed competent. Why? What'd he do? My God, you think maybe he killed Gus?"

"I don't know," Buker said, heading for the door.

"We'll be back." Fred grabbed the basket and followed her.

Buker started the car, a little red sports job that went with the dress. "Funkhouse got a dishonorable discharge in September."

"What'd he do?"

"I don't know, but he was convicted in civilian court of something that put him in prison for a year or so. Gus testified against him, and the colonel says people heard him swear revenge."

"So he came here."

"Looks like he waited for Gus to come home, and then killed him."

"Except that it didn't look premeditated," Fred said.

"No," she agreed.

"That's not to say he couldn't have wanted to have it out with Gus, and then in the heat of the argument picked up a big stick."

"And gone too far."

FIFTEEN

WALT AND RUTHIE were busy with paying customers, and
Joan and the kids weren't finding it all that easy to comfort
Oscar. She was glad Walt had put them in a quiet nook in
the back of the restaurant. She sat next to Oscar, with Kierstin on his other side.

"He's got her!" Oscar said again. "I know it." Big tears
ran down his cheeks.

Joan reached out and took his hand. "Fred and lots of
others are out there searching for her. They'll find her, Oscar. They'll protect her." Scant comfort. She wished she
could believe it herself.

"Not if he's hiding her." His voice trembled.

"Maybe she's the one doing the hiding. Remember, in
the woods, she outfoxed him."

"Well…" He brightened. "She did, didn't she? My
Helga knows a thing or two, even now." He took a forkful
of Ruthie's potato bologna. "She taught Ruthie how to
make this, you know."

"I'm not surprised. Fred always has bragged on her
cooking. He said she won prizes almost every year."

Kierstin spoke up. "Farmor and Ingrid Friberg competed
for years. But they stayed friends."

Joan was glad to see Oscar continue to eat instead of
wailing. But it left her own mind free to worry. The voice
on the phone had scared her down to her toes. Suppose

Helga had recognized that voice while she was out somewhere, even in the familiar bakery. How would she have felt?

Is she terrified now? No wonder we couldn't find her. I'd hide from that guy, too. "And if she saw him…"

"What'd you say?" Andrew asked.

Oops. She hadn't meant to say that out loud, but it didn't seem to have bothered Oscar. "I was just thinking."

"Have another roll, Farfar?" Kierstin asked quickly, holding them under Oscar's nose. "And some of our special Lundquist preserves?" He reached for a crusty roll and accepted the jar she offered, chunks of strawberry sticking out of the top.

Joan smiled at her. It didn't make up for their carelessness, but Kierstin was doing her best to distract him. "Any special reason you went to the bakery this afternoon?"

"Oh, we always do," Kierstin said. "Whenever I take a walk with Farmor, she makes a beeline for it. She thinks it's still in the family. So that doesn't mean anything."

"Probably not," Joan said. "And you're sure she didn't see anything to alarm her while she was there?"

Kierstin blushed. "I didn't notice."

"I should have watched her better," Andrew said. "We should have gone inside with her."

"Never mind that now. Neither of you noticed anybody scary? A big man who looked angry at her? Or just stared at her? Like a stalker?"

They shook their heads. "No," Andrew said. "Just regular people."

"Old friends," Kierstin said.

"And a busload of Swedish tourists, all speaking Swedish," Andrew said.

"Farmor told them the King of Sweden came here."

"He did?"

"Oh, yes, in 1976. It was a big deal. Farmor says King Carl was really handsome. He didn't stay long, though. It rained a lot, and he was mostly under an umbrella. And his sister, Princess Christina, came when I was a little girl. They tell me I saw her, but I was too little to remember. She helped dedicate the art museum—you know, the one with the Olof Krans paintings of the old colonists."

"All this was after Helga went into the bakery? When she talked to the tourists, I mean."

"No, before," Kierstin said. "That's how I heard what she said. She followed some of them in. The rest wanted to practice English with Andrew and me. We talked quite a while. They said they were hanging out while someone pulled their bus out of the ditch over by the cemetery— that's how I know they had a bus. And they asked me about Bishop Hill's history."

Maggie had said Helga was looking out the front window.

"Think hard. Could she have seen you talking to the tourists?"

"I suppose so," Andrew said. "And the friends, too. But I don't think she was paying much attention. She didn't even come out to say hello to the Fribergs."

"Ingrid and Nels were there?"

"Yes, and both their daughters and sons-in-law. While Kierstin was talking with Nels and Ingrid, Tim told me I didn't have to worry—he'd take care of getting a tree for the old folks this year, the way he always did when their fair-haired boy didn't show up."

"He called Gus that?"

"Words to that effect. He's the one they made all the fuss about, he said, not their daughters, even though the daughters are there all the time. And Bengt said his wife was always taking her mom places, but she hung on every word she ever got from Gus, who hardly ever showed up.''

Joan raised her eyebrows at him.

''That's what they said, Mom.''

''Hmmm.'' Both those men were big enough for Helga to have described them as big. Had one of them resented Gus enough to kill him?

''You think those girls expected to inherit from their parents?'' Andrew asked.

''And their husbands thought Gus would get it all?''

''Maybe.''

''What would there be to inherit?'' Joan wondered. ''A house in this little place?'' Nice enough, but hardly a mansion. And no signs of wealth. She couldn't see it as a motive for murder.

''Who knows how much is enough to set someone off?'' Andrew said. He was reading her mind. ''Especially someone who's struggling to make ends meet.''

''Oh?'' she said. ''Is one of those guys struggling?''

''I don't know.''

''And even if he is, would that mean he'd be willing to bump off his wife's parents next? And maybe his sister-in-law, too?'' The more she thought about it, the less likely it seemed.

''Maybe not. But it wouldn't be too hard to check where Tim and Bengt were that afternoon.'' Andrew glanced over at Oscar, who was letting Kierstin put tidbits on his plate, and dropped his voice. ''And Helga probably saw them today.''

She probably saw them last night, over at Ingrid and Nels's, too, Joan thought. But she was so stressed out yesterday that by then she wasn't remembering much of anything. Maybe the intruder jogged her memory. Besides, it's going to come and go no matter what. Hard to tell who or what would make her run away like that.

"Anybody else you can think of?"

"Not that I knew, but yes, there were several others who stopped. Kierstin didn't introduce me to everyone. And she didn't know all the customers who went into the bakery."

Just because Kierstin didn't know someone doesn't mean he didn't know Gus—and have it in for him.

"Did she speak to a man named Mark Balter?"

"The one Gerri Balter was talking about after she attacked Debbie?" He *had* been listening.

"Yes."

"I don't know. Kierstin, did Mark Balter come by the bakery?"

She looked up from her attentions to Oscar. "No, I didn't see him."

"You know him?" Joan asked.

"I know who he is. We don't have a lot of ex-cons in Bishop Hill. I feel sorry for his mom. You know it has to hurt when people talk like they do, but old Mrs. Balter holds her head up high."

Oscar pulled a big white handkerchief out of his pocket and blew his nose loudly. Kierstin patted his back. "It's okay, Farfar. I'm here, and I love you."

Not the same thing as his Helga, Joan thought, but Oscar smiled through his tears. "You're a good girl," he said.

They managed to hold it together through the rest of the meal. Walt and Ruthie stopped in occasionally, but there was no word from Fred or Kate Buker. Early on, Walt had reported that he'd gone off with her, but after that, nothing. How could Oscar stand it? If this were Fred, or Andrew…

The conversational buzz in the rest of the restaurant faded. Joan looked at her watch. Half past eight. She wasn't sure when Lundquists closed, but Oscar's eyelids were drooping. Maybe he'd be able to sleep, if he didn't yield to a nap right now.

"Oscar, it's time to go home," she said gently.

He looked startled. "Do you really think…?"

"Helga won't expect to find you out gallivanting at this hour, will she?"

"No." He didn't need any more persuasion. He stood and pushed his chair back in one smooth motion that belied his age. "I'd better be home for her."

Leaving Kierstin at her parents' restaurant, Joan and Andrew walked him home. Overhead, a helicopter flew low over Bishop Hill, and they met a pair of mounted policemen as they walked. Odd. Could they have to do with Helga? She didn't want to distress Oscar by asking. He didn't seem nearly as surprised to see them as she was, though.

Back at the house, Andrew climbed the stairs to keep Oscar company while he changed for bed. Joan heard them up there, talking softly. At one point, she thought Andrew even got a chuckle out of him. But she was surprised to see her son appear alone at the foot of the stairs.

"Where's Oscar?"

"I told him we'd sit up in shifts, watching for Helga. He might as well sleep first, while it's easy for us to be up. And if Helga comes home and finds him in bed, she can crawl in beside him. He liked that."

"I heard."

Andrew stretched out in Oscar's chair. There was something she'd meant to ask him. Joan tried to let her mind go blank, almost impossible when she was so worried. She and Fred had been talking about something, but why did they think Andrew would know? No, not Andrew. Then why… ah, Kierstin.

"I need to ask Kierstin something." She hadn't meant to say it out loud.

"What?"

"Fred and I were wondering whether Debbie York missed any school this week." No point in asking leading questions.

"Isn't she a little old?"

"Seriously, Andrew. She teaches at Kierstin's school. English, I think. It probably doesn't matter, but it might help to know."

"Why don't I run back and ask Kierstin?"

"Fine. It's not as if we were protecting Helga anymore."

"No, we messed that up but good. I'm so sorry, Mom."

Seeing his face fall even lower, she said, "I'm sorry, Andrew. I know you thought she was safe."

He dragged himself out of the recliner. "I'll probably take the long way home. I could use a little exercise."

I don't blame you, Joan thought. I'd rather not be around me, either.

The phone rang, and Andrew went to answer it. Joan hoped it might be Fred, but Andrew came back from the kitchen shaking his head.

"They hung up."

"Oh." She tried not to let her disappointment show, but it must have. Not only was it not Fred, but it might have been the killer. She should have picked it up. Then maybe he would have said something that might have helped them find him. Even as she beat herself over the head about it, she didn't really believe it.

"Did you see the note by the phone?" he asked.

"What note?"

"The one by the tape recorder."

She went to look. Sure enough, the phone now had a microphone stuck to the receiver, and a note from Fred asked them to record any incoming calls. Good.

"There was nothing to tape," Andrew said. "You want me to hang around?"

"No, you go ahead." She didn't really suspect Debbie York, or any woman, for that matter. But she was glad to give him an excuse to hang out with Kierstin a little longer, if he wanted to. "And, Andrew, if I'm asleep when you come back, go on up to bed. No need to worry about Oscar or me. The killer's not interested in us."

When he left, she moved over to Oscar's recliner, put her feet up, and opened his newspaper. It was filled with pictures of Gus and his family and a somewhat garbled story of how she and Fred had discovered the body. She recognized some of the pictures Ingrid had shown them in her album of Gus as he grew up, but not the sober wedding photo showing Ingrid in a suit and Nels in Navy bell-bottoms, or the whole family posed in front of their house when Gus was still a baby in his mother's arms. Nels and the girls were smiling, but Ingrid already had that timid look. Had she always been so timid? Until now, Joan had thought it might be her reaction to her son's violent death.

The article didn't mention Helga, but now it was too late for that to matter. The killer had found her and followed her. It was impossible not to think what he might be doing to her at this very moment. Maybe, Joan told herself, maybe if he talks to her, he'll realize how little Helga can remember. But she didn't believe it. She made herself fold the useless paper neatly for Oscar instead of throwing it across the room.

Nothing to read, no one to talk to, and in spite of what she'd told Andrew, no way in the world she could fall asleep. The silent house closed in on her, though in the distance she could hear the chopper blades again. It was going to be a long night.

SIXTEEN

DAYLIGHT WAS filtering into the room when the phone woke her. Stiff in spite of Oscar's comfortable chair and the blanket Andrew must have thrown over her, Joan hurried to answer it, hoping against hope that Fred had found his mother unharmed. Only at the last minute did she remember to hit the record button.

Horrified, she recognized the same spooky half whisper. "Don't tell them. Don't tell what you saw. Don't tell anyone." Again, he hung up before she could answer.

Then her horror turned to jubilation. He doesn't have her! He doesn't even know she's missing.

Almost as quickly, she realized that Helga was still in danger. Where had she gone? And why hadn't she come home yet?

"Was that my Helga?" Wide awake, Oscar stood in his nightshirt at the bottom of the stairs. "Is she all right?"

"Oh, Oscar! I think maybe she is." Joan went over to him and took his hand. "Come sit down."

He followed her to the sofa and sat down beside her. "What do you mean, maybe? Did she call?"

"No. It was the man who killed Gus—I'm sure it was. He's called before—when Helga couldn't hear, and maybe last night, too, when Andrew answered and no one said anything. But yesterday afternoon and this morning he thought I was Helga. He warned me—her, really—not to tell what she saw. He just called again and said the same thing.''

Oscar's eyes lit up. ''He thinks she's here. That means he doesn't know where she really is. He didn't get her!''

''Yes.''

''Thank God.''

The tears running down his face didn't worry Joan.

''You better tell Fred,'' he said.

Someday I have to learn that cell phone number, she thought. She leaned against the kitchen wall and dialed 911. ''Can you get a message to Greg Peterson, please?''

''Ma'am, this number is only for emergencies.'' The 911 dispatcher's voice sounded bored. Joan wondered how many personal calls she had to field. Probably plenty.

''Yes, I know. Please tell him we've heard from Gus Friberg's killer, and he doesn't have Helga.''

''The old woman they're looking for?''

''Yes. This is her daughter-in-law, calling from their house.''

''Yes, ma'am, I'll tell him right away. Stay on the line, please.''

''Oh, I will.'' Joan waited for a few moments of silence, and then she heard not Peterson's voice, but Fred's.

''Is it true? He called again to warn her off? Just like the first time?''

''Yes!''

''Did you get it on tape?''

''I hope so.''

''Thank God. Rustle me up a quick breakfast, would you? Kate's bringing me home. She'll take the tape back.'' He hung up.

''Oscar, he wants breakfast!''

But it was Andrew who stood at the bottom of the stairs

now, in fresh jeans. "Oscar went up to put some clothes on," he said. "I'll help."

Oscar came down in time to grind the coffee beans and squeeze fresh orange juice. Then he said, "Someone's out there."

It wasn't the sheriff's van in front of the house, though, but a well-worn, lipstick-red convertible with the black top up. As Joan watched, Fred unfolded himself from the passenger seat, and a young woman in basic black came around from the driver's side to join him. Joan barely recognized Kate Buker with her hair down, but it was clear that Fred and the deputy had made peace overnight. She held the door for them.

Fred kissed her quickly. "I wasn't sure I'd find you here."

"I couldn't leave your dad. Besides, it was just possible she'd come home while you were out there."

"I'm glad you stayed."

"It's good of you to have me," Buker said.

Joan couldn't resist. "After you've spent the night with my husband?" At the look on the young woman's face, she took pity on her. "Seriously, thank you so much for hunting for Helga."

"Of course. But we haven't found her yet."

No, Joan thought, but at least we know he hasn't, either. Fred hung up their coats. "Dad, Andrew, you've met Kate Buker."

Oscar wiped his hands on Helga's apron. "I don't think so."

"The deputy, Dad."

Oscar recovered. "Of course. Please, come in."

"This is great," Buker said and let Oscar seat her at the table. "I thought we were going to grab something and run."

"At this house, you sit at the table like a lady," Oscar told her. "None of this grabbing business."

Andrew carried in a skillet of scrambled eggs, and Joan followed with coffee and juice. Oscar's fresh bread, butter, and some of Walt's strawberry preserves waited on the table.

They both seemed too tired to talk. No one said much until after Andrew had refilled the coffee and Joan had showed Buker where to find the bathroom.

"What will you do now?" she asked Fred.

"Sleep." He yawned hugely. "I don't seem to have much choice. I'm dead on my feet."

No wonder, she thought. He'd been up more than twenty-four hours, and he wasn't as young as Andrew. "I can't believe how calm we all are," she said.

"Yeah," he said.

"Even though your mom's been lost a lot longer than the first time."

"Yeah." This time he muffled the yawn.

"I just feel relieved," Joan said. "I was so sure he'd—"

"Contrast effect," Andrew said. "I learned that in psych."

"Yeah."

"Fred, go to bed," Joan said.

He took another slug of coffee, which she was sure wouldn't make a bit of difference. "Kate, you going home?"

"Not yet. I have to take that tape back." She popped it out of the recorder and slid another in. "Call the office when you wake up."

"Isn't anyone looking for Helga?" Oscar said plaintively.

"Yes, sir," Buker said. "I promise you, we'll have people out there as long as she's missing. We're going to find her. And from now on we'll see that she's protected." She collected her coat and drove off.

"I hope she can drive in her sleep," Joan said. "Let me walk you down to the bed and breakfast."

"Okay," Fred said.

"I'll stay right here," Andrew said. "I'm wide awake." As guilty as he was feeling, Joan didn't doubt it.

"Call me if anything happens," Fred said.

He didn't dare say "if she comes home," Joan thought. Her eyes met Andrew's, and he nodded.

"I may take a little nap, too," she said.

"Andrew and I can manage," Oscar said.

"Oh, Mom?" Andrew said. "I forgot to tell you. Debbie's in the clear. Kierstin says she hasn't missed any school this week."

"WHICH TRANSLATES TO not missing any of Kierstin's classes," Joan said to Fred as they walked back to the bed and breakfast. "We already know she took some time yesterday morning, when she and Gerri had that big fight."

"It's a man," he said.

"Your mom always said it was. But I had to ask."

He yawned again. "Yeah."

In their room at last, Joan lay in bed and watched him sleep. Her own mind kept churning. The killer—it had to be the killer who had made that call—hadn't known Helga was missing. But with all the people out there searching for her, he soon would. He knew who she was. Did he know her well enough to guess where she'd hide?

If he did, they'd better beat him to it. They had to find her before he did.

SEVENTEEN

TWO HOURS LATER, Fred's phone rang, and Joan was instantly alert. Fred fumbled for it on the bedside table. "Yeah?" He listened. "Thanks, Andrew. I'll call her."

"Who?"

"Maggie. She thinks someone was in the bakery last night." He was already punching the buttons. "Hello, Maggie? What's up? Uh-huh. We'll be right over." He sat up and pulled on his pants. "Maggie's missing some milk."

"She's what?" Joan, too, was reaching for her clothes.

"You know, the milk she keeps for customers who use it in their coffee. Last night she had almost a quart left. This morning it's gone."

"Anything else missing?" she asked.

"She says not. Just the milk."

"Your mom likes milk?"

"Yes," he said. "That's why Maggie called. But she looked all through the place last night."

"All through?"

"Bathroom and everything. Unless Mom got back in later, after we thought she'd left."

"You'd think Maggie would have checked again before calling us," she said. Looking at his haggard face, she knew she was going to hate it if he'd been dragged out of bed for no purpose. Still, after his long night searching for his mother, it would have been worse if Helga had been in the bakery and Maggie hadn't called.

"Come on!" He held her coat for her, locked their room door, and slammed the outside door on their way out.

Joan hoped the other guests were already awake. If not, they probably were now.

Her side hurt when they rounded the park, and she had to slow down. Out of shape. "Go on. You don't want to wait for me."

But he'd slowed, too. "If Mom's in there now, she's perfectly safe."

"Probably not hungry, either, if she drank Maggie's milk. We know she had a couple of loaves of bread."

Andrew was waiting for them outside the bakery. "I hated to call you."

"You did the right thing," Fred said. "Let's go in."

As before, there was no sign of Helga in the bakery. "But I think she's been here," Maggie said. "She left the empty carton in the fridge." She held it out to them.

Joan looked in and saw only a film of milk coating the bottom of the carton.

"And she used the toilet, too," Maggie said. "Last thing I did yesterday was clean up that little room. I don't mean she left it dirty, but when I came in this morning I could see someone had been in there. At first I thought Charlie had finally learned to put the seat down, but he says he hasn't used it yet."

"I believe you. Has she ever done anything like that before?" Fred asked.

"Not that I noticed," Maggie said. "Has she ever been missing overnight before?"

Fred won't know, Joan thought, and let the question hang in the air. "What time did you come in this morning?"

"About eight, when we opened. But the baker was here

before six. Charlie!'' she called behind her. ''Come out front a minute.''

A short, bald man in white emerged from the back room, wiping his sweaty head with his apron. No, he said, he didn't see or hear anybody when he arrived to bake the day's loaves. Yes, of course he unlocked the bakery. Maggie brought the cash for the till, but even so, you didn't leave the place open overnight, even in Bishop Hill. Who knew what could happen? Especially with all the strangers in town this weekend.

''Thanks, Charlie,'' Maggie said, and he disappeared behind her.

''But it was unlocked when we were here yesterday?'' Andrew said.

''Sure,'' Maggie said. ''We were open for business.''

''What about the cellar?'' Andrew asked. ''The old coffin factory?''

Fred smacked his forehead. ''Of course.''

''Of course what?'' Joan asked. What did the coffins have to do with Helga?

''Kierstin told me all the kids used to hide out in the old coffin factory when she was little,'' Andrew said. ''She said it was great for hide-and-seek.''

''But if Helga was locked in down there, how did she get to the milk?''

''Through the trapdoor—where they used to bring the coffins up when they were finished.''

Even as Andrew said it, Fred was heaving up a section of the bakery floor by some handle Joan couldn't see. ''Mom?'' he called down into the darkness. ''Mom, are you down there?'' Silence.

''We put a light down there,'' Maggie said. She knelt beside the opening and flicked a switch just below the floor.

A single bulb flooded the area below the trapdoor with light.

Now Joan could see the steps. With one lithe movement, Andrew swung himself over the edge to climb down. "Be careful!" she called to him and then felt silly. If Helga could negotiate those steps with her hands full of bread, Andrew shouldn't have any trouble.

"Helga," he called softly. "It's me, Andrew. Want to go up and get some breakfast?"

"Go away," said a muffled voice from some dark corner. "Leave me alone." Unmistakably Helga. She *was* down there! Joan squeezed Fred's hand, but kept silent. So, wisely, did Fred. Helga was spooked enough with one person invading her hideaway.

"I can't," Andrew said, still softly. "Your family is worried about you. Fred's upstairs, and Oscar is at your house. They're afraid you're hurt."

"Oscar's afraid?" For the first time, Helga came blinking into the circle of light. She was dirty, but unharmed. And she was wearing her winter coat.

"He sure is." Andrew held his hand out to her. "He sent us to bring you home."

"And *he's* gone?"

"Who?"

"Yes," Joan called down to her. "He's gone. It's just your family here, and Maggie. You know Maggie."

"Come home, Mom," Fred said.

"All right, if you're sure he's really gone." Helga avoided Andrew's outstretched hand and climbed up by herself.

So, she had indeed seen the man, and whoever he was, he hadn't alarmed Andrew, Kierstin, or Maggie. The killer who'd frightened her in the bakery had to be someone who could move among them invisibly. Or was it the killer she'd been hiding from at all? How could they trust the memory of a woman who had been so sure the victim was Fred, even when he was there talking to her?

Andrew followed her up the steps. At the top, he flipped off the light and turned the trapdoor back into a dark square on the bakery floor.

"Want any more milk?" Maggie asked, her wrinkles broadening into a big smile.

"No, thanks, I had some," Helga said. "Let's go home."

"Thanks, Maggie." Fred wrung her hand.

"I'll know where to check next time," Maggie said. "I can't believe it never occurred to me to look down there. It's so musty, all we keep down there is old stuff that's too crummy to use and too good to throw away."

"You wouldn't throw away that good blanket!" Helga said. "It kept me warm all night."

"No, I won't," Maggie promised. "I'm glad it was down there for you. But we don't want to scare Oscar again."

"Oh, that's right," Helga said, and headed for the door. Andrew trotted past her and opened it for her.

A young couple Joan had seen in the bed and breakfast came in. "Thank you," the woman said to Andrew, and then pointed at the shelves under the counter. "Oh, look, honey! Swedish cheesecake!"

Joan waved to Maggie and left with Fred. "You going to let them keep hunting for her?" she asked.

"No." He pulled out his phone and was quickly connected with Peterson. "Greg, we found her. Hiding in the old coffin factory, would you believe it? Down in the basement of the bakery—I doubt she ever left the building. We don't know. She thinks she saw him, but can't tell us any more than before." He listened. "We're walking her home right now." He looked around. "We'll appreciate that. And

I can't tell you how grateful we are for what all of you did last night.''

It seemed that he'd hardly pocketed the phone when a squad car passed them and slowed to follow a car length behind Helga.

"They're going to watch her more closely now?" Joan asked.

"You better believe it."

"So you can relax a little."

"We still haven't located Roy," he said. "At least, they hadn't when I came home."

"Who's Roy?"

"A mechanic who was in the Army with Gus. The Army kicked him out after a civilian court convicted him of stealing car parts from the Army and selling them in a police storefront operation where they were buying stolen parts and then arresting people."

"A sting," she said.

"Exactly. Gus testified against him in court—identified stuff stolen from his unit. Roy made noises about revenge. He served a couple of years, and when he got out, he moved near Bishop Hill, which is pretty suggestive. He's worked on Walt's car, so he might recognize Mom."

"Do your folks still have a car?" She hadn't heard anything one way or the other.

"I still don't know. I've got to ask Dad."

"Or Walt, maybe," she said. "In case it's touchy."

"Getting them to quit driving?"

"Could be. I hear both sides of it at the senior center— a lot of older people just don't want to quit, and sometimes their children try to talk them into signing over their car while they're still competent. But families involved with the adult day care people have to go through all kinds of shenanigans to try to keep the people who really shouldn't be driving anymore from taking off in their own cars.''

"I don't see any sign of a car," he said.

"Maybe it's all settled. So, what else do you know about this Roy?''

"His name is Royal Funkhouse," Fred said. "And there's something you have to promise not to talk about.''

She shot him a look.

"I'm sorry," he said. "I don't mean sign it in blood. But I promised to keep this quiet for now. Don't even tell Walt. It seems there may be a different kind of connection between Roy and Gus's family. The sheriff's people have their eyes on Bengt Swanson's used car lot.''

"Christina's husband?" Joan said, less as a question than in amazement. How awful, if after losing their son, the Fribergs would find out that their daughter's husband was a criminal.

Fred nodded. "Uh-huh. There's been a series of car thefts in that area. They've spotted Mark Balter hanging around there and suspect Bengt of dealing in stolen cars. With Mark's previous conviction, they think he's supplying cars to Bengt and maybe driving some of the stolen vehicles out of state. They don't have enough evidence to make an arrest yet, you understand. But Roy has been seen there, too. If what they suspect is true, Bengt needs mechanics who aren't above bending the law. Roy would know how to change odometers, obscure vehicle identification numbers, and such. That's if Bengt sold the whole car pretty much as is. If he moved parts from one to another and disguised them…''

"I thought you said Bengt was honest.''

"I doubt that he pulled anything on family friends. Though how would Mom and Dad know if he sold them something with stolen parts in it, as long as it ran?''

"You better describe Roy to Andrew, in case he was at the bakery yesterday."

"Better yet, I'll show him a police photograph the sheriff got from the cops who convicted him. Why don't you swap places with Andrew?"

She ran ahead of the squad car to catch up with him and Helga, feeling that stitch in her side again after only a few feet. She was getting soft. "Andrew, Fred wants to ask you something."

"Okay." Andrew turned and walked back to him.

"What does he want to ask?" Helga pounced on it. "Or don't you want me to know?"

Joan had heard that kind of suspiciousness at the adult day care. No wonder. To people who couldn't remember or understand what was going on, it had to seem as if they were being kept in the dark intentionally—and sometimes they were, she knew. "It's no secret," she said. "He wondered whether Andrew knew that mechanic Walt uses."

"Mechanic?"

"Guy named Roy, I think." She made it as casual as she could.

"Oh." Helga sounded totally indifferent, and began walking again. If she knew Roy, she at least didn't respond to his name. "Why, is Fred having car trouble?"

"No, he has a good car."

"It looked new. A Chevy, isn't it? We had one once. But I always wanted a Buick. Mostly we had Fords."

"And these days?"

"Walt and Carol drive us. They think we're too old to drive." She grinned an impish grin. "I don't mind. It's kind of nice having a chauffeur. They unload the groceries. Does your boy unload your groceries?"

"Sometimes. Sometimes he cooks, too."

"Fred's a good cook. You should let him cook for you."

"I know. He does sometimes. Oh, look, Helga." Joan pointed ahead at Oscar, standing on the front porch in his shirtsleeves. Of course—Maggie had called the house before Andrew called them at the bed and breakfast. Oscar must have been watching for them the whole time.

"Oscar Lundquist! You're going to catch your death!" Helga ran toward him, and the squad car pulled up to the house.

Joan watched them embrace while she waited for Fred and Andrew. No sign of memory loss in Helga this morning. Oh, she hadn't called Joan by name, but she'd remembered the make of Fred's car, which she'd seen only once. And she seemed to understand that he and Joan were married. She didn't react to the name Roy, if she'd ever known it. Not that he would have been wearing his name in the woods.

Fred and Andrew caught up with her.

"I asked your mom if she knew Roy, Walt's mechanic," she told Fred. "She didn't even blink, and she's pretty with it today. Is he big?" Helga had been plain about that.

"Yes. Six-three, 220, according to the Army. I'm not going to show her the photo. That would poison her as a witness— not that I think she'd ever be called as a witness."

"He's big enough, anyway."

"We can't rule him out," Fred said.

"But we can rule out tourists, people who wouldn't know her name to look her up in the phone book."

He agreed. "That narrows it some." They'd both smiled when the baker had made Bishop Hill sound invaded by hordes of tourists, but he had a point. The bed and breakfast had a full house this weekend, and cars were already filling up the on-street parking spaces. Tonight, Friday, would be the first Lucia Night.

Helga and Oscar had gone into the house.

"Did you see him near the bakery?" Joan asked Andrew.

"No. That doesn't mean he wasn't there, though. So, what do we do now?"

"We're back where we started," Joan said. "But we know the killer knows who she is, and Fred's exhausted."

"You and I could stick with Helga while he gets some sleep. I promise not to let her out of my sight this time." Andrew looked determined to redeem himself.

"I believe you." Fred's eyes drooped with fatigue. He pointed a thumb at the squad car, which had pulled up beside the house. "Those guys aren't going to keep their distance anymore, either."

And I'm not Kierstin, Joan thought. "Go back to bed. We'll be fine. And maybe she'll tell us something today."

He kissed her. "Don't hesitate to call me."

"I won't." But she had no intention of calling.

EIGHTEEN

"WHAT SHOULD WE DO with her today?" Andrew asked.

"You think we're in charge?" Joan said. "Let's find out." They went in and shed their coats when they didn't find Helga right there in the living room, determined to leave again.

She was upstairs taking a bath, Oscar said. "She needs it. I got the worst of it off her coat, but she'll want to wash that, too. She said something about an old blanket. Where did you find her, anyhow?"

They sat down beside him, and Andrew explained about the coffin factory.

"Been talking to Kierstin, have you?" Oscar grinned at him. "When I had the bakery, the kids were always messing around down there. I was always afraid some kid would break a leg in the dark, but they never did."

"Kids are tougher than grandmothers," Andrew told him. "But Helga's tougher than a lot of kids."

"You get out of her why she did it?"

"I'm not sure," Joan said. "But I think she thought she saw Gus's killer."

"In the bakery?" Oscar asked.

"We don't know."

"Maybe outside," Andrew said. "There were a lot of people out there yesterday. Fred was asking whether I saw some guy the Army knew about. But I didn't."

"Walt's mechanic," Joan said.

"You mean Roy," Oscar said.

"You know him?"

"Oh, sure. But I don't think Helga would."

So she could have seen him, known he was the killer, but just not known his name.

The phone rang. "I'll get it," Oscar said, and before Joan could stop him, he did. If a man answered, the killer would hang up. But Oscar talked with this caller. When he came back, he looked somber. "That was Ingrid wanting Helga, but she settled for me. Gus's funeral is tomorrow morning at ten, in the church. She wanted to know if Fred and Andrew would be pallbearers. I told her I'd ask. I'm too old to carry the coffin down those front steps."

"You know Fred will be glad to," Joan said.

"I'd be honored," Andrew said. He'd been too young when his father died, but Joan was sure he remembered the sober men of the church who had done that service for their young minister.

"Tim and Bengt will do it," Oscar said. "And some of the younger neighbors."

Andrew just barely didn't make a face. He hadn't thought much of Tim outside the bakery, Joan knew. "Should I call her back?" he asked.

"Helga can do it when she comes down. Ingrid wanted to talk to her anyway. Did you bring a dark suit?"

"I don't even own one," Andrew said.

"We'll borrow one for you. How about Fred?"

"He brought dark gray pants and a charcoal sport coat," Joan said. She had packed her favorite blue wool dress for herself, not that she'd been thinking of wearing it to a funeral. It would do. Nobody would be looking at her anyway.

"Give me their sizes, and I'll see what I can round up."

"Thanks, Oscar."

"And I'll need a shirt and tie," Andrew said.

"That's the easy part. You have any idea how many years Walt, Carol, and Helga have given me shirts and ties? I have a shelf full of shirts I haven't even taken out of the package." He smiled. "Helga says I age them before I wear them."

"So does Fred." Joan made a mental note never to give either of them shirts or ties. Buying for the men in her life had just become that much harder.

The door opened, and Kierstin came in.

"What are you doing out of school?" Oscar frowned at her, but the growl in his voice sounded more put on than genuine.

"I asked Dad if I could come over and help you and Farmor. I felt so bad about yesterday, you know? He said I could. She's more important than school!"

And you'd have trouble concentrating in school today anyway, Joan thought. But I'm not about to trust her to you two again.

"Not much to do right now," Oscar said. "But don't worry. We'll put you to work."

When Helga came downstairs, she was wearing clean clothes and toweling her short hair briskly with one hand. The other held a hairbrush. "That feels better," she said. "I don't know how I got so dirty."

"Would you like me to brush your hair for you?" Joan offered.

"Not much to it."

"I thought it might feel good."

"Aren't you sweet? Sure, go ahead." Helga sat on a straight chair and held out the brush. Joan brushed through the short white tangles, careful not to pull.

"Helga, Ingrid called you," Oscar said.

"Oh? What was on her mind?"

"Her boy Gus's funeral is tomorrow morning at the church."

Helga sat still for a long moment while Joan brushed. "Gus died? Did I know that?"

Joan stopped brushing.

When Oscar nodded, Helga covered her face. "That scares me to death," she said through her fingers.

They didn't push her.

She looked up at them. "When did he die?"

"Day before yesterday," Oscar told her.

"What did I do?"

"You did everything right," Joan said. "Oscar made some rolls, and you baked a ham and took it over."

She swiveled around and looked up at Joan. "You're a good girl."

"Thank you." Joan started brushing again. She could see Helga's shoulders relax. "We could go over there again this afternoon."

"No." Helga shook her head so vigorously that Joan had to hang on to the brush. Where did that come from? Never mind. It was nothing if not definite.

"Maybe Ingrid would like to come see you, then, to get out of her house."

"He won't let her."

"Who, Nels?"

Helga nodded. "People think she's afraid of her shadow because she stays home, but she's not."

Joan looked at Oscar, who shrugged. "Nels never did want Ingrid to work outside the home. Said he made enough to support his family."

"Did you want to work, Helga?" Andrew asked her.

"Three children were enough work. I didn't need to go looking for more!"

Oscar laughed. "And if I'd told you not to, would you have listened?"

"You wouldn't have!"

His eyes crinkled down at her, just like Fred's. "That's right. I knew better."

Joan laid the brush down. "You going to call Ingrid now, Helga?"

"Call her? Why?"

"To—never mind, it's really about Fred and Andrew. Why don't I call?"

"The phone's in the kitchen," Helga told her.

"Thank you." So was the slim phone book, but the Fribergs' number was one of half a dozen taped to the wall by the old phone. Taped beside it was a snapshot someone had taken of her and Fred and Andrew the day of her wedding to Fred. Beneath them someone had printed their names in a slightly wobbly hand. Joan didn't remember having seen the picture the last time she'd used the phone. Chalk one up to Oscar. He'd recognized Helga's confusion over the strangers in her house and figured out a way to help her sort them out.

Joan dialed and got Nels. "This is Joan Spencer, Fred Lundquist's wife. Both Fred and Andrew will be honored to serve as pallbearers."

He thanked her and promised to tell Ingrid.

"We were wondering whether she might not like to come over for a little while. In fact, Andrew and I were going to let Helga show us some of the Lucia girls in the shops and museums later this afternoon. We'd love to include Ingrid, if you think she'd feel up to it."

Nels didn't pause to think what Ingrid felt up to, but said that it wasn't proper for her to go out like that before the funeral. Joan apologized and hung up.

"That was odd," she said.

"Did he say no?" Andrew asked.

"Yes, Helga was right about that. He said it wasn't proper to go out before the funeral. But you and Kierstin saw them all out walking yesterday."

"Maybe it doesn't count if they're together," Andrew said.

Helga humphed.

"It doesn't matter," Joan said. "Want to come with us this afternoon, Oscar? Helga promised to show us the town."

"I did?" Her eyes sparkled.

"When we come back we can turn on the Lucia candles," Kierstin said.

"Let's do it now," Helga said. "Then we don't have to worry later."

Good strategy for a person who can't remember, Joan thought. "How do we do it?"

"I'll get them." Oscar hauled a cardboard carton out of the coat closet. "We put one of these on each windowsill and plug them in. I have a few extension cords here for the ones that don't reach. And be sure the bulbs are screwed into the sockets." He plugged in a light and set it on the front window in the living room. "Like this."

Joan screwed the bulb in snugly, but with no results. "It didn't turn on. Must be a bad bulb."

Kierstin laughed. "These candles are light activated. When it gets dark enough out there, they'll turn on automatically."

"What if we have lights on in the room?"

"They don't seem to matter. I think you'd have to have a light very close to the windowsill to make a difference."

"Which windows get them?" Andrew asked.

"All of them," Helga said. "Even the bathroom! Come on, Oscar, let's do the upstairs."

"No rest for the wicked." He pulled another box out of the closet and followed her up.

"So who all does this?" Andrew was untangling extension cords.

"Everyone," Kierstin said. "All the houses in town, and the restaurants, stores, and museums. Even the old buildings you can't go into. And we put out luminaries on the sidewalks."

"Are they electric, too?" They'd have to have batteries, Joan thought.

"No, those are real candles, standing in cat litter inside jars, and the jars are inside white paper bags. The jars keep the candles from blowing out, and they keep the bags from catching fire, too. You don't see them unless you're looking right down into the bags. It's really beautiful when all the sidewalks are lit up like that."

"Who puts them out?"

"All the businesses and museums, so they're not all exactly the same. I promised to walk over and help set up the ones by the restaurant."

"Walking reminds me," Joan said. "Helga said she and Oscar don't drive anymore."

"Dad persuaded them to quit. They're not safe out on the road, and Bishop Hill is so little, you don't need a car here. Mom and Dad and Aunt Carol drive them everywhere else—for groceries, to the doctor, and all that. Once in a while I drive them, too."

"So would your dad's mechanic know them?"

"You mean Roy? Sure. He lives just outside Bishop Hill. Hangs out in The Filling Station."

"Where he works?"

"No, you know, that restaurant by the volunteer fire department. I think he's a volunteer, too."

"He's made himself at home here, then."

"Roy's okay. Kind of old, though." She batted her lashes at Andrew, probably also an older man from her perspective, but not old enough to warrant that disparaging tone.

Oscar and Helga finished first and came down, with Oscar making noises about lunch.

More food? Joan could hardly imagine eating again, but it was indeed lunchtime, and they went through the ritual.

"Where's Fred?" Helga asked when it was time to sit down.

"He had to work late last night," Oscar told her. "We're letting him sleep."

"Fred's a policeman, you know," Helga told Andrew.

After they had washed and dried and put away every last dish, Helga proposed taking a walk.

"Not without me, you don't," Oscar told her.

Was Oscar going to be afraid to let her out of his sight? Certainly understandable.

"Where do you want to go?" Helga asked him.

"Church. While you were playing hide-and-seek in the basement, I was baking pies for the chili supper."

She sucked in her breath loudly. "I didn't make anything for it!"

"Good thing you have me." He opened the pierced tin doors of the antique pie safe that stood in the kitchen and lifted out two cherry pies with crusts of a perfection Joan didn't expect to achieve in her lifetime.

"Chili supper?" she asked humbly. "With pie?"

"It's a church fund-raiser," he said. "Even though the restaurants serve supper on Lucia Nights, they can't feed everyone who comes to Bishop Hill. We get so many people this weekend, the sheriff sends over the Mounties to keep them in line."

Was he putting her on? Kierstin seemed to take it at face

value, though, and it was true that everyone and his horse had been out looking for Helga.

"Guess the church figures it might as well get a piece of the pie." This time he grinned.

So they paraded down the street with Oscar and Andrew carrying the two pies, past the bed and breakfast and onto Main Street. The squad car followed decorously behind them. Oscar and Kierstin pointed out the historical buildings along the south side of the park. The sidewalk traffic had increased considerably, and Joan could almost hear the cash registers dinging in the little shops. A sign across from the corner of the park pointed them to the chili supper at the church.

Three short blocks from the park, the white frame building had stained-glass windows. Beside it, a big bell hung low in the yard, and a white wooden nativity scene stood in front, almost invisible against the snow. The sign in the yard called it United Methodist. But the old letters fanned over the door said Swedish M. E. Church—that had to mean Methodist Episcopal—with the dates 1869 and 1900. It must have been founded about the time the Jansonists dissolved the colony, Joan thought. She wondered what had happened in 1900. Thinking of Fred and Andrew carrying Gus's coffin, she was relieved to see only a few steps from the door to the front sidewalk. A ramp led to a door at the rear of the building that looked like a snug fit for a coffin, but a sign told people to use that door for the chili supper.

"The old cemetery's just across the road over there." Oscar pointed with the hand that wasn't carrying a pie. "We could walk through it, if you'd like."

"Don't you go anywhere with those pies," Helga said. "We're taking them right in."

"Yes, ma'am."

Helga led the way into the church basement, where women were stirring huge pots.

"More pies," one said. "Great. You can put them right in there on the table." In the next room, the pie table was already filling up. Other long tables with white paper cloths and small poinsettia decorations were set up for the coming crowd.

After doing as he was told, Oscar told the women, "This is Joan, Fred's wife, and her son, Andrew. They're visiting us."

"I used to have a crush on Fred," one of them said. "But he didn't know I was alive."

"I hope you didn't wait very long for him," Joan said.

"Heavens, no! I have six grandchildren."

"You do this supper every year?" Andrew asked her.

"Every year."

"I didn't know chili was Swedish."

They laughed. "You want Swedish food?" a younger woman said. "Ask Helga to make you some blood pudding."

"Yuck," Kierstin said, scrunching up her nose. "Sorry, Farmor, but I hate that stuff. It's worse than liver."

"What's in it?" Joan asked.

"Blood, onions, salt, and rye flour, mixed up and dropped in boiling water," the woman said. "But these days the EPA won't let you catch blood at the slaughterhouse the way they used to."

"I won't make it anymore, then," Helga said.

"Thanks, Farmor."

"I'll make you lutefisk, instead."

Kierstin made another face, and the women laughed. "Okay," she said. "I can stand lutefisk. If I have to."

"What's lutefisk?" Joan asked.

"Fish," Kierstin said. "Farmor makes it with boiled potatoes. Everything's white."

"I make a roux," one of the women said. "And a white sauce. You can serve that over the lutefisk or mixed in with it."

"How do you cook the fish?" Joan asked.

"It's pretty fragile. Put it into boiling water and immediately remove it from the heat. You don't want to overcook it."

I'd have to add something that wasn't white, Joan thought. I will, if Helga makes it for Kierstin. Though maybe she won't think of it if we don't bring it up again.

"Are you going to serve the funeral lunch tomorrow?" Oscar asked.

"Afraid so," the woman who knew how to make blood pudding said. "We'll have to do double duty. We may use your pies then instead of with the chili tonight. We'll get some more pies for tomorrow night anyway. Poor Ingrid. Ordinarily, she'd be here working today."

"Gus was just a kid when Fred and I were in high school," the one with a crush on Fred said. "I never knew him much. His sisters were closer to my age. But they married so young and never spent much time in Bishop Hill after that. So I feel closer to Ingrid. I hate it that this happened to her."

"What happened to Ingrid?" Helga asked Joan softly.

"Her son died," Joan said, just as softly.

"Oh, no, that sweet little boy?"

"You knew Gus when he was a little boy?" Joan asked.

She nodded. "Poor Ingrid. I think she always loved him best."

"You going over to the cemetery tomorrow?" asked the woman who'd had a crush on Fred.

"Yes," Joan said. "Fred and Andrew here will be pall-bearers."

"Then you'll be too busy to see much else. But sometime when you're not so involved, you might want to look at it. There's a lot of history there—it's been the cemetery since the beginning. Eric Janson, the man who founded Bishop Hill, is buried there, and so is the man who shot him. Look for the gate, just past the trees."

NINETEEN

When they left the church, Andrew insisted on touring the cemetery.

"I'll show you the Lundquist plot," Helga said. "That's where we'll go when we die."

"I'm in no hurry," Oscar said. "But those old graves are kind of interesting."

So they walked across the street and down a bit, past Cemetery Street and past some kind of big green gun standing in the snow near the entrance to the cemetery. From the Civil War? Joan wondered, but it wasn't marked, and she didn't want to display her ignorance by asking. Sure as I do, it'll turn out to be from World War II or even Vietnam.

"The oldest part is up here," Oscar told them, and led them between brick posts where a sign proclaimed the Colony Cemetery Site, established 1846.

The squad car, which had parked in front of the church, made a U-turn to park beside the posts. Joan wondered whether it would follow them into the cemetery, but it didn't. The deputy probably thought he could see well enough from the street. She hoped he was right. Not that she expected the killer to jump out from behind a tombstone, but she couldn't help feeling a little jumpy herself.

The cemetery was edged with evergreens, and they walked in between two rows of tall trees Joan thought were cedars. Modern granite stones rubbed shoulders with old, worn ones of all shapes and sizes, a few leaning. Oscar showed them the graves of Eric Janson and John Root, the man who killed him. Janson's simple stone was tall enough for his brief history to be carved on it:

ERIC JANSON
FOUNDER
OF THE TOWN OF
Bishop Hill.
BORN IN
Biskops Kulla,
SWEDEN,
Dec. 19, 1808;
MURDERED
May 13, 1850.

John Root's name and death date, 1862, were not on a gravestone, but on an iron gate set into stone. So that's what the woman had meant about a gate. Joan had expected to pass through one. Other plots were surrounded by iron fences. Either the iron on the gate and fences was rusting, she thought, or it was painted with some kind of red paint. Or both.

"Up at the north end are mass graves," Oscar told them. "So many people died the first year they couldn't dig separate ones. And a few years later, when the cholera epidemic killed a lot more, men worked day and night to bury them."

"Makes you appreciate backhoes," Andrew said.

Swedish names abounded on both old and newer stones: Nelson, Lindblom, Ericson, Arnquist, Norstrom, Olson, Swanson, Malmgren, Quanstrom, Naslund, Anderson, Osberg, Wahlstrom, Bergland. Some old stones were too worn to read, and Joan wondered about others. Wexell, Cady,

Bonesetter, Lock, and Rosen didn't sound Swedish to her, but that didn't mean they weren't. When they came to a Kennedy stone, though, she didn't even wonder.

Helga proudly showed them the Lundquist plot. Fred wasn't the first Fred in his family, Joan saw. Fredrik Lundquist, 1866-1901, was buried in a plot with smaller stones for "wife," "son," and "daughter," who didn't rate their own names or dates.

And down the hill a tent with two open sides had already been erected over what had to be Gus Friberg's open grave. Like some of the others, it would be shaded by pine trees. Would that comfort Ingrid and Nels? Could anything?

"Is that for Ingrid's little boy?" Helga asked. She remembered that much, Joan thought.

"Looks like it," Oscar said. "We'll bring him here tomorrow."

Subdued, they followed the drive where it curved past the tent and out to Main Street, and there was the Cemetery Street sign they had passed on their way.

"What now?" Andrew asked.

"Now I'm going home to take a nap," Oscar said. "Helga and Kierstin can show you and your mother a good time without me. But what say we all go over to the church about half past five for the chili supper? Everything will be open until nine tonight. There are even some concerts— Christmas carols, I know, and I think someone's playing hammered dulcimer."

"Will you wake up in time?" Andrew asked.

"Oscar always wakes up to eat!" Helga said.

"If you're afraid I won't show up, Andrew or Kierstin can come for me."

"Could you stop in at the bed and breakfast on your way home and tell Fred what we're doing?" Joan said. "He must be awake by now, probably wondering where we all are.''

He promised and headed back toward the park, where they parted company. The rest of them were immediately distracted by the first shops.

"The Colony Store looks neat," Andrew said. "Let's go in there."

"It's old," Helga told him. "And it has lots of Swedish things."

Inside, she and Kierstin bent his ear about the Lucias and *tomten* on the shelves. "*Tomten* are house elves, kind of like Swedish leprechauns," Helga explained.

"And on Christmas Eve you're supposed to give the *jul-tomte* a bowl of rice pudding," Kierstin said. She pronounced it "Yule tomte." That figured.

"Do you?" Andrew asked.

"I used to." Her dimples showed. "I'm getting a little old for that. I have several of these little guys at home, though."

"Talked me into it," he said, and picked out a small one.

They wandered back into the depths of the store, leaving Joan and Helga alone, if it was possible to be alone among so many other shoppers. Helga seemed relaxed, which had to be a good sign. She clearly hadn't spotted anyone who frightened her. Was no one dangerous around? Or could Helga simply not remember the man she was afraid of? At least the deputy who was following them had come into the store.

"I want to find something really Swedish for a friend," Joan told her. It was only partly true. She was intrigued by the things in the store and wondered what Helga would suggest.

"How about hardtack? That's what they used to have instead of bread. The old Swedes dried it on a broomstick."

"Really! Show me." She didn't know who would get it, but that sounded like the kind of thing she could give to anyone. When she saw the big round blue, white, and red packages and could even feel the broomstick-size holes in the middle through the paper, she knew they would be perfect. "That's just the thing, Helga." The package called it *knäckebröd* and said it was the original Swedish recipe for traditional whole rye crisp bread. They might break their teeth on it, or they could circulate it like the proverbial fruitcake. Who knew, maybe it even tasted good. She hoped they'd at least get a smile out of it. She and Helga stacked the packages, which leaked a little grainy flour, on the counter. Joan could feel the edges of half a dozen or more big rounds inside each paper.

"You find what you want?" It was Vicki Holm again, if not friendly, at least courteous. She stretched her sagging face into some kind of a smile.

Relieved not to be facing open hostility, Joan dug out her wallet. "Yes, I did. I hope it tastes okay—I'm going to give it to people for Christmas. I thought it would be fun to give them something genuinely Swedish."

"It is, even though it's actually made in Finland." Vicki showed her on the back of the package. Her many rings sparkled above her poor, bitten fingernails.

"Wouldn't you know it? Never mind. That's all right."

Vicki reached for a bag. "And how are you, Helga?"

"Fine." Helga smiled, but Joan suspected she didn't have any idea who had just called her by name.

"It's Vicki Holm, isn't it?" Joan asked.

"That's right."

"You met her daughter, Gerri, yesterday," she reminded Helga. "Over at Ingrid's."

Helga's eyes lit up. "She was in that big fight! I had to pull those girls apart."

Vicki had already tucked the *knäckebröd* into a bag and reached for the money Joan had put on the counter, but at that she stopped dead.

"You did what!"

"I pulled those girls apart." But the light in Helga's eyes faded. "I don't remember what they were fighting about."

Vicki stared. "My daughter, fighting in a house of mourning?"

"That's what I said to both of them. They should have more respect."

"I don't believe you." Vicki's mouth was so tight, it was amazing she could squeeze the words out.

"It was a misunderstanding," Joan said quickly. "I'm sure your daughter can explain."

"First you tell me she was going to marry Gus Friberg, and now you say she was fighting in his mother's house."

Joan took a chance. "Did you ask her about Gus?" Who knew what Gerri would have told her mother?

Vicki wilted, and the fight went out of her. "She said that was true. They were about to tell me when he got killed."

"Ohhh." Joan made it as sympathetic as she could. The last thing she wanted was to say, "I told you so."

"She couldn't tell me why, though. I didn't see much of Gus after he left Bishop Hill, but he's the last man I'd expect my Gerri to want to marry."

"There's no accounting for love," Joan said, but she wondered what the woman could be talking about. No one had mentioned dark secrets in Gus's past.

Vicki sighed. "Who am I to talk? Gerri's father was no prize."

"Who was Gerri's father?" Helga asked.

"Eric. Eric Holm, and a little too much like Eric Janson

to live with, only I had four little girls before I figured that out.''

"I remember him,'' Helga said, and shook her head as if the memories weren't good ones.

"What happened to him?'' Joan asked, not sure whether Helga meant Eric Holm or Eric Janson. Maybe Helga wasn't, either.

"I took as much as I could,'' Vicki said. "Finally I divorced him. Then I had to support those children, and it wasn't easy, let me tell you.''

"Working in the store?'' Joan looked around at it, stocked with everything from candy to candlesticks. Charming as it was, she doubted that a salesclerk could support four children.

"Heavens, no. The Colony Store was just an old building back in those days. And I could never have made it on what I earn here even now. I put the girls on the school bus every morning and worked in the glove factory in Kewanee.''

Helga leaned over and patted her hand. "You did the right thing. I'm proud of you.''

"Why, thank you, Helga. That means a lot to me.'' Vicki's defensiveness had completely disappeared. "Anyhow, you can see why I worry about my girls.'' She looked around at the crowded store, perhaps feeling uneasy about talking so long about her personal life, even though there was no one in line behind them. "Now, will there be anything else?''

There wasn't. After paying for the *knäckebröd*, they connected with Kierstin and Andrew, and with the uniformed deputy.

"I'm going to have to stick a lot closer from now on,'' the young man said quietly. "I'm afraid we've had some more trouble.''

"Trouble?" Joan asked, but in her bones she knew what was coming.

"They found another body in the ravine."

"A body?" Kierstin was wide-eyed. "Who?"

The deputy shook his head. "Not until they notify the next of kin."

"Was it someone from here?"

"I'm sorry, miss," he said.

Behind him, Joan saw Greg Peterson and another deputy, both looking grim, and both headed straight for Vicki Holm. If Vicki was the next of kin, Joan dreaded what was coming.

"Come on, kids," she said. "Let's get Helga out of here."

Helga tuned in. "What do you mean, get me out of here? Why shouldn't I be here?"

"I'm sorry," Joan said. "I shouldn't have said it that way. It's not about you. I'm afraid someone else is about to get some bad news."

"What are you talking about?" Helga planted her feet firmly.

Then Vicki screamed. "No! Oh, God, no!" Couldn't they have told her in private? Joan wondered.

Customers were whispering among themselves and staring openly at Vicki, who was weeping wildly.

"What happened to her?" Helga asked, not bothering to whisper.

"She just got some bad news," Joan said.

The deputy nodded. "That's right."

"Does that mean you can tell us who it is now?" Kierstin asked him.

"Kierstin!" Andrew looked embarrassed.

She's a child, Andrew, Joan thought.

"Come on outside," the deputy said. "I'll tell you out there."

This time Helga didn't object.

"The people who live in the old meat storage building at the eastern edge of the ravine thought they saw a body down there. It turned out to be that woman's daughter. Name is Gerri Balter."

"Didn't I meet her?" Helga asked.

"Yes," Joan said. "When we visited the Fribergs."

"She was in a fight?"

"That's right."

Helga nodded in satisfaction. "That's what I thought. And I stopped them."

"Yes."

The deputy had whipped out a notebook. "Who was she fighting?"

But Helga looked vacant. "I don't know."

"Debbie York," Joan said.

"What about?"

"They both expected to marry Gus Friberg."

"When was this?"

"The day after he died."

His eyebrows rose. "These two women were fighting over a dead man? Why?"

Joan shrugged. "You'd have to ask Debbie."

"We will."

She felt guilty. She'd just added Fred's old girlfriend to the list of suspects, though he'd probably already told Peterson all that. "Gerri's ex-husband wasn't too happy, either," she said. "He was furious at Gus. But he was crazy about her. You think he'd go after her, too?" She supposed it was possible.

"What's his name?"

"Mark. Mark Balter."

He wrote it down. "Stranger things have happened. I'll pass it on."

"How was she killed?" Kierstin asked with the blood-thirstiness of a normal teenager who knew she would live forever.

"They didn't tell me," the deputy said.

Or they told you to keep it to yourself, Joan thought. She knew from Fred that the police intentionally avoided releasing some of the details of a crime, so that a person who mentioned those details could be suspected of guilty knowledge.

They were still standing on the sidewalk outside the store. Now Peterson emerged with Vicki Holm and the other deputy, who went around to the driver's seat of a squad car parked in front. Vicki had herself under control, or maybe she had gone into shock. Joan wasn't sure she could tell the difference. Peterson opened the car door for her and helped her find her seat belt before they drove off.

Hard to imagine shopping after that. But Helga asked, "What shall we do next?" In her mind, at least, none of it had happened.

Andrew and Joan exchanged looks. "Might as well keep going," he said. "There's no way we can keep her at home."

To give them a destination, Joan asked the others to go with her to the quilt shop to pick out something for Rebecca.

And so they set out again. Instead of resuming the crawl after them in the other squad car, the deputy meandered along a few feet behind them on foot, keeping an unobtrusive and flexible presence. It wasn't as if Helga would run away from him. Joan wondered what their escort could do if the murderer suddenly whipped out a gun, but then she reminded herself that the man feared discovery. That's why he'd called Helga to warn her not to tell what she'd seen rather than risk approaching her in public. Fred was probably right; he wasn't likely to attack her in plain view of a crowd, much less the law.

"We could stop at the bakery on the way," Helga said, and no one argued with her. They had crossed the street toward the Steeple Building. Joan and Kierstin followed Andrew and Helga. Whatever she was telling him, he was giving her his full attention. Good.

Joan remembered what Vicki had said before getting the terrible news that her daughter had been killed.

"Kierstin, what can you tell me about Eric Janson?"

"Like what? I mean, we learned about him in school."

"What kind of man was he?"

"Well, that's the question, isn't it? He founded this place as a commune, with him in charge, and he led a religious movement. Those people believed everything he said. They thought he was divinely inspired, even when he told them they'd understand English the minute they set foot on American soil, or that they wouldn't catch cholera if they truly believed in his teachings."

"Was he a prophet? Like the Mormons and Joseph Smith?"

"I don't know much about them. There was a lot of grumbling about Janson, though. Some people thought he threw his weight around."

"Uh-huh. The man who shot him, you mean?" Joan swerved to avoid kicking a luminary, its white candle still untouched by a match. A woman a few feet in front of her bent to set a candle into the next one.

"He wasn't the only one."

"Was it really about a woman? That's what Fred told me."

"Kind of," Kierstin said. "Not the way you're probably

thinking, though. Janson told people what they could and couldn't do, where they could and couldn't go. Sometimes he even told them who they could and couldn't marry.''

''He told this woman she couldn't marry the man who killed him?''

''No, he let them get married. She was Janson's cousin Charlotta, see, and Root married her. Later on, Root wanted her to leave Bishop Hill with him. It gets complicated, and I don't remember all of it, but Janson threw his weight around the way he tended to do and got her back. Then he hid her and her little boy. Root accused Janson of kidnapping them, and finally he shot him. I guess some people thought Janson had it coming.''

And Vicki Holm thought her husband had something in common with Eric Janson. Did she think Gus did? Was that her problem with him? But how would she have known what he was like, if she hadn't known him after he went off to the Army?

Did Vicki think Gus had it coming? Did anyone else? But who thought Gerri had it coming? And why? Even in a big city, it would be hard to imagine that both of them would be killed in one week by two entirely different people. In little Bishop Hill the coincidence was impossible to believe.

And if it was the same man, there could no longer be any doubt about whether he would kill a woman—whether he would kill Helga.

TWENTY

WHEN THEY REACHED the bakery, Andrew had Helga deep in conversation, and they sailed right on by. Good for you, Joan thought. But The Filling Station, just past it, reminded her that Kierstin had said that's where Roy Funkhouse liked to eat. Maybe she could learn something about Roy there. It looked like a local hangout, not a place that catered to the tourist trade.

"How about a cup of coffee, everyone?" she called out.

Andrew turned and raised his eyebrows at her, but Helga said, "Just what I was thinking."

"My treat," Joan said. She held the door for Helga, and they paraded in. A far cry from the elegance of Walt and Ruthie's restaurant, it smelled like home cooking. The locals must like it—even in the middle of the afternoon, it wasn't empty.

The deputy followed them in.

"Hi, Joe," the man behind the counter greeted him.

"Hi," the deputy said. He appeared to be studying the menu on the wall.

The menu offered Swedish pancakes, but Joan didn't think she could face any more food. "Can we get some coffee?" she asked the counterman.

"Help yourself," he said, and pointed to the mugs and coffeepots clustered between the counter and the tables where people were sitting.

"What do you want?" she asked Andrew and Kierstin.

"I'll have a Coke," Kierstin said.

"Me, too," Andrew said. "Why don't you and Helga sit down, Mom? We'll bring your coffee."

"Offer some to the deputy, too," she told him. She slipped him a ten and showed Helga to a table big enough for the four of them. They draped their coats over the backs of the chairs. At the next table, close enough to reach out and touch, a little girl in a white Lucia robe and crown was making quick work of a dripping burger and fries, while an older woman—her grandmother, maybe?—dabbed at her chin. "Don't get ketchup on your robe, honey," she said.

The candles in the Lucia crown were electric, thank heaven. They had to be battery operated, because there wasn't a wire in sight.

Andrew carried over two mugs of coffee, and Kierstin followed with their Cokes. She pulled up a chair and helped herself to golden popcorn from a basket on the table.

Several men sat together at a long table farther from the door. Joan leaned over to Kierstin. "You see Roy?"

She shook her head. "He's not here."

"Who?" Helga asked, pouring sugar into her coffee until it made Joan's teeth ache. Maybe she wouldn't stir.

"Roy, Walt's mechanic. You don't know him."

"You lookin' for Roy?" asked a man at the long table with "Buddy" stitched on his pocket in red script. "He's working today."

"What's he like, anyway?" Joan reached for the popcorn and was surprised at the taste, almost like caramel corn.

"Roy's all right," Buddy said. "Picks a fight if you look at him crooked, but he don't mean nothin' by it. Just a big kid at heart."

"He ever pick one with Gus Friberg?" Joan asked, but Buddy shook his head and turned away from her. Amazing, really, that he'd told her that much already. He didn't know her from Adam. But she'd gone too far. They'd close their ranks and their mouths now, she was sure, especially in front of Joe the deputy.

Then they surprised her.

"Roy's no killer," said a man with big bones, big ears, and a John Deere cap. "He likes a few beers after work, is all. Best poker player I ever met, till he gets too drunk to play."

"Why do you want Roy?" Kierstin asked Joan.

"I heard he and Gus were in the service together," Joan told her, sure now that the whole room would be listening. "I just thought he might know more about Gus than people who hadn't seen him for years."

Buddy dived back into the conversation. "If he does, you'll hear all about it."

"Roy's a talker, that's for sure." The second man dunked a couple of fries in a puddle of ketchup. "He'll tell you plenty."

"Gossip?" Andrew was catching on.

"Nah, mostly about himself. All his big plans."

"Like what?"

"What's Roy planning now?" Buddy asked the others. They laughed. "You mean the house he's building?" said one.

"And the Stingray he's gonna buy?" said another. They laughed again.

"Can I bring you something else?" A waitress with a warm smile appeared from nowhere and set a fresh basket of popcorn on the table. She stood, pad and pencil in hand.

"I don't think so, thanks," Joan said. "But this popcorn is great!"

"It's kettle corn—they're making it in that tent out

front.'' She waved her pencil at the door. ''They'll sell it all evening.''

''Maybe later, then.''

The waitress smiled again and went back toward the counter.

''I keep thinking Fred will connect with us,'' Joan said. ''Oscar was going to tell him where to look for us.''

''Say,'' Buddy said. ''Aren't you the one married to Fred Lundquist, the one found the body?''

''Yes.'' This could be useful, but she hoped he wouldn't say something to set Helga off.

''Hell of a thing.''

''A shock,'' she agreed. He obviously hadn't heard about Gerri yet.

''Half Bishop Hill was there that night, but they wouldn't let anyone close enough to see anything. Is it true his face—''

''Put a sock in it, Buddy!'' the John Deere cap said. ''Bad enough she had to be there.''

''Thanks,'' Joan said. ''The Lundquists and the Fribergs are old friends.'' She nodded in Helga's direction. ''You can see why I was asking about Roy.''

''I don't know what he'd know,'' Buddy said. ''Sounds like someone pretty much went berserk. Roy's not that kinda guy.''

The others nodded. If they'd heard about any bad blood between Roy and Gus, they weren't giving much away. From what Fred had told her about Roy, Joan thought he hadn't blabbed everything to these men. He'd covered his tracks well in Bishop Hill.

''Is it true Gus was engaged to Gerri Balter?'' the man with the ears and the John Deere cap asked.

Joan wasn't sure whether to answer that or not.

While she hesitated, the waitress answered. ''I wouldn't doubt it. They came in here that morning, you know. He got here first, and then she joined him. I hadn't seen him for years, but we went to school together, so I knew him right away. He never gave a girl the time of day back then—made us kind of wonder about him. But if those two weren't in love, they gave a good imitation.''

"Man, her ex must've split a gut," Buddy said. "Talk about berserk. I can see him going after Gus when he found out."

"Did he come in, too?" Andrew asked. "Her ex?"

"Not while they were here," the waitress said. "But word gets around. People talk, you know?"

Joan almost choked on her coffee. They certainly did.

"Anyway, they left holding hands," the waitress said. "I wouldn't be surprised if Mark heard about them from someone who saw them. Everyone knows how crazy he was about her."

"He's your man," Buddy said.

Case closed, Joan thought. She wondered what he'd say when he heard about Gerri.

"Are we going home now?" Helga said. "I have to go fix supper, you know."

"Is she the one they were looking for last night?" Buddy asked. "The old—"

"Buddy," his friend warned.

"Sorry. But we were all worried about her, you know?"

"Thanks," Joan said. "We're all fine now." She steered Helga out, grateful again for her ability to tune things out at least some of the time.

"Are we going home now?" Helga asked.

"Not yet," Joan said. "You promised you'd come with me to pick out a gift for my daughter, remember? She's the one who quilts." She wondered whether Rebecca's sexy sleeping bags would shock Helga. The double one that made the sleepers look like Adam and Eve entwined sans fig leaves had set one old lady at the Oliver quilt show on her ear. Hard to tell about Helga.

"We should go to the quilt shop, then," Helga said. "It's right down there." She pointed.

"Good idea."

They were on their way out the door when a man opened it and yelled inside, "Hey, Buddy, Jim! You hear what just happened? They found Gerri Balter in the ravine, just like Gus!"

Behind her, Joan heard the chairs scraping across the floor. Buddy and the man with the cap were out of sight before they reached the quilt shop.

The sign called it the Village Smithy, but Kierstin followed Helga in without hesitation. Andrew and then Joan went next, with the deputy close on their heels. Joe, who looked about fifteen, though he had to be considerably older, had passed up coffee for a bag of kettle corn, into which he reached as he walked along. Why not? Joan thought. He's probably still growing. She was glad to see him stop inside the door. Nobody selling fabric and such would welcome sticky fingers coming in. She'd have to watch her own, though she had dipped them in water and wiped them with her paper napkin.

Inside, there was no question that's what it was. A person could buy everything from books about quilting and about Bishop Hill and Swedish traditions to handcrafted items and quilts themselves. There was even a long quilting machine. And a rainbow of fabric bolts waited to tempt quilters, who painted in fabric.

A bolt of deep crimson lay unfolded on the cutting table, its color and subtle, almost invisible pattern crying out to her. "She'd love that red." Joan resisted stroking it. "Don't you think she would?" she asked Andrew.

"Looks nice," he said, and shrugged.

"Nice! Look at the sheen of it. It's all cotton, isn't it?" she asked the pleasant older woman who had greeted them when they entered. Rebecca had taught her that much.

"Of course," the woman said. "Quilters prefer it."

"It's for my daughter, who designs her own quilts."

"We have a good assortment of batting, too."

"I'm sure she can get that in New York. For that matter, she might find this stuff, too, but it will feel more like a present than batting." Not to mention being easier to mail.

"How much did you want?"

"Five yards, I think." She had no idea, but surely Rebecca could do something with that much.

The woman smiled and flopped the bolt several times before measuring off the yards. "She must really like red."

"I hope so. Mainly I know she tends to quilt on whole fabric, rather than piecing or appliqueing designs. She designs sleeping bags." How long was a sleeping bag, anyway? Two yards would be six feet—Fred's height. Maybe five wasn't a bad guess, at that.

She watched the woman tear it expertly across the grain and flip the yard goods into neat folds. I didn't even ask the price, she thought. Too late now. Even after she agreed to matching thread, though, the total was lower than she had feared. Before marrying Fred, she never would have risked letting anyone cut it without asking the price first. Her finances had been too tight. Her widow's pension from the church hadn't come to much, and the high-sounding jobs of director of the Oliver Senior Citizens' Center and manager of the Oliver Civic Symphony paid more in glory than in money.

A little book on the Lucia tradition caught her eye, mainly because the sweet-faced blonde illustrated on the cover wearing a crown of real candles might have been Kierstin. Flipping through the pages, she found not only something about the history of the tradition, but what looked like workable recipes for *luciakatter* and *pepparkakor,* among other traditional cookies for Lucia Day, and even a source for crowns with batteries for the candles. There were also tips for how not to catch your hair on fire if you used real ones.

"I'll take this book, too," she said. "I could get used to blowing money like this."

Kierstin had been letting Helga tell her all about quilts, and she'd shown no impatience to leave. But when Joan signaled to them that she was ready, the woman who had helped her caught on that she was connected to Helga, and then, like Buddy, realized the rest of it.

"You're—you—" she stammered.

"I'm Fred's wife, and yes, we did find Gus," Joan told her quickly, before Helga reached them.

"I'm so sorry. People probably haven't let you alone since. I don't imagine you got much rest last night, either. I'm glad to see they found her. It's such a worry when people you love get old."

"Thank you."

"And poor Ingrid. Will you go to the funeral?"

Joan nodded. "Fred and Andrew, my son over there, are going to be pallbearers."

"I'll probably close the shop for the funeral."

"Your boss won't mind?"

"There isn't any boss." She smiled. "I'm it."

"Oh, of course." What did I expect? In a place this size, how could a little shop like this afford employees?

"Besides, the whole town will be there. I wouldn't do any business anyway."

That day and another day, Joan thought. She'll find out soon enough.

"You want help carrying?" Andrew asked at Joan's elbow.

"If you're offering." She gave her purchases up gladly. Five yards of cotton fabric plus all that *knäckebröd* would have weighed on her by the time they reached home. "I think we'd better go back to the house. Collect Fred and Oscar, and see whether Oscar has found you something to wear tomorrow. Not that I know what we'll do if he hasn't."

"Are you going to the church tonight?" the shop owner asked.

"Tonight? You mean the chili supper?"

"Sure, if you like chili, but that's not the church I meant. There's a concert at seven in the old Colony Church, over there across the street." She pointed. "You'll want to go early to get a seat. They start singing at seven, but I'd go by half past six if I were you. And be sure to dress warmly. That's a historic building. No heat. But it's worth it. The Nova Singers are really good."

"What will they sing?"

"Christmas carols, usually. I hear they've learned something in Swedish this year."

"Farmor, that should be fun," Kierstin said. "Let's go!"

"Why not?" Helga said. "But we'd better hurry home and fix supper first."

For once, there was no need to distract her from her destination. They could deal with the supper part later. Picking up their escort outside the door, they marched him past the Colony Church, where people were setting out unlit luminaries along the sidewalk. The road curved around past the ball park to the ravine.

For the first time, Joan noticed the house with a flag flying and a historic sign at the top of the east side of the ravine. The sign out front said that it was now a private residence, but that the building had been the meat storage building of the original colony. So many ordinary-looking houses in Bishop Hill had signs about what they'd been during the colony days. In some ways, walking around the village felt like walking through a full-scale museum exhibit.

Could the people in that house have seen Gus's murder, too? Suppose the killer ran off in their direction? Mightn't they have seen him and not thought anything about it? After all, if he was local, why shouldn't he be going down the road? Joan turned around and gestured to Joe, the deputy, who was keeping enough distance to give them some privacy.

He jogged up. "You need something?"

"I was just looking at the old meat storage building."

"Uh-huh."

"You think anyone asked those folks what they saw the other afternoon?"

"I'm sure they did. It's routine. Far as I know, though, there's only one witness." And he jerked his head at Helga.

She supposed it was too much to hope for.

Beyond the house, emergency vehicles clustered at the burn site, lights flashing and radio traffic blaring. Deputies held back the onlookers. It all felt painfully familiar.

"What's going on?" Helga asked.

"A woman died," Andrew told her.

"Down there?"

"That's what they told us."

"Don't all those people have something better to do?" Helga shook her head at the gawkers.

Right, Helga, Joan thought. But it was asking a lot of human nature to expect them to go do it.

Something looked different to her today. Something about the burn site, though she hadn't been paying much attention the first time. Probably different vehicles, or maybe they were arranged differently.

And I'm not all torn up about it this time. It makes a big difference, not seeing what he did to her.

TWENTY-ONE

THEY HAD ALMOST reached the house when Joan heard her name. Looking back, she saw Fred coming up behind them. He must have been talking to the sheriff's people at the ravine. She waited for him, watching Andrew, Kierstin, Helga, and the deputy to the house. She had just reached the spot at which they had left the road to enter the ravine, not that it was possible to see any of their footprints anymore. The snow had been thoroughly trampled by all the sheriff's people. Probably by many curiosity seekers as well, she thought, if not that day, then today. She was glad to turn her back on it and toward Fred.

His eyes smiled down at her. "Dad said you were out spending money again."

She blessed him for not starting right in about Gerri. He'd surely been talking with Peterson. "Did he say whether he found a suit for Andrew?"

"A what?" No wonder his eyebrows rose. Except at their wedding, he'd probably never seen Andrew in anything much more formal than clean jeans. And there certainly wasn't a men's clothing store in Bishop Hill.

"Ingrid wants you and Andrew to be pallbearers tomorrow morning. Andrew was willing, and I said you'd do it."

"Of course."

"In a pinch, you could wear what you brought, but he

doesn't have a thing. Oscar was going to look for something appropriate.''

"He didn't mention it. I could ask Walt.''

"Andrew's such a string bean. He'd swim in anything of Walt's. And your dad's not tall enough.''

Oscar met them at the door. "Ingrid invited us to eat supper over there.''

Joan thought of that bulging refrigerator. If the church was going to feed people lunch after the funeral, Ingrid probably had more food than she knew what to do with. "What do you think?''

"I think she means it,'' Oscar said.

"Then let's go,'' Fred said. "Why go to the chili dinner when there's all that food over there?''

"My thoughts exactly,'' Joan said. Not to mention that people at the chili supper would probably be talking of nothing but murder. Maybe it didn't matter, now that there could no longer be any doubt that the killer had it in for Helga, but she hated the thought of sitting through it. "And I suspect Ingrid wants the company. Her daughters haven't exactly been hanging around. We can't stay long, though. Your mother promised Kierstin we'd take her to the old Colony Church tonight for a musical program. I'd like to hear that myself.'' And you don't talk during concerts.

"I'd better take off now,'' Kierstin said. "I promised to put the luminaries out in front of the restaurant. I'll meet you at the church at half past six, at the bottom of the stairs.''

"Okay,'' Andrew said. "I'll wait for you.''

"I'd better tell Helga,'' Oscar said. "She's probably already forgotten about the chili supper and gone in there trying to figure out what to fix.''

"Actually, she's been pretty clear this afternoon,'' Joan said. "But you're right, it's that time of the day.'' How would she defend her own kitchen if the killer wasn't caught before they had to leave, and they ended up taking Helga home with them to protect her? Don't borrow trouble, she told herself, but it didn't feel like borrowing. More like wishing she could see a way to dodge.

Oscar sorted out the details with Ingrid. They were to go over as soon as they could, he reported.

While waiting for her turn in the bathroom, Joan looked out the window at Joe standing on the porch just in time to see a squad car pull up. Kate Buker, in uniform this time, stepped up to the porch, and the two deputies spoke briefly. Then Joe, the young man who had stuck with them all afternoon, trotted down the steps and jogged off toward where he'd left his car. Kate returned to hers. She had put her hair back in its bun and looked totally professional. Also wide awake. She'd evidently had a chance to get some sleep.

Joan was glad to see her. Young Joe had been attentive enough. But Kate had been there. She had seen the violence they hoped would not be turned on Helga. She knew firsthand what they were up against. Rightly or wrongly, Joan felt more confident with her on duty.

Eventually, they all bundled up again for the short walk to the Fribergs' house. The light was beginning to fade, but not enough to trigger the automatic electric candles.

Oscar distributed flashlights. "You'll need them after supper," he told Joan. "Especially if you go over to the Colony Church. Over by the park and the shops and historic buildings, you can see to walk, but no one bothers with luminaries this far away."

Halfway there, she remembered that no one had mentioned funeral clothes for Andrew. She asked Oscar what luck he'd had.

"Nels has something he can try on."

"Good." She no longer cared how well it fit, as long as he could get into it.

Nels flung the door wide. "If it isn't the Lundquists! Come in, come on in!" He was smiling broadly, and waving a mug with his free hand. "Join the party!"

Joan exchanged a look with Fred, who moved closer to her as they went through the door.

"I wondered when he'd snap," he murmured in her ear.

Hanna was there, after all, and took their coats to hang somewhere, or maybe throw on a bed. Maybe their other daughter was in the kitchen, helping Ingrid. The big table was set for all of them to sit down to supper, Joan was glad to see.

"Have some *glögg*!" Nels cried.

"Watch out for that stuff." But Fred smiled as he said it.

The house smelled like cinnamon and orange peel, plus some spices she couldn't identify that easily. Cloves, she thought, and maybe even cardamom. Great Christmassy smells.

Nels ladled a mugful out of a covered crock on a side table, spooned blanched almonds into it from a dish beside the crock, and left the spoon in the mug. "Best I ever made. You have to taste it." His words were fuzzy around the edges, and he reached for his own mug again.

"Don't mind if I do," Oscar said and sipped cautiously. "Ahhh!"

"What's glug?" Joan asked Fred. "Is it Swedish?"

"It's *glögg*," he corrected. She could just hear the difference. "And yes, it is. The Norwegians drink it, too. All those people up where it's cold do."

"Do I want to try it?"

He grinned wickedly. "It'll put hair on your chest."

"I'll try it," Andrew said. Accepting a mug from Nels,

he took a big swallow and nearly choked. At last, whispering, "Why didn't you warn me?" he set the mug back down.

"Try a few almonds," Fred told him. "They don't soak much up."

"What's in that stuff?" Andrew asked, his voice still hoarse.

"Wine, spices, and raisins," Fred said. "The liquor is pretty much up to the cook. Dad's old recipe calls for aquavit, but some folks use cognac or even vodka. I hate to think what all Nels put in this batch."

"Want to try mine?" Andrew offered.

About to turn him down, Joan decided his pride needed an excuse to give it up. She accepted the mug, took a careful little sip as she'd watched Oscar do, and felt the steam come out her ears. "Gee, thanks, Andrew," she said when she could talk again.

Fred took it from her and spooned up some almonds and a few sodden raisins. Even the raisins were probably potent. Joan wondered how much of the stuff Nels had drunk.

Ingrid came to the kitchen door. "Everybody sit down, please. Supper's ready." She looked like the competent woman Fred had described as his mother's rival in cooking, not the pitiful creature who couldn't find her way around her own kitchen the day after Gus's murder.

"Have some more *glögg*!" Nels roared again, waving his mug.

"Nels Friberg, you're drunk. Sit down to supper."

He whirled on her, a little unsteadily. "Don't tell me what to do! I'm the man of this house, and don't you ever forget it. Now shut your mouth and put the food on the table."

She glared at him, but turned back into the kitchen and emerged with a platter of baked ham. Hanna followed with bowls of vegetables, and Christina with a plate of fresh fruit salad and a basket of rye bread. No husbands tonight, it seemed.

"Nothing fancy tonight," Ingrid said. "Except for your wonderful ham, Helga. But we are so grateful to you, dear friends, and we wanted to share a family meal with you before tomorrow."

The meal went pleasantly enough. No one mentioned Gus, or the murder, or the funeral. It was as if he simply weren't home for the occasion. Hanna and Christina swapped news of old schoolmates with Fred, but without mentioning Mark or Gerri Balter, though surely they knew about her by now.

"I hate to ask now," Joan said while they were finishing the ice cream and gingersnaps Ingrid gave them to celebrate the first Lucia Night. "But Oscar said Nels might have something for Andrew to wear tomorrow."

"That's right, son," Nels said. "After supper I'll take you upstairs and fix you right up." He downed the rest of his *glögg* and ladled more into his mug.

By the time they went upstairs, he was weaving visibly. Feeling uneasy, Joan watched them go, but Andrew, after all, was in control of his faculties. It was Nels who might be too sozzled to make it back down those stairs safely.

She and Helga automatically joined Ingrid and her girls in the kitchen, but Ingrid wouldn't let them touch a dish. "You did so much before. Look at all the help I have tonight."

She was almost bragging, but Joan was glad to see her family finally giving her some support. Maybe she was selling them short. Maybe Ingrid's daughters came around more often than she thought. She hoped Vicki Holm's other children were comforting their mother.

She screwed up her nerve. "Do you stop in often?" she asked Hanna.

"Not as often as I should, I know. It's just one thing after another, you know?" She didn't meet Joan's eyes.

And you're all of five miles away, Joan thought. She didn't bother to ask Christina. "I'm glad you're both here tonight."

When Andrew appeared in the kitchen doorway, she hardly recognized him. Nels's charcoal suit fit his lanky body as if it had been made for him, and his dark curls gleamed above a white shirt and black tie. He even wore black socks and black dress shoes.

"Whaddya think, Mom?"

"You look wonderful." And he did. So grown-up that tears stung her eyes. She hadn't expected them, but there they were.

"He does, doesn't he?" Nels stood behind him, matching him inch for inch. Somehow she'd always thought of Nels as a little old man.

"It's Nels's, all but the shoes. They were Gus's. He had a black suit, too, but it was too short for me."

"You're going to wear those shoes in the snow tomorrow? You'll be walking in the snow in the cemetery."

"You're right," Andrew said. "I shouldn't wear the shoes, Nels. I'll wreck them." He looked down at them as if sorry to have to give them up.

"A little snow isn't going to hurt 'em. They're polished by a military man," Nels said, pride oozing from his slurred words. "You go ahead and wear 'em."

Gus brought a suit and shoes for his wedding, Joan thought.

"You might as well keep them," Ingrid said in a small voice. "No one else in our family has feet that size."

Andrew looked at his mother, who nodded and smiled at him. Why not?

"I'd be honored," he told Ingrid. "But I'd better change back fast if we're going to meet Kierstin at the church by six-thirty." Taking the steps two at a time, he looked closer to Kierstin's age than twenty.

"Church?" Helga said. "Why are we going to church at night?"

"We're not, really," Joan said. "Not your church, anyway. There's a special concert at the old Colony Church. People singing for Lucia Night."

"I hope they sing Christmas carols," Helga said. "I like Christmas carols. Did you know it's almost Christmas? I need to do my shopping."

Ingrid and her daughters came back out of the kitchen.

"We talked Mom into letting the rest of the dishes wait," Christina said. "We're going to the concert, and she's coming along."

"It's not fitting," Nels told Ingrid. "You don't have any business going out yet."

"But, Nels," she pleaded. She stopped right there.

He advanced on her grimly until his face was only inches from hers. "I'm your husband. What I say goes."

Joan held her breath. What would he do? Would their daughters stand up for their mother? Would Fred intervene if Nels got physical?

The room was silent. No one moved.

Ingrid paled. Her chin trembled only a little. Then she raised it. In a clear, firm voice she said, "I'm going with the girls. Tonight more than ever I need to hear the music and see the candlelight." She stood very straight. "You could come, too."

He didn't respond, but faced her for a moment that felt

like hours. Then he turned his back and left the room, his empty mug dangling from his hand.

For the first time, Joan noticed that the candles in the window had lit themselves.

TWENTY-TWO

WHEN THEY STARTED up the hill from the Fribergs' to the Lundquists' house, they needed the flashlights even with candles in all the windows of the houses. Then the squad car started up behind them, and its headlights took over the flashlights' job.

There were candles in the windows of the Janson house, too, and then darkness until after they passed the ravine and burn site. The emergency vehicles had left now, taking the thrill seekers with them and leaving only dirt and piles of branches and brush. Whatever snow had still been on the ground was gone. It looked different, Joan thought again.

"This is the darkest way to go," Oscar said. "But it will get us there fastest. On the way home, you'll want to walk through the village and see all the lights."

If not for the danger threatening his mother, Joan would have enjoyed walking in the dark with Fred along what felt more like country roads than village streets. They came to more buildings with candles in the windows. Cars were parked all along the side of the street. Just before the Colony Church, luminaries lit their way, and they turned off the flashlights.

A steady stream of people flowed up both sides of the double stairway at the end of the white frame building to the open doors on the second story. Ingrid and her daughters went up the steps first.

"If the church is upstairs, what's downstairs?" Andrew asked.

"There were apartments down there," Ingrid said. "And in the basement, too. Back in the colony days housing and the church were the first things they built. That first winter, people had to live in sod dugouts in the ravine." She said it without blinking, as if her son hadn't been murdered in that very ravine.

Was it possible that she could separate the history from her own pain? Or had she forgotten for the moment where Gus died? Joan didn't think she herself ever could forget, but then, Ingrid hadn't seen him there.

"Later on, they built a big dormitory back there," Hanna said, pointing toward the ball park. "They ate communally, so they didn't need as much living space as individual families do. But that still was a big building."

"The biggest brick building west of Chicago," Christina said proudly. "They made the bricks right here in Bishop Hill."

"What happened to it?" Andrew asked.

"Burned down," Oscar said.

"I guess it wasn't all brick," Andrew said.

"Not inside," Oscar said. "And they didn't have electric candles."

"Is that what did it?"

But nobody seemed to know the answer to that one. A woman at the top of the stairs counted them as they went inside. "There's only so much space in here," she said. "No standing room. When I count enough to fill the pews, we close the doors. The rest of the people can come to the second performance."

Helga wouldn't last that long, Joan thought. She was moving along and seemed oriented, but she had stopped talking. They'd need to sit near an aisle, in case she wanted to leave before it was over.

"I'd better wait out here, then," Andrew said.

"Why?" Joan asked.

"Kierstin said she'd meet us at the bottom of the stairs, but she's not here yet. If she doesn't make it this time, I can sit with her at the late show."

"Sure."

Helga hadn't reacted to Kierstin's name. Oscar caught her when she stumbled over the wide doorsill from the dark entry hall to the old sanctuary, but inside, with more light, she held on to the pews as they walked up the aisle. Looking back over her shoulder, Joan was glad to see Kate Buker standing by the door. The no-standing rule wouldn't apply to a deputy sheriff in uniform.

"It's beautiful," she said to Fred, sitting on her left. Simplicity itself, with dark, box-like pews and light walls. Overhead, electric candles hung in what must be something like the candleholders that had hung there back in the colony days.

"Keep your coat on," Fred reminded her. "No heat, remember?"

"All these people ought to put out some," she said. "Especially if we sit close." She put her arm around Helga on the other side. "You warm enough, Helga?"

"It's cold in here. Someone ought to turn the heat up."

"We have to make our own heat in here," Oscar said, and they squeezed Helga between them until she laughed. "Good thing they don't make Fred and me sit on the other side of the church from you girls. In the colony days, you know, all the women and children sat on one side, away from the men."

"I wouldn't like that one bit," Helga said.

"Me, either!" he said, and hugged her.

They had most of half an hour to kill. Sure enough, in the next ten minutes or so, the pews filled up. Joan looked around for Andrew and Kierstin, but didn't see them—Andrew would be glad of an excuse to cozy up to Kierstin without his mother there, watching. Ingrid, Hanna, and Christina were right in front of them. Not talking, they sat close together, letting the chatter of the crowd go on around them. Joan wasn't surprised. The dinner had to have been a strain, especially on Ingrid.

Over to her left, she saw a man reading a book with one of those little portable lights. He held it low, behind the pew in front of him, almost like a child hiding a book in bed after lights out.

Now several young girls came down the aisles, handing out programs about the Nova Singers. Joan would tuck the program into her collection of such programs, in hopes it would give her ideas for the Oliver Civic Symphony.

"What are they going to sing?" Helga asked, not looking at the program in her hand.

She's really alert for this late, Joan thought. And calm. Good. "Looks like Christmas carols, mostly. Oh, and it says here they're going to do something special for Lucia Night."

Finally the singers came out, and the program began. They sang a mixture of traditional carols, mostly sacred, but beginning with the Wassail Song. The songs were in interesting arrangements by composers as diverse as William Billings and Zoltan Kodaly. One of the carols was sung in Latin, and then the leader announced that for the first time, they had added some songs in Swedish, especially for Bishop Hill. "You probably know this one as 'Lo, How a Rose E'er Blooming,' but in Swedish, it's *Det är en Ros Utsprungen.*'"

From the German she had studied at Oberlin, Joan could

understand something about Jesse's stem in the first line, but after that she couldn't guess at the meaning and simply had to listen to the beautiful harmony.

Next came "*Kitsch, Katsch, Filibom-bom,*" a bouncy Swedish song about a Fru Söderström, full of what sounded like nonsense words.

Finally, the leader invited the audience to look inside the program for the printed words to some carols for a sing-along, and they sang several traditional favorites together. Helga, who paid no attention to the program, sang out in a strong, clear soprano without missing a word. The last song, on the back of the sheet, was "*Sankta Lucia,*" in Swedish.

"Do your best with the Swedish," the director told the audience. "But I'm sure you all know the tune."

She was right about the tune—it was the old Neapolitan boat song Kierstin had sung in the restaurant. Joan stumbled over the Swedish, and Fred didn't sound much better, but to her surprise, Helga sang these words as confidently as she had sung "Joy to the World." Maybe she had learned them in school, or maybe when she was a Lucia, as Kierstin had been for them the first night.

Natten går tunga fjät, rund gård och stuva
kring jord som sol'n förlät skuggorna ruva.
Då i vårt mörka hus stiger med tända ljus,
Sankta Lucia, Sankta Lucia.

Natten var stor och stum nu hörs det svingar
i alla tysta rum sus som av vingar.
Se, på vår tröskel står, vitklädd me ljus i hår,
Sankta Lucia, Sankta Lucia.

No translation was provided. "What does it mean?" Joan asked. Helga and Oscar didn't know, but Ingrid turned around. "It's not the same words as the old Italian song. This one's all about dark on a farm, and Lucia coming to bring light with her candles. Those winter nights are long in Sweden, and she brought breakfast to the family."

Then it was over, and they were making their way back down the stairs outside the church. The two staircases rose from different sides of the building to meet at the double entryway on the north end of the church. They had come up from the west, but now they were facing east, toward the shops rather than their houses. Below them, other concertgoers fanned out from the building on the candlelit sidewalks.

"Is it my imagination, or is this staircase wider than the one we went up?" Joan asked.

"It's real," Oscar said. "They made this side wide enough to carry coffins in and out of the church."

The few steps Fred and Andrew would have to negotiate from the Methodist church tomorrow were nothing by comparison with this full flight. She couldn't help wondering why the colonists hadn't put their church downstairs and the apartments upstairs.

Andrew and Kierstin were waiting at the bottom of the steps, to be allowed in for the second concert of the evening. "How was it?" he asked.

"You're going to need Kierstin," Fred said, letting him wonder why.

Also at the bottom of the steps was Tim York, Hanna's husband, his dark, bushy eyebrows creased in a frown and his arms crossed on his chest.

"We missed you at supper, Tim," Ingrid said. "You coming back to the house?"

"Sure, Mom, if you want us," Hanna said. "We—"

Tim cut her off. "Hanna and I will walk you home if no one else is going there, but we need to take off right away."

His rigid stance told Ingrid to turn him down. He had to know the Lundquists would walk her home.

Hanna appealed to him with her eyes, but he didn't budge. "All right," she said finally. "I guess we'll see you in the morning before it's time to go to the church."

"I have to leave, too," Christina said. "I promised to be back home early tonight to close up Bengt's office."

"We'll take you home, Ingrid," Fred said quietly.

Probably just as well they're not going back with her, Joan thought, considering the shape Nels must be in by now. But she felt for Ingrid.

Ingrid seemed to deflate. The hostess persona that had sustained her throughout dinner was gone now. And her daughters were leaving her to cope by herself with Nels and the cleanup.

"Walk through town with us to see the lights, won't you?" Joan urged her. "Then I'll come help you do those dishes."

"Me, too," Helga said. "I can help." Joan wasn't sure she'd still have it in her by then, but she was holding up amazingly well.

"Oh, I couldn't ask you to," Ingrid said.

"Sure you can," Fred said. "We'll all help, won't we, Dad?"

Shaking her head, Ingrid looked defeated. "Nels won't like it."

"We won't ask Nels," Oscar said. "He's probably asleep by now, anyway. He was hitting the *glögg* pretty hard."

"Take them up on it," Christina said. "Don't let Daddy dictate your life." She looked at her sister, but stopped short of telling Hanna to defy her husband.

Ingrid squared her shoulders. "You two go on home. I'll be fine."

Her daughters stood there, as if uncertain whether she meant it. Tim was saying something in Hanna's ear, but she didn't respond to him. For a change, Joan thought, they were concerned about their mother.

Ingrid turned her back on them and linked her arm in Helga's. "We're old friends, aren't we, Helga?"

"We sure are," Helga said. "Remember when our children were little? I'd take yours or you'd take mine, and we'd have a little time to ourselves."

"I remember," Ingrid said.

The wonder, Joan thought, is that Helga does, especially this late at night.

"And now we're glad when they come to see us," Helga said, and they both laughed.

Ingrid wiped away tears. "Oh, Helga, I'm going to miss him so much!"

Helga looked blank. "Miss him? Did someone go away?"

Ingrid couldn't answer her.

"Ingrid's son, Helga," Joan said softly. "Gus died." She couldn't make herself say murder. As if by not using the word, she could erase the deed.

"I'm so sorry," Helga said. "How could I forget a thing like that? When did he die?"

Ingrid had her voice back. "This week. His service is tomorrow morning, in the church."

Helga looked up at the old building, into which the second audience was climbing. "Here?"

"No, in our church. The one you go to."

"Good. It sure would be hard to carry him up and down all these stairs."

Ingrid laughed just a little too long, but stopped short of hysteria.

"You sure you're all right, Mama?" Hanna asked.

"Yes, I'm sure. You both go on. This is good for me." She gave each of them a quick hug and shooed them off. This time they left.

Joan couldn't help wondering what kind of marriages they had. Even while lecturing her, they seemed as quick as Ingrid to knuckle under to their husbands' desires. Christina was closing Bengt's office. Would she even know whether what the sheriff suspected about him was right? Would she hide the truth from herself?

Tonight Ingrid had taken a stand that seemed to be unusual in her household. Could she sustain it? What would happen when she wasn't surrounded by supportive family and friends?

TWENTY-THREE

LEAVING KIERSTIN AND Andrew at the Colony Church, Joan, Fred, his parents, and Ingrid walked toward the park. Now the sidewalks were crowded, and on-street parking spaces were clogged. Good thing they were on foot. Charlie the baker hadn't been exaggerating, after all.

At the far end of the park, a small evergreen blazed with white lights. Luminaries lit the sidewalks, but the brick walks along the park provided uneven footing, even though they were fairly clear of snow. As she had in the woods, Helga walked more steadily than Joan, who grabbed Fred's arm after slipping. He took pity on her, and they all crossed over to the ordinary concrete sidewalk in front of the shops and the post office.

Ahead of them, two little girls in Lucia robes and crowns were trying to sing Christmas carols as they walked. "Silent night, holy night," they sang, and then they got stuck.

"Maybe we'd better choose another one," one Lucia said.

"All is calm, all is bright," Ingrid sang behind them.

"Oh, that's right," the other Lucia said, and they went on from there, with Ingrid, Helga, Oscar, Fred, and Joan harmonizing through the rest of the first stanza. It was probably too much to hope that the girls knew any more of it, if they got stuck so soon. Sure enough, without further prompting they moved on to "Rudolph, the Red-Nosed

Reindeer.'' Hardly a traditional Swedish carol, but they sang with great enthusiasm and didn't stumble over the words.

When a couple of uniformed men rode slowly down the street, the girls ran over to pet the horses. But they didn't beg for rides, as Joan thought she might have been tempted to do at their age, even in a Lucia robe.

"I'm glad I came," Ingrid said.

"Me, too," Helga said. "We should do this more often."

"Let's stop in at the Steeple Building. They usually have something hot to drink."

"*Glögg?*" Oscar said, and laughed. He pointed up to the steeple that gave the building its name. "You notice the clock up there?" he asked Joan. "There's only one hand."

She saw it now, a single hand pointing between eight and nine on the dial. "What happened to the other one?"

"There never was another one. The colonists thought only the hours were worth watching."

"That's a joke, right?" she asked Fred.

"I don't know if that part's true, but there really is only one hand—you can see it on all four sides of the steeple."

Looking back at it, she saw he was right.

Inside, the building was full of tourists studying historical displays, which clearly bored Helga. Joan's nose led her to a side room. "Look in here," she said.

Another young Lucia stood at a table in the corner. Under the supervision of her mother she ladled hot, spiced cider that reminded Joan of *glögg*. "We didn't have time to bake *luciakatter*," Mama said. "But have some of our home-made *pepparkakor*—gingersnaps."

They all accepted free cider and cookies from Lucia, whose crown stood on the table beside the cookies.

"Is it heavy?" Joan asked.

"Itchy." The girl reached up and rubbed her forehead.

Joan could imagine that the imitation greenery wrapped around it would itch after a while. The hot cider warmed her all the way down to her toes. She hadn't thought she was cold tonight, but she welcomed it, after all.

"Am I almost done?" Lucia asked her mother.

"Not until nine. Keep smiling, dear."

Lucia heaved a big sigh and ladled more cider. She looked about twelve.

"Do they pay you for doing this, or do all the Lucias volunteer?" Joan asked.

"Oh, they pay us." The little girl's face lit up. "It's kind of fun at first, too, but it's a long night. I'm glad someone else will be here tomorrow night."

I'll bet no one pays her mother, Joan thought, and smiled at Mama. She didn't ask who had baked the cookies, but the odds were on Mama.

After the Steeple Building, they stood outside a gift shop to hear a couple of singers standing on the front porch. These women stuck to secular music—"Chestnuts Roasting on an Open Fire," "Walking in a Winter Wonderland," and "Let It Snow." Beautiful as the snow was, Joan wasn't sorry that it had been melting or evaporating or whatever it did in cold weather to shrink to only a couple of inches. The light dustings they'd had since the murder hadn't amounted to enough to worry about, though they had added to the beauty of the evening. She thought the temperature might even have risen. Her toes would have been numb by now if it hadn't. Instead, they were comfortable.

"I think it's time to go home," Ingrid said when the singers took a break.

"You worried about Nels?" Oscar asked.

"No, but I think Helga's ready."

"You want to go home, sweetheart?" he asked. Helga nodded, and he put his arm around her. "Then let's go."

Ingrid took her other arm, and Joan and Fred followed behind them. Looking back, Joan saw the squad car start up again. It crossed her mind to ask for a ride for Helga, but so far, she seemed to be holding up all right.

They walked west on Main Street across from the south side of the park, past the Colony Store, the Colony Administration Building, and the historic Bjorklund Hotel. Lagging back a little, Joan asked Fred whether Peterson had learned more about Bengt.

"He hasn't told me anything."

"I can't get it out of my mind. I keep thinking what it would mean to the Fribergs."

"Yeah."

"Fred, what if Gus stumbled on it? If he saw Mark or Roy drop off a car at Bengt's, you think he'd know enough about them to suspect what was going on?"

"Maybe."

"We know Gus testified against Roy. If he was worried about his sister, don't you think he might tell her husband he'd testify against him, too, unless he stopped? Or turn him in, or something?"

"He might."

She was on a roll now. "So what if that set Bengt off, and he lured Gus into the woods and killed him?"

"You figure out how he lured Gus into the woods?"

"Well, no," she said. "I don't have any idea how he'd do that."

"Me, either," he said. "But someone did. Why would Gus just wander in there and wait for a killer?"

"Like Bengt." But even she had trouble believing in it.

"Why would Bengt even come to Bishop Hill in the middle of a business day?"

"I don't know!" The whole idea sounded silly to her

now. And what would Bengt have against Gerri Balter? "Why are you always right?"

"I'm not," he said mildly. "But I'm pretty good at picking holes in the other fellow's idea."

Oscar looked back over his shoulder. "You two okay back there?"

They looked at each other.

"We get a little loud?" Fred asked.

"A little. You don't want to upset anyone." He inclined his head toward Helga.

"I'm sorry, Dad. We're fine."

They'd come to the last of the luminaries. Fred pulled out his flashlight, as did Oscar, up ahead. For a few moments they needed them in the sudden darkness around their feet. Then the squad car came close enough that Fred clicked his off again. They turned north on Olson Street now and walked past the bed and breakfast, where Lucia candles were burning in their room.

"I didn't do that," Joan said.

"I know," Fred said. "I did. All I had to do was tighten the bulbs. After that it was automatic."

"It's really a lovely holiday. I could get used to the candlelight."

"No law says we can't do it in Oliver."

"No," she said. "But what makes it special here is that everyone does it." Through the leafless trees, she could see the lights on Main Street, and even some on the far side of the park, where the crowds were.

"We may have to come back."

"Fine with me. Only maybe next time we can sleep the whole night in the same bed."

He tightened his arm around her. "I hope we don't have to wait that long."

"You do want to do shifts again tonight, don't you?"

"Afraid so," he said. "As long as he's out there."

And if they didn't catch him before it was time to leave? She hoped Carol and her husband would be as flexible as she and Fred. Not my problem, she told herself. But she knew it was. More and more, she was afraid they'd have to take Oscar and Helga home.

"It's getting to you," Fred said.

"No. Yes. Not if it stops soon."

"But you're borrowing trouble, as Mom says."

"Can't help it."

He reached down and stroked her face with a gloved hand. "Dad's right. I picked a good one."

"Oh, Fred, I feel so lucky."

"In spite of all this?"

"In spite of all this." She stretched up and kissed him. She didn't have to stretch far—he bent to meet her and tipped up her chin.

Then she saw that they had an audience. Helga, Oscar, and Ingrid had waited for them at the corner before turning down the hill to Ingrid's.

"You two just planning to stay out here and neck?" Oscar said.

"It crossed my mind," Fred told him. His eyes crinkled down at her. "But we didn't forget where we were going."

Speak for yourself, Joan thought. Washing Ingrid's dishes had been the last thing on her mind just then.

The mood broken, they followed the rest of them down the hill. As they had the night Gus died, the neighbors' dogs set up a ruckus, but tonight they hushed when Ingrid called them by name.

"I hope they don't wake Nels," Joan said.

"I wouldn't worry," Fred said. "That *glögg* is powerful stuff."

"And you let Andrew drink it."

Fred grinned. "He knew enough to stop."

"He did, didn't he?" An encouraging thought.

There was no sign of Nels when they first entered the house, but *glögg* still perfumed the air. "He forgot to turn it off," Ingrid said. She went over to the crock and turned a dial. "At least it's not burning dry on the stove." She shook her head, picked up half a dozen mugs, and carried them out to the kitchen.

Joan's heart went out to her. How many women faced what she faced with Nels? And how bad did he get? Tonight he'd been expansive before he tried to throw his weight around—like Eric Janson and Eric Holm, she thought. Was that why Vicki Holm didn't want her daughter to marry into this family? Was his father what she had against Gus? It didn't seem fair, but who said life was fair?

Following Ingrid into the kitchen, Joan wanted to kick her daughters. They had talked her into abandoning the dishes for the concert, and then abandoned her, tonight of all nights. Had they always been so selfish?

Ingrid ran water into the dishpan. "I'm so glad we went out together," she said. "It was just what I needed tonight, of all nights."

Maybe they were more tuned in to their mother than Joan had given them credit for. "I'm so glad you came," she made herself say, and then realized that it was true. It would have been a shame for Ingrid to stay home to watch Nels descend into his *glögg* instead of doing what she really wanted to do.

"Okay, you guys," Joan called into the living room. "You said you'd help."

Fred appeared at her elbow. "We're going to carry Nels up to bed, instead. He's out cold in there." He jerked his head back at the living room.

"Is he all right?" Ingrid asked, but she didn't turn around.

"He's fine now, but he'll pay for it in the morning." He left.

Ingrid washed and Joan and Helga dried and put away until Joan couldn't bear the silence. "Does this happen often?"

"Often enough that the girls knew better than to come back home."

"It would upset them to see him like that?"

"Not like that, no. But he isn't always like that."

Uh-huh. "I'm so sorry."

Ingrid jabbed at some bit of dried-on food. "I should have left years ago. At first I told myself I was staying for the children. Then I couldn't. They left instead."

"He threatened them?"

"He didn't need to. They had eyes and ears."

"So you're still together."

"Where could I go, an old woman like me?"

"You can come to my house," Helga said. So she had been listening. Joan hadn't been sure.

Ingrid threw her soapy hands around Helga's neck. "Helga, you're a good friend."

Helga hugged her back. "So are you."

Andrew and Kierstin rolled in just when the others were ready to leave.

"We timed that well," he said.

"It's all right," Ingrid said. "I had plenty of help."

"So I see," Andrew said. Indeed, the kitchen shone, and everything had been put away. "What happened to Nels?"

Ingrid was blunt. "Fred and Oscar put him to bed."

"Oh." What else could he say? "Tell him thanks again for me. I really appreciate the loan of his suit. And thank you both for the shoes. I wish Gus were here to wear them himself.''

Ingrid's eyes filled up. ''Me, too.'' She reached out, and Andrew walked into her arms and hugged her.

Joan felt tears gathering in her own eyes. Bless you, Andrew, for responding to her like that. How could I ever have worried about letting you come on this trip?

''It's time to go home,'' Helga said.

''Yes, dear,'' Ingrid said. ''I'll see you all tomorrow.''

Helga let it go, and they were spared telling her what would happen then.

On the walk home, Fred asked Andrew, ''Can you stay awake again tonight?''

''Sure. I'll make a pot of coffee after I come downstairs.''

And so, after he came back from walking Kierstin home, they left him with the old people. But Fred stopped to greet Kate Buker, sitting in the squad car with its motor and lights off. ''You need to use the facilities?'' he asked her.

''I'll be fine for the rest of my shift,'' she said. ''I had a turn at the public rest rooms a little while ago, when another car came by here.''

He hesitated. ''Would you mind spending your shift inside? Andrew's sitting up, but after this morning, and then this afternoon…I'd feel much better to know you were in there, too.''

''Sure. And I'll ask the man who follows me to do the same. I think you're wise.''

''Thanks, Kate.''

Joan didn't think Andrew's feelings would be hurt. He'd probably be relieved, and of course having someone to talk to would make it easier for both of them to stay alert.

She was glad to be alone with Fred. The candles still burned in all the windows they passed, but they didn't meet anyone. Walking down the middle of the street, they didn't bother with a flashlight.

It was tempting to keep going, just the two of them. If they hadn't both been so worried, if Fred hadn't faced another all-too-short night—if, if, if. As it was, they unlocked the door to their room in the old hospital bed and breakfast, washed, and fell into bed. The candles in all their windows were perfect night-lights.

But sleep didn't come easily.

Listening to Fred's breathing, Joan decided she might as well ask what she'd been thinking. "Do you think it's the same man?"

"Who killed Gus and Gerri? Probably."

"Mark Balter?"

"Sure looks like it," he said.

"I can't imagine how he'd get her down there—unless he didn't. Maybe she went down there on her own to see where Gus died, and Mark followed her there."

"Only he didn't."

She pushed herself up on one elbow and looked down at him, staring at the ceiling with his arms behind his head. "What do you mean? Isn't that where she died?"

"Nope. That's where they found her."

"You think someone killed her someplace else and took her there?"

"Something like that."

"Why?"

He looked at her. "You could see marks all over her body and broken branches all the way down the ravine."

"He threw her down there?"

"Yeah. But her cuts and scratches didn't bleed. She was already dead."

"So either he killed her somewhere else and took her there or he killed her at the top of the ravine." She thought for a minute, hesitating to ask the next question. "What killed her?"

"Some blunt object. Blow to the head. Didn't break the skin, but it did a job on her skull."

"Nothing like Gus. Doesn't that suggest a different killer?"

"Only if it was planned ahead of time. In Mom's kitchen he opened the knife drawer before he heard me and ran."

She shuddered. It still could be Mark. Whoever it was, his only interest in Helga lay in what she had seen. The phone calls made that clear. The real question was why Gus and Gerri had been chosen.

At last Fred snored gently. But Joan lay wide awake beside him, dreading the day to come.

TWENTY-FOUR

THE MORNING OF Gus Friberg's funeral dawned clear. Only a little frost decorated the windows—maybe by the time they had to go to the cemetery, they wouldn't feel the cold.

Fred had been gone for some time when Joan woke and took a leisurely shower with one of the fragrant soaps made in a little shop in Bishop Hill. She brewed coffee in her room and brought her muffins and scones in to enjoy at the old table between brushing out her wet hair and blowing it dry.

The service wouldn't be until half past ten. By the time her hair was dry, it was almost nine. Checking the clothes rack, she saw that Fred had left his pallbearer's clothes. She didn't know when he'd come back to dress, but decided she'd better be ready. She pulled on a fresh pair of panty hose—what a strange feeling, after this week—and everything but her dress. In her bathrobe again, but ready underneath, she pinned her hair up into a French twist. Then she carefully slipped the soft blue wool over her head. No pearls today, she thought. For all I know Bishop Hill may be offended by light blue at a funeral.

In spite of her best efforts, she hadn't finished all the scones. She considered taking the rest upstairs, but decided she didn't want to face the other visitors today. If Fred didn't want any, and it was hard to imagine that he could, after eating at his mother's, they could return them to the hall table in the basket. Or save them for a bedtime snack, she could hear him telling her. She was sure she had never in her life eaten as much as in the past few days.

All right, Fred, she thought. You can come anytime now. She wasn't even tempted to turn on the television news. After all the intense family visiting, she welcomed a little quiet time to herself, but a week like this one made her miss music. She wished she'd thought to bring along a portable CD player or even a radio. Fred's car had both, but she wasn't that desperate.

Instead, she leaned back in the big rocking chair and opened the book she'd brought to read in the car. Fred's key in the room door startled her awake.

"Is it time to go?"

"Almost," he said, and bent to kiss her. "Glad you took some time off. I've been feeling guilty. This isn't how I pictured this week."

"Me, either. But it's good we came."

"Yeah." He tossed his coat over the back of a chair and began changing clothes.

"How are they doing?"

"Dad and Andrew are dressing. Mom's fine. Once she got it that we were going to a funeral, she dressed appropriately. We'll drive up and give them a ride to the church. Don't want Andrew to get his shoes dirty."

"He's really going to wear them?"

"He said he was. Nels sounded so proud of Gus. I think he'd be disappointed to see Andrew in anything else. But I talked Mom into her boots, for the cemetery." As he spoke, he put on his own boots, and Joan did the same.

When they pulled up to the house, Helga came out the front door fully dressed. "Come on, you two!" she called to Oscar and Andrew. "They're here!"

Andrew offered her an arm, and Oscar gave her one on the other side.

"You'd think I was an old lady," she said, but she let them tuck her into the car.

The parking lot was already half full, a silver hearse near the entrance the only vehicle pointed toward the cemetery. Fred dropped them near the door. "Find out where they want us," he told Andrew.

"You do what you have to do," Oscar told Andrew. "Helga and your mom and I will stick together."

This morning, Joan saw, the signs for tonight's chili supper had been removed. She followed Oscar and Helga into the dim sanctuary.

An usher greeted Oscar and Helga by their first names and smiled at Joan before he led them halfway down the red-carpeted center aisle and handed them each a program. Ruthie and Kierstin were already in the pew. The usher had known the family well enough to seat them together. Ruthie smiled and nodded. Kierstin, her face solemn, looked angelic. Oscar went first, so that Helga sat between him and Joan, who ended up on the aisle.

The church was decorated for Christmas. At the end of every pew a slender white pole supported a lantern with a candle burning inside and greenery and red ribbon outside. Two green trees stood in the chancel, and an Advent wreath with its first two candles lit rested on a stand near the lectern. A wooden manger promised the birth of the Christ child. Banners on the walls proclaimed love, joy, hope, and peace.

But the closed casket below the manger overshadowed their message. A spray of red roses lay on it. Around it stood traditional funeral bouquets. Joan tried not to think of how the body under the roses had looked when she had seen it.

She thought the little church with stained-glass windows, warm and lovely in its own way, probably would have shocked the Swedish colonists. The simple white walls and clear windows of the Colony Church were more like Shaker architecture.

She was relieved to see that most of the gathering congregation seemed to know one another. They weren't talking much, but their occasional murmuring sounded like the greetings of old friends, not the kind of thing she would have expected from thrill-seeking tourists.

Whiffs of chili escaped the basement kitchen from time to time. Joan wondered whether the cooks would stop stirring to attend the funeral. Some would, she was sure.

Now the family was escorted through a door at the front of the church and seated in the second row. Nels, Ingrid, Hanna, and Christina filled the pew, with Ingrid on the aisle and Nels beside her, their heads bowed. Hard to tell whether in reverence or grief, but Joan's money was on grief. Debbie York, if she had come at all, was not near the family, and Gerri Balter, who might have sat with the family, couldn't. The congregational murmuring increased.

Then the pallbearers paraded in to fill the front pew. Joan recognized Fred, Andrew, Walt, and the Fribergs' two strapping sons-in-law, Tim York and Bengt Swanson. There was another young man about Andrew's age. Six ought to be enough, she thought. They all looked plenty strong.

Helga seemed peaceful inside the church, but now she leaned over to Joan. "Isn't that Walt down there? And do I see Fred? Why aren't they sitting with us?"

"They're pallbearers. They're going to carry the casket out of the church."

"Oh. Who died?"

"Gus Friberg. Ingrid's son."

"That's right."

Good, she remembered.

"And we went to their house last night," Helga said.

"Yes."

"Didn't we sing in the old church?"

"You're right. We did."

Helga looked pleased with herself. "I hope we sing today, too."

"Sometimes people sing at funerals. I don't know what this church does."

A piano played several familiar hymns and Bach chorale tunes. The congregation hushed and waited expectantly. When the minister went to the pulpit, the pianist brought "Jesu, Joy of Man's Desiring" to an ending midway through.

Pastor Vincent began with a prayer and scripture readings. Then he talked some about this good family, and how much they had meant to the church over the years. Joan was sure by now that he meant Ingrid. He'd probably never known Gus. She didn't envy him his job. Her first husband had always hated officiating at funerals. The ones he did for friends hurt, he said, and the ones for people he didn't know were so hard to make meaningful.

Vincent seemed to be doing well at that impossible task. He spoke about the need to find peace in their hearts in the face of the evil that had invaded their village and hurt their son, their brother, their friend, and the people who loved him. He had to know about Gerri, but he didn't mention her by name, though she supposed he had covered her in that general list.

What would he say, Joan wondered, if he knew that the evil he meant still threatened another member of his flock?

He described Gus as his family remembered him, telling little stories he must have learned on the day he visited them to plan this service. He promised them that a loving

God would keep Gus safe now. He read more scripture, ending with the Twenty-third Psalm. Finally he invited the congregation to sing an old Swedish hymn that the family had requested.

"Sing the Swedish if you know it," he said. "Or sing it in English. You'll find both versions in your order of worship."

The piano began playing a tune Joan recognized. Choosing the alto line of the music as usual, she sang along with the congregation, glad not to have to attempt the Swedish, but fascinated to see it next to the old version of the English translation she knew. Beside her, Helga stuck to the melody and sang the Swedish words as if she had sung them many times before.

Tryggare kan ingen vara	Children of the heavenly Father
Än Guds lilla barnaskara,	Safely in his bosom gather
Stjärnan ej på himlafästet,	Nestling bird nor star in heaven
Fågeln ej i kända nästet.	Such a refuge e'er was given.
Herren sina trogna vardar	God his own doth tend and nourish,
Uti Sions helga gårdar;	In his holy courts they flourish.
Över dem han sig förbarmar;	From all evil things he spares them,
Bär dem uppå fadersarmar.	In his mighty arms he bears them.

Joan was particularly touched by the third stanza. She supposed it could mean not only Gus and the family who mourned him, but the child of God who had committed this terrible deed. But she didn't expect anyone else to hear it that way.

Ingen nöd och ingen lycka	Neither life nor death shall ever
Skall utur hans hand dem rycka.	From the Lord his children sever;
Han, vår vän för andra vänner,	Unto them his grace he showeth,
Sina barns bekymmer känner.	And their sorrows all he knoweth.
Vad han' tar och vad han giver,	Though he giveth or he taketh,
Samme Fader han dock bliver,	God his children ne'er forsaketh,
Och hans mal är blott det ena:	His the loving purpose solely
Barnets sanna väl allena.	To preserve them pure and holy.

By the end of the last stanza, she heard people all around the church weeping. She couldn't help wondering how many of them had known Gus as the "sweet little boy" Helga remembered. How many thought of him as a real person, however little time he had spent in Bishop Hill in recent years? A person they thought God had forsaken? And which of them had murdered him and still was a danger to Helga?

A witness—that's what that man worried about. Had Gerri seen him, too? Not killing Gus, or she would have turned him in long ago. What, then? What could she have seen him doing at the ravine? No, above the ravine.

At the burn site, it had to be. And someone *had* done something there, something that changed the burn site.

Closing her eyes and bowing her head with the others, Joan didn't hear a word of the final prayer. Instead, her mind's eye saw the burn site as it had looked the night before, after everything had quieted down. Just dirt and piles of brush and branches waiting to be burned, but somehow different from the way it had looked after Gus's death.

The piles! They'd moved! And they'd changed shape— at least one of them had. She was absolutely sure of it. A big pile of branches that had been near the road had been moved closer to the ravine. A person with something to hide—the man who murdered Gus—could do a lot worse than hide it under a pile of wood. He might bury it, but he wouldn't have to if he covered it with what would become a bonfire. When the pile was burned, probably under the supervision of the volunteer fire department—and hadn't Kierstin said Roy Funkhouse was a volunteer firefighter?— anything burnable under it would be destroyed. Roy would be on the spot and could be sure that's what happened.

If the thing was worth destroying, it must be something that would give away who he was. He killed Gerri and threw her body into the ravine because she saw him hiding it under the wood.

Nobody will bother it during the funeral, she thought. I'll have time to tell Fred.

"Are you all right?" Helga asked her.

Joan looked up. The minister and the pallbearers were already following the casket, on silent wheels, down the aisle. "Thanks, Helga. I'm fine."

Now the funeral director came down the rows and dismissed the people a row at a time. He began with the family, but his body kept Joan from seeing Ingrid's face as she went by. Just as well.

Like a wedding, she thought, only without the congratulations. Their row, halfway down, wouldn't be out in time to watch the pallbearers carry Gus down the steps, but she had looked up in time to see Fred and Andrew walking down the aisle side by side. Andrew looked so tall and adult in Nels's dark suit. If it were Andrew instead of Gus, she thought as she had before, how could I bear it?

"Can't we go now?" Helga asked. She was right. The man had reached their pew. Slipping into her coat, Joan started down the aisle after the people who had been sitting in front of them. She recognized some of the people still waiting for release. There was Debbie York with an older woman—her mother, perhaps? The woman from the quilt shop smiled at her as she went by. Mark Balter scowled from a corner, and she thought she recognized the men she'd talked to in the restaurant. A man with them looked like the picture Fred had shown her of Roy Funkhouse. Was Roy there to make sure he was dead? Or to keep an eye on Helga? Or was it Mark? Why else would either of those men attend Gus's funeral? Especially Mark, if he'd loved Gerri as he'd claimed. Not that he'd be welcome at her funeral.

Sitting together near the back of the church were Greg Peterson and Kate Buker. Peterson wore a darker suit than usual. Kate, not in uniform, had dressed soberly and put her hair up.

Outside, the silent parade broke up, and people sorted themselves out. But instead of getting into cars and parading miles to a cemetery, they were being directed to line up on foot behind the hearse. In pairs, the pallbearers waited behind it, the family right behind them, and the rest made scraggly rows behind the family.

At last someone gave a silent signal to move. The funeral director and his assistants stood in the street like school crossing guards and stopped traffic from either direction while the mourners followed the hearse on the short trip down and across the street. They walked slowly between the posts into the cemetery and its tree-lined corridor.

"Is this what they usually do?" Helga asked softly beside her. "I don't remember this."

"No, this is special," Oscar said. "This is how Ingrid wanted it."

"It's not Ingrid!" Her mouth puckered up.

"No, no," he said gently. "Ingrid's walking up ahead. It's her son, Gus."

"Oh, that's right. I knew that." Helga beamed up at him as if she'd passed a test.

Whew. Joan hated to think of her getting upset right there in the cemetery. It could only distress everyone more. She debated calling her attention to Fred and Walt, but decided to leave well enough alone.

As they passed familiar tombstones, she was glad they had walked through the cemetery ahead of time. The women in the church basement were right—there was no time today to linger over an interesting word or shape. Still, the procession moved slowly. It seemed that everyone who had attended the church service had decided to walk across to the cemetery. Rain or sleet might have shrunk the crowd, but in this beautiful sunshine, cold as it was, why not see the whole show? No, that wasn't fair. Nobody was acting like a tourist or a thrill seeker. These were the Fribergs' friends and neighbors.

If they all showed up at the church for lunch, the cooks would be tired before they even started tonight's chili supper. That crew probably hadn't come to the cemetery. They might have turned down the heat under the chili long enough to attend the funeral in the church, but they'd have to stay in the building now to get ready for this onslaught.

"Where are we going?" Helga asked.

"Down there," Oscar said and pointed to the tent below them.

A good question, as they had walked the full length of
the cemetery now, and were about to curve around the end
and down to the lower level. Why, Joan wondered, hadn't
the hearse driven in that way and shortened the walk? Had
Ingrid chosen the long march? Or, if the driver was accus-
tomed to being followed by a line of cars, had he simply
taken his usual route through the main entrance?

At least they would walk downhill from here on.

The hearse, already at the lower level, pulled up at the
tent. Joan could see Fred and Andrew and the others carry
the casket with slow, careful steps over the uneven, snowy
ground to the open grave, where they set it down to rest on
something that kept it up at ground level.

While the mourners walked the rest of the way to the
grave, the undertakers set out flowers. Then the hearse
pulled a short distance away, making room for people to
stand where it had been. The family and a couple of dozen
others crowded into the tent, some seated and the rest standing. By the time the Lundquists arrived, the tent was full.
With everyone else they clustered around facing Pastor Vincent, who stood at the open end of the tent, beside the
grave.

Eventually, when they were assembled, he began to pray,
but his voice didn't reach the people beyond the tent.

"I can't hear him," Helga complained, right in the middle of the prayer. Before Oscar or Joan could stop her, she
circled around to the far side of the grave. They both followed her and ended up facing the family and pallbearers
inside the tent and the larger crowd outside it.

Joan felt self-conscious, but Helga had a point. Now that
he was only a few feet away, Mr. Vincent's words were
soft, but clear. Helga's expression crossed piety with smug-

ness. She didn't interrupt again, but gave her full attention to him and what he was saying.

The committal service was brief. After "dust to dust" and the final amen, the funeral director and his assistants lowered the casket slowly into the grave, and the pastor offered a small, clean shovel to Ingrid. Weeping openly, she shook her head and waved it away. Nels leaned over to her and gave her a fresh handkerchief.

Christina accepted the little shovel. She dug into a small pile of loose dirt beside the grave and threw some into it before passing the shovel to her sister, who did the same and passed it to Tim. When it was Bengt's turn, he filled it fuller and threw harder than the others, almost as if he were still envious of poor Gus.

Ignoring the shovel again when Bengt offered it to her, Ingrid scooped a small handful of dirt with her gloved hand and threw it in.

As each little shovelful of dirt landed, Helga seemed more and more uneasy. Joan began to wonder whether it had been a mistake to bring her. But she decided it would most likely be as disruptive to leave now as to let her fidget for these last few moments. She took Helga's hand in hers and squeezed, hoping to offer some comfort.

"They're almost done," she whispered.

Bengt was handing the shovel to Nels when Helga cried out in terror.

"Don't let him get me!"

TWENTY-FIVE

OSCAR GRABBED Helga's arm. "Who? Who's going to get you?"

"The big man. There." Sobbing and twisting in his grasp, she pointed at the crowd facing them. "Let me go!"

Joan tried to follow her pointing finger, but everyone seemed to be coming at them at once. Fred, Walt, and Andrew were pushing between Tim, Bengt, and the other pallbearer, all of whom were big men. On the far edges of the crowd, Greg Peterson and Kate Buker were shoving and shouting at the people in their way. Even Mark Balter and the man she thought was Roy Funkhouse were running toward them. But Ingrid and Nels Friberg already were closest to Helga—Nels with fire in his eyes and the shovel in his hand.

Pulling away from Oscar, her eyes wild, Helga tripped on the lumpy, frozen ground and sprawled on the pile of dirt at Nels's feet. He raised the little shovel high above her.

"No!" Ingrid cried and threw herself across Helga's exposed back, knocking her face into the dirt. "Haven't you done enough?"

The blow crashed down on Ingrid instead of on Helga. Then Fred crashed into Nels. He twisted Nels's arm up behind his back, and the shovel hit the ground. Peterson and Buker ran up with weapons drawn, but all they needed to do was handcuff him.

"Ingrid, I'm sorry!" Nels cried out. "I never meant to hurt you! I'm sorry!"

Ingrid scrambled to her feet, but she looked shaky. Averting her eyes from her husband, she looked down at Helga.

Joan knelt in the snow by Helga, who lay silent, her eyes tightly shut. Oscar was already kneeling, holding her hand. Fred and Walt stood over them.

"Nels Friberg, you're under arrest for the assault of Ingrid Friberg," Peterson said.

He's being careful, Joan thought, even though most of us could see that Nels really was going after Helga, not Ingrid. And some of us knew why. Very few, though, she realized. Only the Lundquist family, Peterson, and Buker. The only other person who knew what Helga meant was Gus's killer. No one else knew she had witnessed the murder. Had Ingrid guessed? From her quick reaction, Joan thought it was possible.

And if Nels hadn't tried to attack Helga, no one might have believed her accusation. Now, though, he'd proved she was right.

"Are you all right?" Peterson asked Ingrid gently.

"I will be," she said, but a bruise already was forming on her cheek and neck, and Joan could see dirt in the raw spots the shovel had made.

Most of the force of the blow, she thought, must have been deflected by the collar of her winter coat. Ingrid probably would be bruised underneath the coat, too. But it could have been much worse.

"I'm so sorry," Ingrid said.

"It's not your fault," Joan told her.

"It's never the victim's fault," Peterson said.

But she was weeping big tears. "Yes, it is." Both her

daughters clung to her now, and she kept repeating "I'm so sorry" to them.

Peterson held her collar away from her neck. "We'll have to take care of that. Don't want it to get infected. I can call another squad car for you."

"No!" Ingrid said. "I'll be fine."

"They have first-aid supplies over in the church," Hanna said. "We'll take care of her."

"All right," Peterson said. "If you promise. And get some ice on it. But she really ought to have it examined."

Helga still lay there in the dirt, her eyes squeezed shut, even though Oscar was stroking her. Joan was sure she was conscious. She couldn't squeeze so tightly if she weren't.

Oscar put his arms around her. "It's all right, sweetheart. I won't let anyone get you."

"You're safe," Joan told her. "They've caught the man. He can't hurt you now."

Helga opened her eyes. "They caught him? The big man?"

Looking over at Nels, as tall as Andrew, Joan saw him for the first time as a big man. At home he seemed much smaller. But the parka gave him bulk he didn't have indoors. Maybe that's why Helga hadn't recognized him indoors. When she'd seen him at the bakery, he'd been outdoors. That was the only other time she had run from him. Had being out in the cold today made it even easier for her to remember something she'd seen when she was out in the cold ravine? Possibly, she thought. Andrew had told her about state-dependent memory, like getting drunk to remember something you learned when you were drunk. Or maybe it was just the coat. His hair was covered now, too. Had it been covered those other times? Very likely.

"Yes," Oscar told her now. "He won't hurt anyone, ever again."

"You're sure?"

"I'm sure." Smiling broadly, he pulled her to her feet.

"Well," she said, and brushed off her knees. "That's good. I'd better go home and make you lunch."

"Better yet, how about if I take you out? I hear they've already fixed a nice lunch for us over at the church."

"Sure," Peterson said. "Why don't you do that? We know where to find you."

Oscar led her through the assembled mourners, turned so quickly now to gawkers. Meanwhile, Buker was reading Nels his rights while she marched him to the squad car out on the street.

"Show's over, folks," Peterson said. "Unless you're in the family or know something, it's time for you to leave."

That thinned the crowd substantially, though a few stayed to watch the next act. Peterson ignored them.

"You think Andrew and I should stay?" Joan asked Fred.

"Sure," he said, and smiled down at her. "You're Mom's family."

She squeezed his hand.

"I'm sorry," Peterson said to Pastor Vincent. "We didn't mean to wreck your service like this."

"You didn't do it. We're all terribly sorry. I can hardly imagine what Ingrid's facing now." He went to her, took her hand, and spoke softly to her and the other family members. Then he went out and spoke to the funeral director. Peterson followed Buker and Nels to the squad car.

Inside the tent, Ingrid sobbed on her daughters' shoulders. "It's all my fault, don't you see? I should have stopped him. I should have known what he'd do."

"Me, too, Mama," Christina said. "I feel guilty for leaving home so soon, leaving you with him. And Gus—he was so young when I got married. But Bengt was good to me, and I couldn't take it anymore. I was afraid someday Daddy would turn on me.''

"We both knew how he was," Hanna said. "We worried about you last night, going home to him when he'd been drinking. We were glad you'd have someone else there. I don't know how you stayed with him all these years—I couldn't have. In between, he could be so sweet, but when he got like that, there was nothing you could do. It's not your fault you didn't stop him. You couldn't.''

"Not your father! Gus!''

"Gus?'' they chorused, and she broke down again.

"But Gus…'' Christina said. She took her mother's hands. "It was Daddy who hit you, Mama, the way he always did, not Gus. Gus is dead.''

Ingrid shook her off. "You think I don't know that?'' Then she turned away from her daughters and quit responding.

The funeral director spoke to two men who had been leaning on good-sized shovels. After making quick work of the ceremonial pile of dirt by the grave, they began to dig into a lumpier pile behind it. In an oddly insistent rhythm, the first clods thudded down into the grave, drowning out what Ingrid's daughters said to her.

"She knows," Joan murmured to Fred and Andrew.

Fred nodded, but Andrew looked confused. "What does Ingrid know?''

"That Nels killed Gus," Joan said. She saw the shock on Kierstin's face. "I think maybe she's known all along. That's why she's feeling guilty.''

"Mom, that's not what she said.''

"She learned how to avoid Nels's abuse—much of the time, anyway," Joan said. "She didn't cross him, didn't assert her independence, was the perfect cook. Nobody had much good to say about Nels, except that he was a good

house painter, and he was. I didn't hear any rumors about
how he abused his wife, but I'll bet Vicki Holm knew.
That's why she didn't want her daughter to marry into his
family.''

"Her daughter?'' Andrew asked.

He probably hadn't heard Gerri's maiden name, she realized. "Gerri Balter, the one Gus was engaged to. The one
whose body they found yesterday.''

"The one who attacked Debbie,'' he said.

"Vicki didn't know about the fight until Helga told her,
when we were shopping with you and Kierstin at the Colony Store. She probably figured Gus would take after his
dad, and she didn't want her daughter hurt again.''

"So Gus was killed, and Gerri got it anyway.''

Walt, Ruthie, and Kierstin had been listening. Now they
came closer, and Ruthie joined in. "Why would Vicki see
that side of Nels, if most people didn't?''

"She said her husband was controlling—compared him
to Eric Janson. Maybe she recognized in Ingrid how she
would have been if she hadn't left him. And she wasn't the
only one. Helga knew what was going on—part of it, anyway. She told us ahead of time that Nels wouldn't let Ingrid
take a walk with us, and she was right. She said people
thought Ingrid was afraid to do anything on her own, but
it was really because of Nels.''

"You think Nels finally snapped and attacked Gus when
he came home and didn't act like Ingrid?'' Andrew said.
"But he wasn't killed at home.''

"No, he wasn't,'' Fred said. "Your mother and I were
talking about that last night. How could his killer, even
Nels, have lured him into the woods?''

"Suppose he killed him at home, and moved the body
to the woods,'' Andrew said. "I know Helga was scared

there, but maybe that's what she saw, him putting the body in the woods, where it wouldn't be tied to him.''

"No." The bloody scene flashed again behind Joan's eyes. She didn't think she'd ever be able to shut it out. "I don't know what Helga saw, but trust me, Andrew, that's where Gus was killed."

Andrew looked past her as if he didn't believe her, but Fred nodded. "Your mom's right, son. There can't be any doubt about that part."

Kierstin was in tears, as if Gus's murder had only now sunk in. "Poor Farmor! She must have been so scared!"

"I know, honey," Walt said. "Shall we go over to the church and love her up a little?"

Kierstin nodded blindly and left with her parents.

A little wind had picked up, and they had been standing in the snow and cold long enough that Joan's toes were cold, even in her boots. Andrew, in his new black dress shoes, must be miserable by now, she thought, unless he's running on adrenaline.

"Any chance there's room for us in the tent?" she asked Fred. She could see some kind of green carpet under the chairs and thought they'd be out of the wind, as well.

"Looks like it," Fred said. "Right now it's almost all family in there."

She hated to intrude, though she didn't see how there could be much left of the Fribergs' private lives from now on. "What do you think?"

"We can ask," Fred said.

"I think we just should go in," Andrew said. "Not shun them, you know? They shouldn't feel embarrassed every time they see us from now on. It's not as if we didn't know. They should know they still have friends."

Out of the mouths of—but he was too old to call a babe. She didn't have any babies, just a family of adults.

She hoped Ingrid's adult children would stand by their mother now.

Ingrid stood up when they went into the tent. She had been sitting with her girls, watching the men finish burying her son. Bengt and Tim were also in there, talking with the pallbearer Joan didn't know.

"Is Helga all right?" Ingrid asked. "Did he hit her, too?"

"She's fine," Fred said. "Dad took her over to the church for something to eat." He took her hands in his big ones. "We're all worried about you, you know."

"I feel so terrible. I don't know why he went after Helga, of all people."

"Don't you?" Joan asked gently. "Then how did you know in time to keep him from hurting her?"

"She saw him, didn't she?" Ingrid's mouth struggled against more sobs.

"Yes."

"Until she cried out like that, he must have hoped she wouldn't remember." Ingrid's sad eyes looked up at Fred. "We all know what's happening to her. It breaks my heart, but what can you do?"

More than Walt is willing to consider, Joan thought. But this was not the time to get into possible treatments for Helga.

"I had no idea," Fred said. "I've been away much too long."

"Well, you're here now, and we're all glad." Her gaze wandered off for a moment, as if she were remembering that her own son had come home after much too long. She dragged herself back. "Thank you, Fred, for helping today. It meant a lot to me."

"And thank you for protecting Mom. I'm sorry you were

hurt. How bad is it?'' He peered at her neck, sliding her collar back to see.

"It's been worse." Those few words said it all.

"Can you manage a little lunch?" Joan asked.

"Oh, I don't know." She shook her head. "All those people."

"They came because of Gus, Mom," Hanna said. "And to tell you how sad they are for you. That hasn't changed. Let them show you they love you."

"Besides, we're getting hungry," Christina said practically. "And we can't very well go off and leave you here. You wouldn't want to starve your children, now would you?" Christina didn't look in any danger of starvation, but she obviously knew her mother.

"You're all waiting for me?" Ingrid said. "I'm so sorry. I didn't think." Turning her back on the grave, she let them lead her out of the tent. Fred stuck with her.

"It was Nels who made those phone calls, wasn't it?" Andrew asked Joan as they walked out a little way behind Fred and Ingrid.

"Probably. He'd been in the house plenty often. He'd know there's only an old-fashioned phone, with no caller ID or star anything. And he never stayed on the line long enough to trace a call the old, slow way. But with the tapes we made, they ought to be able to prove it's his voice. They say voiceprints are as good as fingerprints."

"I still can't see how he got Gus to go to the woods with him."

"Something tells me Ingrid knows. She blames herself, and then she shuts up. But you know, Andrew, she's kept the secret of Nels's abuse for many, many years. It's not going to be easy to give up now, even after we all know."

"Even after we saw him for ourselves? Did you see how fast Fred grabbed him when he tried to hit Helga? I'll tell you, Mom, if Nels had been going after you, I would have beaten him to it. Only I'm no cop, like Fred. Anybody who beats on my mother, I'm not just going to grab him. I'm gonna beat him to a pulp.''

From his clenched fists and the fierce expression on his face, Joan was inclined to believe he'd try, anyway. Then she stopped dead in the snow. ''Andrew, that's it!''

''What's what?''

''Nels didn't go after Gus for standing up to him. Nels laid into *Ingrid*, as he'd been doing for years, and this time Gus went after *him*. Gus wasn't a little kid afraid of his father anymore. He was a big man, and a master sergeant in the Army. You heard yourself just now. Gus would have charged at anyone who hurt his mother. Nels didn't lure Gus into the woods—Gus chased him there.''

''That would explain why Helga was there, too,'' Andrew said slowly.

''What do you mean?''

''Helga doesn't miss much. If they ran from their house to the woods, they had to go right past our house.'' He sounded as if he'd grown up there himself. ''She'd see them from the kitchen.''

''Of course! She must have been curious, and Oscar was asleep.''

''So she went out to see where her neighbors were running, and why.'' His voice rose as his excitement grew.

''And saw a murder, instead.'' It all made sense, once you started from the other direction. And then she had to wonder. ''Only maybe it wasn't murder.''

''Come again, Mom? You told me yourself, he battered his face in!''

''If a strong man is after you with blood in his eye and you grab the only weapon you can see out there and succeed in hitting him with it before he hurts you, is it murder, even if you kill him? Or self-defense?''

"Either way, he killed his son. All Gus did was try to protect his mother. I hope I'd do the same.''

"No!'' Now she understood why Ingrid had said she should have stopped Gus, not Nels. But how? Could Ingrid have kept Gus from defending her any more than Nels could keep from defending himself? Still, all Nels had to do was not hurt Ingrid in the first place. Then Gus wouldn't have gone after him.

Thank God I won't be on that jury.

Then she remembered Gerri Balter. If she was right, Nels had killed Gerri to hide what he had done. He was as guilty as if he'd killed Helga.

She called ahead to Fred, who had reached the street with the Fribergs. "Fred, we have to go over to the burn site!''

When she explained to him what she expected to find, they left the Fribergs and set out with Andrew for the burn site. Fred called Greg Peterson on the way. He said Peterson would drive back from Cambridge, leaving Buker to book Nels into the jail. "We don't want anyone claiming later that we planted evidence.''

"Why would we plant anything? You think like a cop.''

His eyes laughed at her. "Remember me, the guy you married? I am a cop.''

"I know, but—''

"But nothing. You can't be too careful about this kind of thing. And we're in no hurry now. Mom's safe.''

She shuddered. "Oh, Fred, he almost got her! And it's all my fault.''

"You sound like Ingrid. It's no more your fault than Gus's death was hers.''

"Yes, it is. If I'd told Peterson what I remembered about the burn site before we all crossed over to the cemetery, he might have found something that would have warned him about Nels in time to keep him from attacking your mother. We were lucky Ingrid moved as fast as she did. Your mom could have been hurt worse than Ingrid.''

''More than likely, he would have posted a guard at the burn site until after the burial. Wouldn't have changed a thing.''

She sighed. ''I suppose.'' And Ingrid would never give herself credit for protecting Helga.

Peterson and several deputies reached the burn site before they did, even without using sirens—Joan supposed because no bodies were involved. This time, she saw, they had parked on the edge of the road, rather than on the burn site itself.

The men circled the pile of branches Joan pointed out to them, but when nobody spotted any signs of freshly dug earth around the edges, they started lifting the heavy wood back to where it had been a couple of days earlier. With several pairs of strong arms working, they soon exposed the earth that had been covered. A uniformed photographer documented the process.

''You were right,'' Fred said, his arm around Joan. ''You can see where he dug.''

Shedding their warm gloves for latex, the men dug carefully by hand in the loose soil where the pile had been. ''Something here,'' one of them said, and the others helped him uncover it.

Joan held her breath. What the man lifted from the shallow hole left no doubt in her mind. The padded denim jacket covered with many colored drips of paint could belong to only one man in Bishop Hill. But over the paint drips were unmistakable spatters of blood. She was sure that when it was tested, it would prove to be Gus's. According to Fred, Gerri hadn't bled at all.

The man pulled several more pieces of clothing from the hole. "That's about it," he said. "This oughtta nail the—" He looked at Joan and stopped.

"He had to have a shovel," Andrew said. "You know he didn't dig with his hands, the way you guys did. You were digging in loose stuff, but he was digging packed earth, maybe even with packed snow on it. If you found his shovel, maybe you could match it to the indentation on Gerri's head."

"We're getting a search warrant for the house and any outbuildings," Peterson said.

"You think he took the shovel home?" Andrew asked.

"Probably put it where he usually kept it. It would have done the job, not like the little one he was going to use on Mrs. Lundquist. Even if he wiped it off, we may find some of this soil, and with luck, there will be hairs or something else we can link to Gerri." He raised his bushy eyebrows at Joan. "You figured all this out in the church?"

"Not all of it. But I knew someone had moved that wood, and I knew Gerri had been thrown into the ravine. If she saw him hiding evidence that could prove he killed Gus, I believed he'd kill her, too."

TWENTY-SIX

BACK IN THE church basement, they were in time for sand-
wiches and homemade pie and coffee. The church workers
had seated everyone at as few tables as possible, so that
they could ready the rest for the chili supper. Fred joined
his parents while Oscar finished a second piece of his own
cherry pie. Joan and Andrew were put with Tim and Bengt,
whose wives sat farther down the same long table, closer
to their mother. Ingrid was at the far end, her neck washed
and bandaged. Someone had filled a plastic bag with ice to
reduce the swelling, but she wasn't using it. Probably shy,
Joan thought, with so many people watching.

People did indeed come over to offer sympathy to her
and her daughters. By now the word about Nels had reached
everyone who had missed seeing him hit Ingrid with the
shovel. Nobody mentioned Helga—they all expressed concern about Ingrid's neck. It was almost a code for their real
concern, the fact that he would attack her at all. They didn't
make the connection with Gus.

"What came over him?" some said, and "He must have
been crazy with grief."

Over and over Ingrid said "thank you" and "you're so
kind."

At such close quarters Joan couldn't tell Andrew the
thoughts that pounded her thick and fast now. Ingrid had
known all this time. She must have seen the fight in the

house—must have seen Gus chase Nels outside, at least. And she must have been there when Nels came home alone—covered in Gus's blood.

Unless somehow he'd changed into fresh, unbloodied clothes before she saw him. Maybe even washed up. So what had he done with the bloody clothes then? He hadn't buried them that night. Gerri was still alive and well the next day. That had to have happened later.

Whatever Ingrid saw when Nels came back, whatever he told her, Gus hadn't come back with him. Joan wondered what they had said to each other. Whatever it was, they'd waited at home until Peterson and Buker notified them officially, and the Lundquists went over. And from that day to this, Ingrid hadn't let on to anybody that she knew. Had he threatened her? Or was not telling on Nels so ingrained in her by now that he hadn't needed to?

Joan couldn't imagine the torment of that day. For that matter, she couldn't imagine living through any of it. Yet there Ingrid sat, thanking people for their kindness, just as she had the night after Gus died.

Tim and Bengt, though technically in the family, seemed out of the sympathy loop and sat talking quietly to each other. Joan heard an occasional word, but not enough to make sense of what they were saying.

She was startled when two men appeared at her elbow and even more surprised to recognize Mark Balter. If the police were right, why would he come anywhere near Bengt?

But he spoke to her. "Joan, Mark Balter. We met when you were out with Fred."

"Yes, I remember. My son, Andrew. Andrew, Mark was a classmate of Fred's." And Gerri's husband.

Andrew chewed before saying hello. Did he remember?

"I don't know if you've met Roy Funkhouse," Mark said. "Roy, this is Fred Lundquist's wife."

"Ma'am," said the man she had recognized from the picture Fred had showed her.

"Roy's a top-notch mechanic."

She smiled. "I understand you work on Walt's car."

"That's right," he said. "Pleased to meet you."

"Have you had lunch?" Given what the sheriff suspected about them and Bengt, she felt odd acting social with these guys.

"Yes," Mark said. "We were just waiting to talk with Bengt. You know, it was Gus who got us both jobs with Bengt."

She choked, and Andrew pounded her on the back until she could speak again. "No, really?"

"You know my story, and Roy—well, Roy can speak for himself. But Gus told Bengt we knew cars, and Bengt offered us both work. Without Gus, I don't think he would have taken a chance on a couple of ex-cons. You know how I felt when Gus went after Gerri, but I have him to thank for my job, anyhow."

Bengt turned around. "Hey, fellows, what's up?"

"Come to pay our respects," Roy said. "I was pretty mad at Gus at first, but he more than made up for it. Told me he'd help me all he could when I got out, and he kept his word."

"I know that," Bengt said. "You ought to speak to his mother."

"We will," Mark said. "But we appreciate what you did, too. We're not going to let you down, you know."

"I know," Bengt said. "You do good work, both of you." He turned to Joan. "Mark's the best salesman I've ever had. And Roy fixes up the clunkers so I know they'll run when I sell them."

"That's great." Joan smiled at them. Wait'll I tell Fred, she thought. Whatever they really thought about Gus, if they were doing something crooked with Bengt, they wouldn't be here talking about it like that.

Mark and Roy went over to speak with Ingrid, and Andrew excused himself to spend some time with Kierstin. Joan finished her meal in silence, not sorry to be left on her own.

She wasn't sure whether to rejoice or mourn. Now Helga would be safe. Life in Bishop Hill could go back to normal. But Ingrid's life would never be the same again. And Vicki Holm was suffering, too.

THE NEWS ABOUT Nels, coming to light a little at a time, turned the village upside down as the murder of his son hadn't begun to do. When Greg Peterson appeared at her door with a search warrant a couple of hours after the funeral, Ingrid finally broke her long silence. She led him directly to her dirty clothes hamper and was startled to find only traces of blood at the bottom, where she had hidden Nels's blood-spattered jacket and overalls before he had moved them in secret.

Some of her neighbors were horrified that she would provide evidence against him. Others couldn't understand why she had waited so long. Everyone had an opinion, she told the Lundquists over supper at their house that night, and no one was shy about telling her what she should have done. "But they didn't live through it."

"When did you first suspect Nels?" Oscar asked her.

"I was afraid when Gus fought with him and they ran off, but I never imagined what was going to happen. When Nels came back alone and looking like that, I knew. I wanted to go out to Gus, in case he was still alive, but Nels wouldn't let me. He said it was no use—Gus was dead. All

I could do was hide his clothes when he told me to. I didn't want to lose him, too, and I knew those clothes would convict him.''

Joan looked at Fred. How could she bear it? And how could she take the word of the man she thought must have killed her only son? How could she protect him instead of trying to rescue Gus?

"You believed him?" Oscar asked.

"God help me, I did. I always believed him. Every time he told me he was sorry, I believed he'd never hurt me again. And he really would be sweet and loving for a long time. He was so torn up about Gus—he probably still is. But it's too late. We lost our boy. If I could have saved him and didn't, I'll never forgive myself for listening to Nels.''

"No," Fred said firmly. "I'm sure Gus died almost instantly. You couldn't possibly have gotten him help in time.''

Joan thanked him with her eyes. Ingrid had suffered enough. She didn't need to torture herself with that guilt on top of what she already felt. Besides, he might even be right.

"Gus was a sweet boy," Helga said.

"Yes, he was." Ingrid blinked back tears and squeezed her friend's hand. "I'm glad I have you, Helga, and you, Oscar." Through the tears, she looked as if a huge weight had been lifted from her shoulders. No longer timid looking, she sat tall and strong.

"We're glad they have you," Joan told her. What a comfort, to have such an old friend living next door. But how much longer would Helga even know who Ingrid was?

DURING THE REST OF their stay in Bishop Hill, they were able to relax, and Joan met more old family friends. She and Fred spent each night in the same bed, untroubled by danger. Helga, thank goodness, seemed to have forgotten her fear of the big man. But she was going to need plenty of help in the months and years to come. They would need to come back to Bishop Hill, and Joan hoped the family could agree on having Helga evaluated. It might not be too late for treatment that would make a difference.

Peterson had said that one or both of them might have to return to testify at Nels's trial, but he had assured them that Helga wouldn't be involved. "She can't testify—we all know that."

Andrew and Kierstin spent more than a little time together in the last few days. The night before they left, he extracted a promise from her to visit them in Oliver as soon as she could. "I leave it to you to persuade your parents," he said.

"I'll tell them it's educational—you're going to show me this great college. If it's all right with you, of course, Aunt Joan," and Kierstin turned the dimpled charm on her.

"Of course," Joan said. "We'd love to have you and your parents whenever they can get away, wouldn't we, Fred?"

"Of course," he said.

Thank you for backing me up, she thought. The last thing I want to do is worry about Kierstin on her own.

Andrew shot her a look, and she smiled benignly back at him. That wasn't the kind of visit he had in mind, she was sure.

"Bishop Hill pretty much shuts down right after Christmas," Kierstin said. "Even the restaurant. And Aunt Carol will be back to help Farmor and Farfar. That would be a perfect time."

The silent laughter in Fred's eyes meant he knew Joan

had been well and truly outmaneuvered. There was nothing to do but give in gracefully.

"I'll speak to your mother." And figure out where to put them all. Kierstin by herself could have slept in Rebecca's bed, but Joan was going to have to hang her parents from nails on the wall.

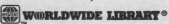

FootPrints
in the Butter

AN INGRID BEAUMONT MYSTERY
CO-STARRING HITCHCOCK THE DOG

DENISE DIETZ

Ingrid Beaumont's high school reunion promises a night of fun and good times. But the wild night brings a deadly morning, with the murder of classmate Wylie Jamestone, local artist and genuine creep. Wylie leaves behind a long list of enemies and a clue challenging Ingrid to find his killer.

A painting of Doris Day and a cryptic note send Ingrid and her dog, Hitchcock, into Jamestone's scandal-ridden life and onto the trail of a killer. But will Ingrid's hunt lead to treasure or tragedy?

> "An exceptional book by an exceptional talent."
> —*Painted Rock Reviews*

> "...a wonderful amateur sleuth tale starring a wisecracking and witty heroine and her beloved dog."
> —*Harriet Klausner*

Available November 2004 at your favorite retail outlet.

WDD511